Repentance

Alison Gibbs was born in Kyogle in 1963 and spent her childhood in the towns and villages of northern New South Wales. She now lives in Sydney, where she runs her own writing consultancy producing copy for United Nations agencies and the not-for-profit sector. Her short stories and essays have been published and broadcast in Australia and the United Kingdom and have received numerous short-listings and awards. *Repentance* is her first novel.

In memory of my parents,
Stan and Vilma

REPENTANCE

Alison Gibbs

SCRIBE
Melbourne • London

Scribe Publications
18–20 Edward St, Brunswick, Victoria 3056, Australia
2 John Street, Clerkenwell, London, WC1N 2ES, United Kingdom
3754 Pleasant Ave, Suite 100, Minneapolis, Minnesota 55409, USA

First published by Scribe 2021

Cover photos by:
Scott Hortop RF / Alamy Stock Photo
banphote kamolsanei / Alamy Stock Photo
Florilegius / Alamy Stock Photo
Antiquarian Images / Alamy Stock Photo

Typeset in 12.25/16.25 pt Garamond Premier Pro by the publishers

Printed and bound in Australia by Griffin Press, part of Ovato

Scribe Publications is committed to the sustainable use of natural resources
and the use of paper products made responsibly from those resources.

9781922310064 (paperback)
9781925938807 (ebook)

Catalogue records for this book are available from the
National Library of Australia.

scribepublications.com.au

And God said, Let us make man in our image, after our likeness:
and let them have dominion over the fish of the sea, and over
the fowl of the air, and over the cattle, and over all the earth,
and over every creeping thing that creepeth upon the earth.

Genesis 1:26

We are stardust
Billion year old carbon
We are golden
Caught in the devil's bargain
And we've got to get ourselves
Back to the garden.

Joni Mitchell

Coleoptera

If the hippies really were going to be eaten alive by insects, as the locals were always predicting, then surely that summer of 1976 was when it should have happened. It's a time you can hardly remember without feeling the nip and sting of things. Swarms and infestations, the flubber of moths in the washing, the arch-aching bite of green ants in the lawn. Already on that humid afternoon in mid-October, the fruit flies were turning the town's tomatoes into putrid sacks dripping on the vine. Things flickered and dived in the air of the place. They were slapped and sprayed and stamped on. Clouds of gnats sent whole soccer teams veering off course during evening training and clogged the gauze on the ventilation fans at the back of the Parmenters' shop.

And every night, across the valley, the rainforest would open its canopy and let its big guns fly: horned beetles and cockroaches, lacewings and leaf-green cicadas, cricket-like creatures with jointed legs and long fishing-rod feelers. Called by the glow of the street lights, they hurtled towards the town and struck against the BP sign at the top of Main Street. Bing zap! went the ultraviolet ring on the wall of the Repentance pub, where men crunched on beer nuts and drank to the hippies' demise. 'I give 'em six months.' Nods all round and a thoughtful pause as they pictured all those men and women sleeping naked in the hills, the hearts of their organic cabbages oozing with caterpillar slime. Even in the noisy pub, you could hear the scream of mosquitoes coming at their bare flesh like needles in the dark.

Chapter One

It was like deja vu, this second tongue-lashing from Melanie Curtis's mother. Joanne clutched the edge of the counter as the woman drew herself up like a furious medusa, shaking her wild red hair and jabbing a finger, again and again, at the cigarette rack on the wall. There was a sharp crack as her hand slapped down on the countertop. She wore so many rings at once, stacked beneath her knuckles. A silver snake was winding around her index finger.

'And how old are *you*? Don't tell me. You're the same age as my Mel. So what the fuck is going on here? You're telling my twelve-year-old daughter that she's too young to come in to your shop and buy tobacco for *me* while *you*, a girl the very same age, is standing here selling the stuff.'

Joanne fought the urge to say that she was now thirteen. She turned and pulled a packet of Drum from the rack and waited for the money, noting the tuft of orange hair growing under the woman's arm and her nipples clearly visible through her singlet. Linda, her name was. Even Melanie called her that. She cracked the coins down, one by one, two dollars thirty, and with a final flounce of her hair, pounded across the linoleum and out through the fly tapes.

Mrs Chittock almost collided with her as she came in. She glanced over her shoulder and raised her eyebrows at Joanne as she and her children made their way to the fridges down the back.

'How are you, Jo?' she called out, sliding open the glass lid of the freezer cabinet.

'I'm good.'

'How's Mum?'

'Okay.'

Joanne pulled a bundle of letters from the pigeonhole as Mrs Chittock returned, holding a fistful of icy poles above the heads of her children, who leapt and skipped around her like overexcited pups. They were exhausting, these kids of hers. Mrs Chittock always looked tired. When they left, the shop felt even quieter than before.

Joanne moved to the window. Melanie Curtis's dirty white car was still parked across the street. Her mother was in the driver's seat rolling a cigarette and you could just make out Melanie sitting beside her in her school uniform, her feet pressed against the dashboard. A truck roared past, heading for the mill, its undercarriage sprayed with mud and its empty chains clanking. Melanie's mother gave a careless laugh and glanced towards the shop. Joanne knew they were talking about her and stepped away from the glass.

Barbara came in from work.

'Saw your little hippie friend out there. Did her mother have another go at you?'

'She's not my friend.'

'She's a bitch, that woman, you shouldn't serve her.' Barbara slung her shoulder bag under the counter and went to the fridge to fetch herself a drink. 'Where's Dad?'

'In town.'

'How's Mum?'

'She's okay. The nurse came, she's had her meds.'

'Did she eat any lunch, do you know?'

'Soup, Dad said. Quite a bit.'

Barb cracked the ring-pull on the can. 'I'll go and see her in a minute. I'm having a shower first, but.' She wiped her fingers down the side of her nose and rubbed the tips together. 'My skin feels disgusting.'

Joanne turned back to the window. Melanie's car was gone. No one else seemed to be coming, so she took an iceblock for herself and went outside to eat it. Michael Phelan drove past in his new ute and she followed him down the hill with her eyes, down to where the footpaths petered out and the main street of Repentance became a country road again, banked by feathery grasses. Half a mile on was the mill. You could see the incinerator stack and hear the descending whine of the saw all over town. All day long it went, over and over, the same sliding note, and then a pause and, if the wind was right, the faint crack and splinter of breaking wood.

But all too often there was no wind. Repentance lay more than a hundred miles from the coast, behind a thickly forested ridge that blocked any hint of a sea breeze. This was part of the vast state forest that ran all way to the border. The larger town of Balbirnie was only three-quarters of an hour away, but sweltering in the still air behind that wall of trees, Repentance could sometimes feel like the town at the edge of the earth. It clung to the side of the valley, its main street trickling down the hill, past the pub, a smattering of shops, the primary school, two churches, and the gates of the showground, to the sawmill at the bottom and the looping ribbon of the creek.

Standing in the street now, Joanne watched a hippie woman packing up her wares and squeezing them into a battered suitcase. She'd been there almost every day for more than a week, selling silver jewellery pinned to a blanket on the footpath. The previous Friday afternoon, Joanne had come down from the bus stop with Tracy Willis and Rhonda McKay — well, not *with* them exactly: she didn't sit with them on the bus; they sat up the back — but she had followed behind them as they got off and dawdled down the hill, the kick pleats of their uniforms bouncing on their ballet-school bums. Tracy was describing the colours of her new Hawaiian shorts and Rhonda was hanging on every word when they suddenly stopped and grabbed each other by the arm.

The earring woman was crouched in the purple shadow of the jacaranda. Every now and then she leant across to flick a fallen blossom off the rug. According to Tracy's older brother, she wasn't wearing undies. When she chucked a spread, he reckoned you could see right up her skirt — hair, clit, everything, deadset.

'Gross!' gasped Rhonda, clutching her chest. Tracy dared her to go and see. And then they remembered Joanne and spun around to face her.

'You go, Jo, go on! You won't laugh. We'll giggle too much, won't we, Rhonda?'

'Yes.'

'Just go and pretend to be looking at her stuff.'

'Her stuff!' spluttered Rhonda.

'Go on,' Tracy said, 'and come back and tell us if it's true.'

Joanne had blundered forward as if pushed into the middle of the street. Ahead of her the blanket of silver trinkets was spread like a sticky trap.

'Hi,' said the woman in a husky voice that sounded faintly American. She was heavy boned, with a thick rope of mousey hair hanging over one shoulder.

'Hi,' Joanne said, crouching down in front of the woman, her eyes carefully averted. She poked at a pair of earrings, silver spider webs.

'You can try those on if you want. Here.' The woman pushed a piece of broken mirror towards her. 'They're seven dollars, those ones. They're sterling silver.'

Joanne noticed the way the woman was crouching. She looked strangely unsupported, the backs of her thighs pressed into her hams and her feet splayed flat on the ground. Leaning forward, Joanne was aware of the rucked-up skirt and the fleshy knees in front of her. 'They're nice,' she managed to croak.

'These ones here are cheaper. Or I can give you one of those cobwebs there for four.'

Fourrr, the accent, like something off *Sesame Street.* Joanne's neck ached as if someone were holding her down. She could feel the eyes of the girls across the street. 'Or there's these ones,' said the woman, leaning across the rug, her weight suddenly shifting from one heavy hip to the other. Joanne's head shot up and she staggered to her feet. But no, it was too dark, she couldn't see.

'I haven't got pierced ears!' she squeaked.

'Oh, that's a shame. I can do 'em for you if you want. Just boil up a needle and bring me some ice and half a potato. Or a zucchini, that works just as well. It's just to put behind the earlobe while you push the needle through.'

Joanne pressed her hands against her burning ears. 'No, thanks. I'm getting studs for my birthday.'

This was a lie. Her family had a thing about pierced ears, that they were woggy or Catholic or something.

'You can buy them now and hold onto 'em,' the woman continued mildly. She peered around Joanne's legs to the girls across the street. 'Do your friends want to come and take a look? Oh, no, they're going.'

Joanne turned around to see Tracy and Rhonda scurrying down the hill, helpless with laughter. She crossed back over the road and went to follow them, but they were well past the shop by then and it was pointless. They had thrown her one last giggling glance and, pulling each other by the elbow, disappeared around the corner of the Presbyterian Hall.

From the deep shade of the shop awning, Joanne watched the earring woman walk heavily up the hill towards the Balbirnie turn-off. There were so many of these hippie people around the place now, more and more of them all the time. She couldn't remember exactly when it started — three, four years ago? It was just the odd one to begin with, but then they started gathering in small groups on street corners. You began to see the same ones twice. And before long you could pick them: the women in their singlet tops and rust-stained satin, with their hard, brown bellies and silver jewellery that dangled and jiggled. The men had beards like Jesus Christ and wore soft cotton clothing that slid off their shoulders and down their hips as though they'd lost too much weight.

Where did these people come from and what was bringing them here? And what set them apart from the funny sorts who had always lived around the place — hillbilly people with their mongrel dogs and way too many kids? People like the O'Connors. You wouldn't call them hippies. They were just poor, people like that. They kept pretty much to themselves. When they did come to town to stock up on stuff, they left again just as quickly. They didn't hang around in the street, talking and playing the guitar. And they weren't the slightest bit colourful. In fact, they were all one colour, the O'Connors: their clothes, thongs, kero cans, the soles of their feet were all stained the same dull orange-brown, the colour of the water they washed in. Joanne remembered how scared the little O'Connor kids were back in primary school. They looked pained if the teacher spoke to them and made tiny coughing noises in their throats. You'd think they'd never been to Repentance, never worn a pair of shoes, before the authorities roped them in and dragged them to the classroom, wild-eyed and blubbering like calves.

The hippie kids were nothing like that. The complete opposite, in fact. They'd been everywhere, they'd seen everything, they were cocky and smart in class. *Knowing* was the word her Aunty Peg used, or *a bit too old in the head*, phrases followed by a slow compression of her mouth and chin. It was a distinction Joanne grappled with as she observed both types from behind the counter of her father's shop. Mrs Phelps, her history teacher, had summed it up for her one day, watching the O'Connor kids follow their dad out the door.

'In the end,' she told Joanne, 'it all boils down to choice. You can live with no electricity at the end of a rough dirt road. The difference lies in where you come from, not where you finish up.'

The air on that Tuesday afternoon was typically warm and still. The smoke from the mill's incinerator hung like a rag in the sky. Women sniffed at their sheets on the line and considered doing a rewash, and all over town people muttered about the need for rain.

Another timber truck rattled past. Joanne watched the heat resettle on the road like puddles of silver jelly. She squinted towards the forest, where thick clouds were often brewing by this time of the afternoon, but today there were none. There was nothing fresh about this spring. It felt tired and stale already. Biting down on her iceblock, she thought about her mother and felt a smarting ache behind the eyes.

Chapter Two

'Da-daaah!'

Linda darted across the hot bitumen and flumped into the driver's seat, clutching the packet of Drum like a trophy.

Melanie was unimpressed. 'You told her off then, did you?'

'Too right I did.'

'Muum, it's not her fault. It's her dad who makes the rules.'

Linda shrugged and tossed the mail on the floor at Melanie's feet. 'It's stupid, that's all. I can't stand the hypocrisy. You know who her father is, don't you?'

'Yeah.'

'He's that dickhead on the Council.'

'Mum, I know.'

'He's a total arsehole, that man. And what's her name, the girl in there?'

'Joanne Parmenter.'

'Parmenter, that's right, Ray Parmenter. Is she in your class?'

'Yeah.'

'She's smart, then?'

'I suppose. She's good at stuff like English, but she's more of a swot than a brain. She's a bit of dag, to tell the truth. I don't think she's got many friends.'

Linda grinned as she dabbed her tongue along the edge of a

cigarette paper. 'It was her father who got Andy and Jane kicked out of their place last year.'

'I know.'

'He's a bigot, that man. He won't want you making friends with his daughter, you can be sure of that.'

'Who said I'm making friends with her? We barely even speak. She's in my class and on my bus, so what?'

Linda lit the cigarette and, settling back in her seat, pulled the smoke gratefully into her lungs. She looked across at the shop and, for a moment, thought she saw the girl watching them through the front window.

'So, what do you reckon she is, then, Mel?'

'What do you mean?'

'I'm thinking some kind of mouse.'

'Don't.'

'Little fat face, pouchy cheeks, definitely some kind of rodent. A bandicoot.'

'Will you stop it?'

'What?'

Melanie turned away in a huff. 'A bandicoot's a marsupial, anyway.'

'What are you saying?'

'It's not a rodent.'

'It can be both.'

'Nope.'

'Kangaroo rats.'

'Marsupial.'

Linda stared at her daughter. What was the matter with her? She liked this game. It cracked her up. They'd been playing it all the way up the coast. Just last week, the Repentance butcher: an alligator — perfect! The two of them had almost pissed themselves as they walked out of his shop. Linda tossed the last of her rollie and leant forward to start the car. It took three jiggles of the ignition to get it going.

'Her mother's dying,' Melanie said as the engine roared into life.

Linda's knuckles tightened on the wheel. 'Who told you that?'

'The kids at school. She's there, in the house, out the back.'

Linda craned to see down the side of the shop. The house behind it jutted into the grassy yard, a plain weatherboard place with ugly aluminium windows. She pictured a woman lying on the other side of that wall. A woman much older than she was, her eyes closed against the light, her temples throbbing in the heat. Mrs Parmenter. Linda frowned. She wasn't sure if she'd ever seen her in the shop. A few different people worked in there; she didn't know their names. What if the woman was dying at this very moment? Would you be able to tell? Linda gazed intently at the sky above the house as if looking for signs of death, rising and spiralling in the warm afternoon air.

'What's she dying of?'

'I dunno. Cancer, I think.'

Linda slapped the gearstick with the palm of her hand and dragged the car off the gravel.

'Well,' she said, with a shake of her head. 'I don't know anything about that.'

They drove up Main Street in silence. Past the butcher and the hardware store with its sacks of smelly chicken pellets stacked on the front veranda. They saw their housemate Jane sitting on her rug on the pavement. Melanie waved to her, but she wasn't looking. Trish's Unisex Hairdressing, the BP station. They idled at the top of the hill, in the beery breath of the pub, before turning onto the Balbirnie road.

'I've got to do a project with her.'

'Who?'

'Joanne Parmenter. The teacher put us together.'

'Why?'

'Because we live close, I dunno. We've got to choose a local industry and study its history. We've got to do a presentation and a display, like a diorama or something.'

'So what are you going to do? Not forestry, I hope.'

Melanie grinned. 'Joanne suggested that. Her sister works at the mill. But no, don't worry, we're not doing it. We're doing the dairy industry.'

'That's not much better in Gerard's book.'

'Who cares what Gerard thinks? It's kind of nice — butter and stuff — and there's heaps of information. We've got an excursion to the museum. You've got to sign a note.'

'I wish you'd learn something useful at that school.'

'You're the one making me go there. Anyhow, I mightn't have to do it yet. It's not due till the end of term. We'll be gone by then, won't we?'

Linda winced and adjusted the sun visor.

'Won't we, Mum?'

'Yeah, okay. But you can't just leave it to someone else, Mel. That's not fair.'

They turned abruptly onto one of the narrow ribbons of bitumen that wound into the hills. These would be dirt roads anywhere else, but this was dairying country and they were sealed for the milk tankers. Not that many milk trucks came out this way anymore. The further you travelled from the main road, the more the soft edges of the bitumen broke away like biscuit and longs wands of lantana whipped you on the bends.

The road ran along the flats beside the creek to begin with, past lichen-tufted cattle yards and the cream-can letterboxes of the farming families living on either side. Hennessy, Gibson, Byrnes, Sneath: their names were painted on the cans. Their houses sat on short stumps halfway up the slopes, surrounded by buckled concrete paths and ugly chain-wire fences. They were unadorned, the farmhouses in these parts, their clapboard walls painted some unremarkable shade of pastel and their front verandas often closed in with fibro and frosted glass.

Gerard's house was one of these old dairying homesteads. Plain and draughty, it sat nestled in a garland of shrubs on the crown of a red-dirt hill, overlooking its disused dairy and stony cattle yards choked with thistles and lantana. The surrounding pasture was a bright acid green. It grew thick in Gerard's front paddock with no livestock to eat it down and drenched you up to your knees in the early morning. Kikuyu, Gerard told them it was, on their first morning there. A grass from fucking Africa, a bastard of a thing. Linda had read the disappointment on Melanie's face. These rolling, folding hills were lush and beautiful. You didn't want to know that they were somehow unethical or wrong. You didn't want to hear about the ancient scrub that used to cover the region before it was supplanted by fucking foreign grasses. Better to imagine yourself rolling down the cushiony slope, over and over, grass and sky, all the way to the creek at the bottom.

Kikuyu grass had become the first entry on a list of 'forbidden things' that Linda and Melanie secretly loved about this place. It would soon be joined by the sherbet clusters of lantana flowers, the billowing camphor laurel trees, and the frothy white crofton weed that lined the creeks in the spring.

Another item on that list was Wayne Mackenzie's farm, but only from a distance, as it appeared looking across the creek from the northern end of Gerard's front veranda. The red iron roof and whitewood fences, the dark triangle of a Cyprus pine rising up behind it. It was picture perfect from that angle, like a farmhouse in a tapestry or children's book, its neat paddocks scattered with placid Jersey cows. But for Gerard, that farm was everything that was wrong with the agriculture in these parts. There wasn't a single native tree growing on the place, and those velvety fields were nothing more than the product of superphosphate. As for Mackenzie's cows, they were a bleeding menace, breaking down the fragile banks of the creek, stirring up the mud, destroying the earth's atmosphere with their voluminous farts. Linda had hooted with laughter when Melanie told her that one. Don't worry, she told her daughter, you can like them if you want. It was really Wayne Mackenzie that Gerard couldn't stand.

He was a known hippie-hater — that was the term they used — a regular on the letters page of the local paper. His pet hate was farmers renting out their unused houses and dairies to the likes of Gerard and his friends. It was happening everywhere, it was a total disgrace, and perfectly good farming land was going to the pack.

Linda had met Wayne Mackenzie just the once, when he came up to the house one day and asked to speak to Gerard. To begin with, the two men had maintained a sneering civility.

'Gerard.'

'Mr Mackenzie.'

'Just a couple of things.'

He'd gone on to list the state of their fences, the cars coming past his place, how someone didn't shut the gate, how their dog was worrying his cows. Gerard agreed to discuss his concerns with the rest of the household and to raise the matter of the broken fences with their landlord, Bill.

But then Wayne Mackenzie had broached the issue of noxious weeds and the need to spray certain ones that were poisonous to livestock. Gerard's response was swift and, in Linda's view, extreme.

'Fuck your bloody cattle,' he bawled. 'You're not spraying that shit around here. Do you know what's in that herbicide? Do you want me to poison the creek?'

Half an hour after Wayne Mackenzie had retreated down the road, Gerard was still stomping around the house, muttering under his breath about that stupid fuckwit and his fucking 2,4-D.

Melanie looked apprehensive as they drove towards the Mackenzies' farm and found the evening milking in full swing. The two gates on the road were shut to form a kind of holding paddock at the back of the bales. Melanie had to open them, one by one, and stand there while Linda drove through. They both disliked this part of the drive home — the stink of fresh manure, the throb of the milking machine.

They didn't like the feeling that Wayne Mackenzie was around the place watching them. Sometimes they caught a glimpse of him through one of the dairy doors, or saw him down in the yards. He would turn his head at the sound of their car and then quickly look away. When their eyes did happen to meet, Melanie gave a hesitant wave, but he never once responded. Today his kelpie barked at her and came and sniffed her hand. 'Get out of it,' he bellowed from somewhere inside, calling the dog away.

'There's your research subject,' Linda said as Melanie opened the car door. Her daughter didn't respond but grabbed instead for the Kodak packet on the floor.

'Oh yeah, I forgot to say. Your photos have come back.'

Melanie tore it open and flipped through the shiny prints as they bumped across the causeway and started the final climb towards the house. She paused and snickered to herself. Linda glanced at the photo on top. It was a bunch of schoolgirls, Melanie's friends at Holbrook Central, all of them laughing and one of them flashing a bright-pink training bra.

'That was my last day,' Melanie said. 'Francine and Margi.'

'They were silly girls.'

'They were not! You didn't even know them.'

'What's that one there?'

'Which one?'

'The one you're covering up?'

Melanie pouted and then lifted her hands. 'It's you in that milk bar in Taree, where you didn't like the man.'

'Hah! I told you that wouldn't work out. Too much backlight, see?'

Melanie crammed the photos back into the packet and folded her hands on top. The road was now two unsteady lines of rotten rock with a central ridge of tussock that brushed beneath the car. As they rounded the final curve, the giant fig tree that stood behind the house rose up before them, its sweeping boughs extended like the arms of the dancing Vishnu. Andy and Jane's little dingo pup came running towards them, yapping.

'I'm going skittle that dog one day,' Linda said as she pulled up on the grass next to Andy's motorbike.

There was no sign of Gerard as they came through the house, but the light was on in the lounge room and his stuff was strewn across the table in the corner. His trouble-making stuff, Linda called it — duplicated documents, topographic maps, numerous cold cups of tea beside his old typewriter.

Melanie headed straight to their room, dragging her schoolbag, with the photos tucked under her arm. Linda went to follow but stopped in the hall to listen for sounds of someone home. There were five people living in the house now and still one empty bedroom. Gerard was keeping that, he said, for someone who could pay full rent. This left Linda and Melanie sharing a room, the closed-in veranda on the fig-tree side of the house. It was unlined and unbearably hot at certain times of the day. Most of the glass louvres were difficult to open, their metal levers gummed up with the sooty fallout from the tree. It wasn't ideal, but then again, they'd arrived here with almost no warning. It was lucky that Gerard had room for them at all. Linda had an idea of about how she'd like the bedroom situation to resolve itself. It might take a bit of time, but she was patient. For now, the two of them had to be content with arrangements as they were — the long, hot, narrow room with a single bed, a wardrobe, and a mattress on the floor.

Linda tapped on Gerard's bedroom door. No answer. She pushed it open and looked inside. It was pretty much as she expected: a futon on the floor, a clothes rack, guitars against the wall, a Doors poster above the bed, its corners eaten by Blu Tack. The room smelt musty and male, like sweaty coins and unwashed sheets. A door slammed somewhere and she jumped. It might have been the wind, but she quickly stepped back into the hall and closed the door very quietly.

Back in the kitchen she put on the kettle and searched for tea in the cupboard. She pushed aside Jane's jars of weird leaves and bits of bark, Japanese green tea, Indian chai, licorice something-or-other. At the back she found a box of Lipton's. Thank God for that. She shook some into the smaller of the two teapots on the bench and poured in the boiling water.

She and Mel were starting to feel more settled here now. The DSS had finally redirected Linda's payments, and in Balbirnie that afternoon she'd managed to withdraw enough money to pay Gerard some rent and a small share of the bond. She hoped this might make her position in the house a little more legitimate and make others less hostile towards her, but then again, those currents ran deep. Jane gave the appearance of being nice but sat in judgement of others. She seemed determined to live like a medieval peasant and expected everyone around her to do the same. Linda had come across her type before, women so committed to returning to the earth that they were prepared to throw away all the gains of women's lib and turn themselves into drudges. Washing by hand, carting water, making their own soap and candles, for God's sake. Jane looked exhausted half the time, much older than her twenty-seven years. There was something slow and ponderous about her, something almost bovine, and those hands of hers, already cracked and roughened by the washing and gardening, were now being further desiccated by the pottery she was turning out on a hand wheel in the dairy. She wore gathered skirts made of a thick and roughly woven cotton that did nothing for her heavy hips and bottom. Her demeanour of weary patience got under Linda's skin. The polite enquiry and tilt of her head, the slow lift of her brow. And all that sage advice on stuff she knew nothing about. Parenting, for instance. Melanie's welfare. She clearly had misgivings about their presence in the house and was always asking about their plans to travel on.

A spade dragged on concrete outside the kitchen window. Was Jane home already? She must have got a lift from town almost straightaway. Or maybe not. Linda glanced at the clock and realised she had lost track of time, sitting slumped in her chair at the kitchen table. She touched her mug of tea and found it almost cold. As she tossed it down the sink, in contravention of house rules, she heard the dragging spade again, and peered through the kitchen window. Sure enough, there was Mother Earth herself, toiling in the vegetable garden.

Jane looked up, and Linda gave her a guilty wave. 'What are you planting?' she called out.

'Come out and see.'

Friendly, yes, okay then. Linda picked up Gerard's mull box and went out the back.

'This is looking really good,' she said, surveying the garden beds. 'You're doing a great job here, you and Andy.'

Jane pushed on the spade with her gumboot. 'Yeah, it's hard work, though. The soil here isn't as good as it looks. You'd think it'd be so fertile, this red volcanic dirt, but the water runs right through it like a sieve.'

Linda looked at the zigzags of pumpkin vine and the raucous bursts of nasturtium. It seemed to her that the garden was thriving.

'Yeah,' Jane drawled, unconvinced. 'Some things do okay, but the pests here, they're really bad. I'm giving up on brassicas.'

'I burnt mine years ago,' said Linda, sitting down on the back steps and opening the box of mull.

Jane gave her a pallid smile.

'Do you want some of this, Jane? Come on, take a break.'

'I've got to get this parsley planted. I haven't had a chance this week. I've been doing the jewellery stall.'

In the tray beside her, the seedlings lay like bits of limp green cotton.

Linda patted the step beside her. 'Sit down for a sec, come on, and then I'll come and help you. I like gardening — I do — and it's better after a smoke, don't you find? You can really get into it then.'

Jane shook her head and leant back into her work.

'I got the money for the bond today,' Linda continued brightly.

'Oh!' Now she stopped. 'So you're staying, then?'

'For a little while, yeah, why not?'

'What about Toona Bay?'

'What about it?'

'Melanie seems to think that you're going very soon. At the end of next month, she told me. I have to say, I was surprised, given what's happened up there, but Melanie didn't mention it, so I gathered things must have settled down.'

'You mean the police raid?'

'Yes, I do. It was pretty ugly.'

'Yeah.'

'They used a helicopter. They burnt people's houses down.'

'It was months ago.'

'It was August.'

'I'm sure it's all right now. I was planning to get there by Christmas, but there's stingers at that time of year and you can't even swim.'

'Maybe you should tell Melanie. She seems a bit confused. She's been telling me all about it: about the fires on the beach and the snorkelling and stuff, all the kids hanging out together. She hasn't mentioned the raid, so I haven't said anything, but I'm not sure it's a good place to be taking a child right now.'

'I'll deal with Melanie, thanks very much,' Linda said tartly. She pulled a clump of sticky brown leaves from the box and crumbled them into the bowl on her lap with a hairy wad of tobacco. 'Also, I was thinking —' She rubbed the mix with her fingers. 'Gerard could do with some help right now, with this forest thing.'

'You're gonna help him with that?'

'I am helping. Did you see the poster I did? We used to do this kind of stuff when we were at uni together. In Hobart, the Student Union, he was president. I used to help with their magazine, and banners, stuff like that. We go back a long way, you know, me and Gerard.'

'So I believe.'

Linda felt a prickle of discomfort. She wondered what conversations happened in this house when she and Melanie weren't there. What did Gerard say about her, about their past relationship, about Hobart and her mother and the events of thirteen years ago up at Toona Bay? Gerard's soapstone box slid off her knee and a small lump of hash fell under the wooden steps. She looked down between her knees and saw Andy's little dingo pup snuffling his way towards it.

'Get out of it!' she hissed, trying to kick him with her toe. 'Shit,' she muttered as the puppy wolfed it down.

Jane couldn't see what was happening, but she heard Linda talking to the dog, and whistled for him to come. He squeezed through a hole beside the tap and bounded over to her. Linda put the lid on the box and pushed it behind her back.

'Have you given that dog a name yet?'

'Donovan,' Jane said.

She rolled the puppy onto its back and rubbed its fuzzy belly. Andy had found the poor little thing on a recent trip to Queensland. It looked like its mother had taken a poison bait. Remembering this, Linda felt a spasm of dismay. What could hash do to a dog that small? It was only a little bit. She decided to go and smoke the joint on the front veranda instead.

This was her favourite place to be at this time of day, when the light grew dusky and the currawongs flew across the valley, gulping at the air. Across the creek Wayne Mackenzie's cows were returning to their paddocks, shrieking for their calves. Linda settled into the grimy cushions on the swing seat and felt something sharp against her thigh. It was the corner of the Kodak packet. Melanie had been out here. Linda tipped the photos onto the seat beside her and sorted through them, smiling to herself.

Mel and her little Instamatic — it was all she had wanted last

Christmas. It was funny to see what a twelve-year-old girl considered worth recording. There were the silly school friends from Holbrook and a nice shot of their friend Louise outside her mudbrick cottage, where they had been staying for much of the past two years. How different the country was down south: the beige-brown fields, the silvered sheds and fences, those enormous skies. And here, again, was the picture of the milk bar in Taree. Melanie had taken meticulous records of their trip up north. She'd made extensive notes each night in an old exercise book, decorating the pages with pictures snipped from tourist brochures and leaving spaces for the photographs she took along the way. Mum in the milk bar in Taree. That would be the caption. You could see the sun-dazzled street outside with its strings of plastic bunting and Linda, silhouetted in the booth by the window, the sunlight blazing in the auburn ends of her hair.

Melanie had got chatting with the man behind the counter, blahing on about Toona Bay and how her mother used to live up there, that it was a kind of community, that they still had a week to drive, that they'd be taking a boat for the last little bit 'cause there were no roads to the bay.

'So, North Queensland,' the man had said, looking across at Linda as he pumped chocolate syrup into a cup. 'And what does a person do for work in a place like that then, eh?'

Melanie had misunderstood him and laughed. 'I'm still at school, you dope.' And then she'd gone on to explain that there were no schools up there, that the parents taught the kids, that her mum had studied teaching at uni, and English literature, and before that she was at art school, but she didn't finish her course.

Linda had called her over then and told her to sit down.

'People ask these questions, sweetie. They don't really want to know.'

Melanie had sat quietly for a while, sucking on the straw of her milkshake, before making a sudden grab for the camera.

And here it was, that photograph, hopelessly backlit as Linda had sourly predicted at the time. And there was another one too, the next picture in the pile. It was taken just a few minutes later, through the cafe window. Linda recognised herself in the phone box across the street. That was her call to Gerard — shit — that's when she made the call. Why on earth had Melanie taken a photo of that? It was a bit spooky really. She'd had no idea at the time who Linda was talking to, or that this was the moment when their plans would change.

Linda went to the bedroom. Melanie was lying on her mattress on the floor, her shoes and socks beside her.

'Get out of your uniform, will you, love? And move this school case before someone trips over it.'

'You mean my *port*,' Melanie said in a sarcastic voice. 'That's what they call them here — *ports*! They've even got a *port* room outside the hall at school.'

Linda perched on the end of her bed. 'That comes from French,' she said, smiling. '*Porter* means to carry.'

'I'll bet no one here knows that.'

'Come on, get that dress off.'

'I hate this uniform. Look at the size of it!' Mel stood in front of the mirror, holding the side seams taut like the pegged corners of a tent. Jane had found it for them. It had belonged to the daughter of a friend of hers, a heavy fourth-form girl called Tess, and it hung ridiculously large and loose on Melanie's lean frame.

'I could take it in,' Linda said. 'Come here, let's have a look.' She steered Melanie towards the mirror and began tugging at the seams.

'What's the point!' Melanie whined. 'I don't even want to go to that school. I don't see why I have to. We're only here for a couple of months. We'll be gone in a few weeks' time.'

'You'll grow into it, sweetie,' Linda replied. 'You're hitting puberty now.'

Melanie stared at her in the mirror, her eyes narrowing. 'What are you saying?'

Linda smiled stupidly and tried to pull her close.

'We're not going, are we?' Melanie snapped, wrenching herself free.

'Yes, of course we are. Just a bit later, that's all.'

Melanie bucked and threw herself onto the mattress, face down.

'Mel!'

Nothing. Just this angry, silent flump. Linda tried to sit next to her but she refused to make room.

'Just a bit longer. Come on, sit up. Maybe a couple of months. Just till the stingers have gone and you can swim in the sea.'

Melanie rolled onto her side, a tear puddling in the crease of her nose. That fierce little face of hers. She had her father's flecky green eyes, exactly the same as his, and his sandy complexion and pointy chin — a meerkat, prone to frowning. Lately, too, she'd been showing flashes of his impatience. The carefree child was giving way to a moody adolescent: unsatisfied and critical of her mother. But then, she was right to be upset. Linda did have a habit of changing course, of getting waylaid. This was their second attempt to go north, the first one having fizzled out with a broken radiator outside the town of Holbrook. But that wasn't so bad, was it? They'd had two great years with Louise, and when the time came to leave, it had been Melanie who was reluctant.

As the girl got to her feet, Linda pulled her into a hug. 'Just a couple of months,' she whispered into the lank blonde hair. 'It's always warm, it's not as though we're missing out on summer.' Melanie resisted and then gave in with a single juddering breath. They stood, holding each other, rocking to and fro, the mattress sinking beneath their feet like sand. A bird scratched in the gutter outside and the fig tree squeaked and groaned as the warm waters of Toona Bay gradually receded.

Chapter Three

A jeep pulled up outside the shop just before closing time. Joanne waited, but no one came inside. Through the window she saw a man pull out a small stepladder and set it up in the street, beside the telegraph pole. Up he climbed, struggling to position his thick leather sandals on the narrow steps while holding what looked like a poster and a roll of masking tape. He flung his arms around the pole, one hand groping for the tape he held in the other. His t-shirt rode up to reveal the top of his drawstring pants and a line of dark hair running down from his belly.

She'd seen this guy before. He used to come into the shop all the time, but not so much these days. He was very good looking, she thought, or would be if he wasn't so wild and hairy. There was something a bit frightening about him — or angry, that's what it was — he had dark, angry eyes. He never bought much, just came for his mail and he seemed to get heaps of that, lots of bulky brown paper envelopes and circulars. They had trouble sometimes, squeezing his letters into the pigeonhole. His last name was foreign, started with A, the kind of name you would struggle to pronounce unless you heard someone else say it.

It was seven o'clock. She was closing up. If he wanted his mail, too bad. She went out the front to retrieve the headline cages.

'Tell your father to leave these alone,' the man shouted at her. 'We know it's him pulling them down.'

Joanne squinted at the poster. It was hard to read in the fading light, the black ink on purple. She might have told him about the community noticeboard, but her dad had recently had the whole thing put behind glass. The hippies were taking it over, he said. The council approvals and fire-brigade numbers were being displaced by rainbow-coloured flyers for meditation classes, personal messages — *where are you Libby? I thought you said the 6th* — signs scrawled on feint-ruled paper advertising rooms for rent, each with a fringe of phone numbers to tear off and take away. Her dad said the whole board had looked as if it were tarred and feathered. He ripped the whole lot down and replaced it with a lockable cabinet.

The man tossed the ladder under the dusty flap at the back of his jeep. When he'd gone, Joanne went and took a closer look. RESCUE OUR RAINFOREST — COMMUNITY MEETING. Someone had drawn a fancy border around it in what looked like thick black texta, a twisted riot of leaves and vines and a butterfly or two. The girly prettiness of it sat strangely with the poster's strident announcement. It didn't look like the handiwork of the angry man. This was the second poster to go up in recent weeks. Barbara had taken the other one down and put it on the pile of newspapers in the corner of the kitchen. Joanne supposed she ought to do the same with this one too, before her father saw it and got all riled up. She fetched the wooden post-office steps and ripped at the masking tape. The paper was a really nice colour. It was thick, like card, and blank on the back. It seemed a waste to throw it away. She thought she might keep it for craft, for making birthday cards and stuff. She looked up the street to see if there were more.

Barbara was in their bedroom, bashing drawing pins into the wall with the wooden heel of her sandal. She was putting up her own poster, a large white one like a scroll with black plastic batons at each end.

'It's called *Desiderata*,' she told Joanne. 'I got it at the gift shop in town. I love it, don't you, and look, it's so old, 1692. They found it in an old church in America somewhere.'

Baltimore, it said at the bottom, Old Saint Paul's Church. Joanne had seen it before and recognised the large G at the beginning.

'*Go placidly amid the noise and haste, and remember what peace there may be in silence,*' Barbara quoted, her eyes closed. 'I'm going to learn it off by heart in bed.'

Joanne decided she would too. It was beautiful and so wise.

'Hellooo!' came a hooting call from the side porch.

'Aunty Peg,' Barb sighed, climbing down from the chair. 'She's bringing dinner. Tuesday. It'll be tuna mornay.'

Joanne flopped down on her bed. 'I hate her tuna mornay. Mum was going to get up, but she won't now, you watch. She never gets up when Peg comes and she's here all the time now.'

'Dad's her baby brother,' said Barbara sensibly. 'She wants to look after him.'

'Why? He can cook. And you can too, sort of.'

Barb laughed and tossed her sandal into the cupboard. Their Aunty Peg considered herself the matriarch of the Parmenter family, dismissing any claims from the wives of her two brothers. It was she who held the reins, as she saw it, who held the family together. But the girls saw her quite differently. In their minds her name dangled alone at the edge of the family tree with no lines, no reins, no nothing connecting her to the next generation.

'Mick reckons that if we were Catholic, she would be the family nun.'

'Mick who?'

'You think about it. She'd make a really good one. She never misses church, she's not married, and I'll bet she's never had sex.'

Barbara moved to the dressing table and began to brush her hair.

There was something in the sway of her hips, in the smugness of her smile, that made Joanne sit up and ask, 'Have you?'

The brushing stopped.

'Oh God, you have!'

'Shhh — shut up!'

'Michael Phelan!' Joanne squeaked, rolling onto her back and kicking her feet in the air.

Barbara grabbed her by the arm and glared at her. 'You tell anyone, I'll kill you.'

'Who would I tell?'

'Mum ... your friends? Oh no, that's right, you haven't got any.'

Joanne hugged her pillow to her chest and looked surreptitiously at the crotch of her sister's jeans. She thought with disgust of *The Godfather* — page twenty-seven. Their cousins had snuck them a copy from their Uncle Bill's study and it was still hidden under Joanne's bed.

'Are you there, girls?'

Barb looked at the door. 'We should go and say hello.'

'No,' said Joanne. She felt like being alone. It had been a trying afternoon. She felt overwhelmed and teary. Aunty Peg, the man with the poster, Melanie Curtis's mother, and now the big hulk of Michael Phelan pushing himself into Barb. *Avoid loud & aggressive persons; they are vexations to the spirit.* She lay curled on the bed after Barbara left, staring at the poster, until their father came and rapped on the bedroom door.

Sure enough, Delia Parmenter did not join the family for dinner. Instead Joanne carried her mother's meal into her room on a tray and set it on the hired metal table that straddled the bed. They were accumulating lots of furniture like this, cold and adjustable. The old spare room where Delia now spent much of the day and all her nights was slowly taking on the appearance of her room in the hospital.

'How are you, sweetie?' she asked from her crevice in the pillows.

There was a white crusty residue at one corner of her mouth, a combination of Mylanta and saliva.

Joanne kicked the brake on the table. 'Are you getting up later, Mum? Dad's made jelly.'

'I don't think so. I'm sorry, do you mind? The nurse has given me something, I think. I'm feeling very drowsy. I will eat some of this, though. It looks nice.'

'Tuna mornay,' Joanne said.

'Your Aunty Peg's very kind doing all this cooking for us.'

'I don't like her mornay. It's sloppy. I like the way you make it.'

Delia winced as she pulled herself upright in the bed. Joanne moved in swiftly to push the pillows behind her back, taking care to avoid the tube hanging down from the drip-stand.

'This could come out now,' Delia said, pressing at the bruised skin around the cannula in her arm. 'It was Judy today, did Dad tell you?'

Joanne glanced up at the bag of fluids hanging from the stand.

'I like Judy, much more than that male nurse they send sometimes. I don't like it when he comes.'

'It's hot in here, Mum. Do you want me to open the window?'

'How was school?'

Joanne blinked. School felt like a long time ago. 'Okay. I'm doing a history project on the dairy industry. I thought Uncle Bill could help.'

'He's got beef cattle now.'

'But still — he worked with Grandma all those years. I thought there might be stuff in the old dairy we could use.'

'You like school, don't you, Jo?'

'No.'

Her mother reached for her hand. 'You do, and you don't want to leave like Barbara did. She was in such a hurry and then she had trouble finding work. They're letting all these men into nursing now. There aren't the jobs there used to be for girls.'

The anniversary clock on the chest of drawers chimed under its fine glass dome. Joanne watched the four golden balls spin this way and that. Turning back to her mother, she found her gazing at a tall flower standing among the clutter on her bedside table. It was a stem of gladiolus, salmon pink, stuck in a block of floral foam and looking set to topple in its flimsy plastic pot.

'That's pretty. Who brought you that?'

Delia shook her head. 'I don't know, but isn't it lovely? Look at that wonderful pink.'

The rapture in her mother's voice made Joanne uneasy. Delia was breathing too quickly and staring too intently at the flower.

'You can't see it properly from there, Jo. Come over here —'

'Mum, I can.'

'That creamy pink inside it, look, like the inside of a shell.'

Joanne nodded. It's the morphine talking, said Aunty Peg's voice inside her head. This had been happening a lot lately, these moments when her mother seemed almost a bit possessed. Maybe it was time to disconnect that tube.

All of a sudden Delia hoisted herself from the pillows and lunged at the flower, knocking the hospital table with her knees and sending her knife and fork spinning across the floor.

'Mum!'

Joanne grabbed her by the shoulders and eased her back to the bed. Delia looked bewildered, wild-eyed, as though she had frightened herself. Her wilting finger continued to point at the place where the flower had been.

'Are you coming?' Ray called from the kitchen.

'Off you go, darling. I'll be fine. Go and have your tea. You can bring me some of that jelly later, if you like. And you can open the window too. It's very muggy, isn't it? Do you think it's going to storm?'

Joanne opened the flyscreen and pushed up the aluminium frame. They were new, these windows, easy care. You didn't have to paint them.

'We could use the rain,' her mother said, her voice suddenly normal as if she were making small talk with someone in the shop. Joanne felt the mild relief of the evening air on her cheeks and smelt the cloying sweetness of the night jasmine. She would have liked to have stood there longer, listening to the tiny chucking of frogs in the grass and watching Mr Blainey next door move his garden hose.

'Joanne!' Her dad again.

She almost stepped on the gladiolus as she went to leave the room. It had fallen from the bedside table and was lying in the middle of the floor, its fleshy stem still fixed inside the concrete boot of sponge, but bent in the middle. Joanne retrieved the plastic pot from underneath the bed and crouched beside the flower where her mother couldn't see what she was doing. Some of the petals were bruised and two of the smaller trumpets were missing from the top of the spike. Her first thought was to take it out to the kitchen. Aunty Peg did the flowers for the church and could put it back to rights. But this was not a good idea. Peg would want to know what happened and Joanne wouldn't want to say. Instead she snapped the stem off at the point where it was broken and pushed the flower back into the pot herself. She decided not to return it to the bedside table. Her mother might see the damage and go all weird again, see the injured trumpets gasping for breath and black beetles crawling from their salmon-speckled throats.

No, Joanne thought, looking around the room. She set the pot on the chest of drawers by the anniversary clock.

The three of them were waiting for her at the kitchen table. Peg's hands were folded, ready for grace. Ray mumbled his way through it, and they began to eat, intently at first and without conversation, their cutlery making paths through the thick beige sauce and scratching on the sandy glaze of the brightly patterned plates.

Peg peered between her knife and fork. 'Where did these plates come from?'

'Big W,' Barbara said. 'Mum got them at the sales.'

'But you have the family china, Ray. What's wrong with that?'

'Nothing,' Ray said, moving quickly to fill his mouth with mornay.

'Mum liked these ones,' Barbara said. 'They're nice, don't you think? Earthenware, just for everyday.'

'That's right.' Ray coughed, reaching for the salt. 'She's keeping the other for best.'

'Oh.' Peg lifted her bread-and-butter plate and inspected the mark underneath it. 'That looks Japanese to me.'

'It is.'

Barbara caught Joanne's eye and smirked.

'Well, I can't say I like them much. A bit gaudy for my taste.'

'Mum loves orange,' Joanne said. It was true, she did. It was her new favourite colour. At the June sales, she'd bought both girls a set of orange sheets and a large burnt-orange pottery vase for the lounge room. Even the last dress she'd bought herself was a mottle of tiny orange and apricot flowers, a flowing maxi dress in a soft, bubbly fabric that the girls considered to be unusually groovy for their mum.

Peg dabbed at her mouth with her napkin. 'I can't for the life of me see what's wrong with your grandmother's Johnson china. It did her perfectly well for sixty-odd years.'

'Speaking of her —' Ray looked at Barb. 'What does Sandy think about this meeting?'

'They put another poster up,' Joanne chimed in. 'I took it down.' She pointed at the newspaper pile in the corner.

'He's thinking of going,' Barb replied.

'You're kidding.'

'No, I'm not. It says *community* meeting on the poster.'

'Where are they holding it?' Peg asked.

'At the Braemar Hall.'

'All the way out there?'

'Yeah, they don't want people like us to go, that's why.'

Joanne looked at her father. 'What's this got to do with Grandma? Speaking of her, you said.'

'He lives in her house,' Ray said, 'the bloke who's organising it. The mad-looking one, what's his name? Gets his mail from here.'

'Gerard someone,' Barbara said. 'He's always phoning the mill. Sandy met with him a couple of times, but he's really sick of him now.'

'He lives in Grandma's house?' Joanne gasped. The man up the telegraph pole.

Aunty Peg sniffed and placed her scrunched-up napkin on the table. 'I said they'd be trouble, didn't I, Ray? I've said that all along. I don't know what Bill was thinking, renting it to people like that.'

'You can't really blame Uncle Bill,' Barbara said. 'No one else would rent the place in that condition.'

'What do you mean?' Peg said huffily. 'It's a lovely old house.'

'Come on, it's pretty basic. It's got an outside bathroom.'

'It has not. It's attached to the house.'

'You've got to walk outside to get there. Remember that, Joanne? How much we used to hate going down that path in the dark? I used to wee in a pot plant so I wouldn't have to go.'

'Barbara!'

Joanne giggled. 'It's true, she did. In Grandma's Chinese jade.'

She remembered the bathroom so clearly: its corrugated-iron roof and concrete floor, its dark, dank atmosphere and the copper in the corner. There was a bathtub on clawed feet that took about an hour to fill. And the thing that heated the water, that gas thing on the wall, the whooof it made when you stuck the match in, it used to scare the life out of Joanne when she was little.

She tried to imagine that Gerard guy standing there cleaning his teeth, to picture him inside the house, moving from room to room. All the details of the place came flooding back to her: the kitchen with its yellow nylon curtains kicking in the breeze and the fluorescent light on the high ceiling that took so long to come on. The lounge room was always dark, even in the middle of the day, closed in by part of the veranda that served as her grandmother's sewing room. Joanne used to sit out there on the rose-patterned lino, playing cake shops with the contents of her grandma's button tin. On the lid of the tin was a photograph of two girls in national dress, with bright-red mouths and long coloured ribbons in their hair. Inside were all the buttons that her grandma had saved over the years, some cut from old clothes and others still bound to their pieces of card. There was a set of yellow duckling buttons snipped from a baby's cardigan, and big pearly ones that served as meringues in Joanne's shop. The flat leather studs were rock cakes, and the swirly red and white ones, cream buns with glacé cherries. She'd arrange them in careful rows, chatting to an imaginary shopgirl, the two of them frantically preparing for the morning rush. When everything was ready, she'd call for the doors to be opened, admitting the crowds of customers waiting outside in the street.

An awful thought occurred to her.

'There's no one living in the dairy, is there, Dad?'

Her father shook his head.

'There could be, Ray, for all we know.' Peg began to collect their plates and scrape them onto hers. 'He's rented the whole side of the hill, all the way down to the creek. Why he did that, I have no idea. It's not like they need it for livestock. According to Fay Mackenzie, the place looks a real mess, all the weeds and long grass. And Bill doesn't have the faintest idea what they're up to. I've told him to go and check on them, but he doesn't, he won't. And Janine doesn't give two hoots about the place.'

Five years before, when Joanne's grandmother died, her Uncle Bill and his wife had divided the deeds of the farm and built themselves a new house on the other side of the hill. Peg and Ray had never been happy with the plan, but there wasn't a lot they could do about it. Bill was the oldest son, Janine was his wife, and that was that, as far as the rest of the family's feelings were concerned. That Janine had never liked the old house was no secret. A dump, she'd called it on that memorable Christmas Day when they had all gathered there for lunch. After the pudding, she and Bill had presented their plans for a new AV Jennings home, brick and tile with a large pebblecrete porch for entertaining. They were getting out of dairying and going into beef instead and building a new driveway up the western side of the hill.

But it was the plan to rent out the old house that really got Peg's wind up. She had blown her stack in the car on their way home. Janine was only interested in money. As though she and Bill hadn't been left enough — the house, the farm, a prizewinning herd of milkers. It wasn't her ancestral home being rented out to strangers. It wasn't her mother who'd collapsed and died on that dairy floor. She had no respect for the Parmenter name, no sense of family history.

Joanne had heard all this many times before, *and* the fact that the tenants were hippies and that was a disgrace. Until now, however, she hadn't known who was living there. No wonder Peg was angry. That Gerard guy was trying to get the mill shut down.

'So why are they having this meeting now?'

Barbara rolled her eyes. 'There's a new section opening up, the northern side of the basin. It's just bush, but the hippies are calling it rainforest and getting everyone all worked up.'

Joanne looked at her in dismay. 'Not the pretty bit beside the creek?'

'No! See what I mean? You're as bad as them. We're not touching that bit. We just had to put the road through there, that's all. This is the shit they're talking.'

'Barbara!' said Peg.

'That's good. I like that bit,' Joanne said. 'All the palms and moss, like a jungle.'

'And even up the top, we're only selective logging. It's not like we're chopping the whole lot down.'

Peg got up from her chair and began to fill the sink. 'It's funny, all this talk about the forest out there. All these people bushwalking, having picnics all of a sudden. No one ever went out there before this trouble started. Now it's become this precious place and we're spoiling it.'

A bubble of sound came wobbling down the hall. Ray pushed back his chair and went to the box of medications beside the fridge. Peg watched, arms folded, lips pursed, waiting for him to leave the room.

'They're not controlling this thing,' she said to the girls over the hissing tap. 'I told your father this morning, she needs to go back to the hospital.'

'No!' Joanne snapped. 'She doesn't want to go back.'

'That's all very well, dear, but the nurse has been in twice today and she's still not comfortable. And the morphine's making her funny. It's upsetting for everyone. I think it's getting beyond us now, that's all I'm going to say.'

'It's got nothing to do with you.' Joanne's voice trembled with rage.

Peg appeared to capitulate. Her hands moved swiftly inside the hot rubber gloves, dunking and scrubbing and rinsing and plonking things onto the draining board. Barbara and Joanne wiped up in silence, their ears tuned to the muffled voices down the hall.

Ray came back to the kitchen and put some jelly onto a plate. 'Never too sick for jelly,' he said, giving Joanne a wink.

Joanne smiled with relief and felt a rubbery slap on her wrist. She nearly dropped the teacup she was drying.

'That's Lena!' Peg snapped, snatching the cup from her and re-placing it, upside down on the sudsy draining board.

'It's the leaning cup,' Barbara said in a sarcastic whisper.

'Where's the washing-up rack gone?' Joanne opened the bottom cupboard.

'You don't need that,' Peg said, shutting the door with her knee. 'Lena works perfectly well as long as no one moves her.'

'Fuck Lena!' Joanne shouted.

Peg and Barbara stared at her. She stood rigid with fury, fighting the impulse to pick up the cup and hurl it against the wall.

'Thank you, Joanne,' Peg said primly. 'I think you should go to your room.'

'And I think you should go and get fucked!' Joanne flung the tea towel onto the bench and blundered down the hall.

Barbara stood at the bedroom door, her eyes wide, her hand clamped over her mouth.

'Shut up,' Joanne whimpered through a slime of tears. 'What's wrong with the way we wash up?'

Joanne buried her head in her pillow and felt Barbara sit beside her on the bed. For a moment she thought that her sister was crying too; she could feel her body trembling. She sat up and stared at her. Barb shook her head. She was, in fact, shaking with laughter.

'What's so funny?'

'Nothing,' Barbara gasped as the paroxysm eased. Out in the kitchen Aunty Peg was opening and shutting doors. Joanne started to giggle too and tumbled against her sister.

'Fuck Lena!' Barbara sputtered. 'God, what on earth were you thinking?'

'Same as you,' Joanne said, wiping her eyes with the back of her hand. She remained nestled against Barbara's chest, breathing the sharp green scent of her Jean Naté.

They were both thinking the same thing, that they had entered the end game and their Aunty Peg was preparing to make her move. Any day now, her Triumph would be parked in their garage, its roof rack piled high with her belongings.

Chapter Four

Linda loved that first part of the forest. They left Gerard's jeep by the side of the road and came in via a narrow path that snaked through a thicket of lantana. Then a warm, still space opened up before them like a grand salon, under a vaulted ceiling of palms. Bangalows, Gerard said, striding ahead of her. She could hear the quiet scratch of their fronds overhead. Sunlight fluttered through them, just a little here and there, piercing the musty gloom and falling in dazzling patches on the empty forest floor. She could hardly see the path at this point, in the absence of undergrowth. It was just a vague compression in the muddy ground and glimpses of Gerard moving through the grey pillars of the palms.

The trees rose up and closed over them, and cicadas screamed above the roar of running water. The path was wet and rocky now, and lawyer canes ripped their skin as they pushed their way through to the creek. Sitting beside it Linda felt a brief sense of relief, the sound of the bubbling water pushing the forest back and freshening the heavy air. But the feeling of menace returned as they set off again, not helped by Gerard's pointing out of the various plants and insects. Stinging trees, strangler figs, those fucking thorny caper things. She panicked every time she lost sight of him, as though some hostile vine was going to hook itself around her and pull her into the spidery hollow of a tree.

The forest opened out a little as they left the valley floor and made their way up the northern wall of the basin. Linda found it less oppressive, although the walking became more difficult without any kind of track and there was probably a greater risk of snakes. Gerard was well ahead of her. From this distance he appeared to be marching up the slope, his knees lifting high inside his khaki shorts, his feet in sturdy elastic-sided work boots. He carried a small canvas bag slung across his chest like a satchel and paused every now and then to extract things from its pockets — a small pair of binoculars, a Spirex pad and pencil stub — struggling all the while to keep his footing in the slipping leaf litter.

Sweat trickled down Linda's neck and stung at the point where the tiny hooks of the lawyer cane had caught her. She stroked the raised welt with her finger. At least the plants up here weren't as vicious as the ones by the creek. Ahead of her, Gerard tipped back his head and squinted into the branches, his ears reaching for the scuffle of a bird. An upward rush of white-headed pigeons, the flip and curtsy of a fantail. Out of nowhere the note of the whipbird swelling and falling through the air like a drop of bright water. Into the notebook they all went, along with the names of the trees. The more notable specimens he marked as crosses on a pencil sketch of the valley to be transferred to his map when they got home.

He was taking her up to what he called the turning bay at end of the new access road still under construction. The bulldozers had been cutting through the basin for weeks already, following the route of an old fire trail that zigzagged up the valley wall, turning in a series of hairpin bends just wide enough to accommodate a jinker. Towards the top, the road levelled out and skirted the neck of the basin, crossing over a series of dry gullies and terminating in a wide, flat, circular excavation carved into the hillside.

Gerard and Linda could have taken the newly graded road — it would have been much easier — or they could have approached the turning bay from above. Gerard knew Joel Spender, the man who owned the land on the other side of the ridge. A walking track led from his flats up into the bush and over the top of the hill. This track had become Gerard's preferred route into the forest since the road-works began, allowing him to avoid the scrutiny of the road crews and forestry workers coming in and out on the gravel road from Repentance.

Today he was taking a different path again, entering the forest down the bottom, just beyond the point where the new road began, and climbing straight up the northern wall of the basin. He wanted to acquaint himself with the terrain on this side of the valley, which included a large section marked for the logging. He needed to explain it to people, to know it like the back of his hand. He wanted to convey the full scale of the massacre to come, to photograph every magnificent tree destined for the chop.

As they climbed he described the changing vegetation: the wet rainforest at the bottom, the buffer zone of sclerophyll forest they were passing through now, blending into the smaller, dryer eucalypt brush at the top. Each time Linda caught up with him, the lecture continued. He pointed out the creamy pink bark of the brush box trees, the bloodwoods, carabeen, and black butt. All of them doomed, every one. In six months they'd be gone. He ranted on about phrases like 'selective logging' and what they meant in practice.

The gradient was almost impossible now. Linda felt herself beginning to fade. She had been progressing in fits and starts, scrabbling upwards, grabbing at saplings, only to feel herself sliding down again.

'It's like fucking Snakes and Ladders,' she whined. 'Did we have to come this way?'

Surely the trees in this part were safe — look how steep it was! But according to Gerard, they'd cleared plenty of hillsides steeper than this one. The entire bloody district, in fact, on both sides of the range, and most of it with axes and a couple of two-man saws.

'Speaking of which,' he said, stopping abruptly.

'What is it now?'

'In front of us — there, to the left, a red cedar.'

He pulled his notebook from his bag and sat down on the ground, leaning his back against a fallen log. Linda sat on the log itself, her hands tucked under her buttocks, the buckles on her dungarees falling slack.

'There's not many left in this basin,' he said. 'That's one of the few I've seen.'

Linda tipped her head to one side and considered the cedar. She'd expected something mightier, an iconic tree with a dark-red trunk soaring up to the sky. This one looked almost straggly, its foliage light and feathery. It had none of the power and gravitas of the buildings it had made: all those town halls and courtrooms and grand staircases. The trunk had a reddish tinge, perhaps, but it was rough and twisted. To be honest, she found it underwhelming. But Gerard seemed energised. He drew a number on his map, circled it in pencil and wrote 'Toona ciliata!' in the key at the bottom of the page. Looking over his shoulder Linda was surprised by his breathless use of the exclamation mark.

'Imagine how many men have stood here and thought about cutting it down,' he said.

'So why didn't they?'

He shook his head. 'It's a pretty pathetic specimen, I s'pose. The fork in its trunk, that's no good. Something's happened there. And they grow a hell of a lot bigger than that, or they did when they had half a chance.'

Linda regarded the tree more sympathetically now. It appeared sad and alone, the last of its tribe.

'*Toona ciliata*,' she whispered. 'Like in Toona Bay. There must have been cedars there as well. Do you remember them?'

Gerard stared distractedly through the trees. For a moment she wondered if he'd heard her and if she should say it again.

'I dunno,' he said at last. 'I don't remember much about that time. It must be, what — eleven, twelve years ago now?'

'Thirteen. I was only just pregnant when I left.'

'When you left, yeah, but I stayed longer.'

'How much longer?'

He shrugged. 'A couple of months.'

'We lost contact there for a while.'

'You were in fucking Bali.'

'For a while I was.'

'Why do you want to go back there?'

'To Toona Bay?'

'Yeah.'

'You mean because of the raid?'

'Yeah, that. And the fact that places are never the same as you remember them.'

'I'm not changing my mind because of a raid. They happen all the time. They happen round here.'

'Did you see the news reports?'

'No, we were on the road. You told me about it, you know that. As soon as we arrived.'

'I thought it might change your mind.'

'Well, it did a bit. I'm not planning to get up there before Christmas now.'

'But you're still going.'

'Yeah, of course. I'm sure it's just as beautiful, and things will settle down. I've been promising to take Melanie there for years, and I'm sure as hell not going to let Bjelke-Petersen stop me. I never wanted to leave, you know. It was Tom who wanted to go.'

'He owed everyone money, that's why.'

'That's not true. His visa had run out.'

'His visa, okay,' Gerard sneered. 'Does he have any contact with her?'

'With Melanie? No. Not since she was about three. He's back in Belfast now, I think. Someone told me that.'

'She's the image of him.'

'Yeah, she is.'

Gerard leant back and folded his hands behind his head. Linda knew from their mutual friend, Louise, that he'd suspected the baby was his. That was sad, but she had told him otherwise. She'd been absolutely sure. And God, there was no doubting it now: Melanie with her sharp little chin, green eyes and freckled skin. A face like the map of Ireland, Linda's mother would have said if she'd ever actually seen her, which she hadn't.

The bush thrummed with cicadas, all holding the same aching note. Gerard's shirt had ridden up to reveal the line of dark hair running down from his navel. Linda followed the trail of it in her mind. She imagined grabbing this moment, wriggling out of her dungarees and straddling him, pushing her hands up under his shirt. There'd been a time up at Toona Bay when he couldn't walk past her without getting hard. He used to tell her that. Couldn't see her at the kitchen bench without coming in behind her. She remembered his hands moving over her breasts and belly, his ragged breath in her ear, and the slow arching of his feet on the floor.

'So what do you want to do for me, Linda?'

'What?'

'The forest campaign. You wanted to help.'

'I don't know, whatever you want. What about this meeting? I could help some more with that.'

She waited for him to respond, but he didn't answer. Leaning forward on the log, she saw that his eyes were closed. A big, black fly thing buzzed through the air between them. Linda wished she'd brought a joint to smoke. It felt uncomfortably intimate, watching him sleep like this, hearing the soft puffs of breath breaking from his lips. How could he fall asleep after that talk about Toona Bay? They hadn't spoken of it since she arrived, not directly to each other. It had left her heart pumping, adrenaline fizzing through her veins, but the effect on him was clearly more soporific than exciting.

A sudden wind stirred through the trees, breaking the unnatural stillness. Did he really remember so little about the time they had spent up there? Did he not think of it as she did, as a golden time of their lives, a significant time against which all other stages of life were measured? Driving north with Melanie, she had pictured her life, her adult life, as a circle that was closing, but here she was in this forest of his, at another loose end after all.

Louise hadn't liked the idea of them dropping in on Gerard. She didn't outright refuse to provide his number but she kept changing the subject and leaving the room. In the end, Linda took it. She copied it from the address book that Louise left by her phone and kept it on a fold of paper in her jeans, unsure of what she'd do with it until the man in the milk bar and that blurry phone box moment in Taree.

She shifted on her buttocks. Time stretched and sagged. She wanted to wake Gerard up, to move him on, to move. She stood up and dusted her bum with her hands.

'Gerard!' she almost shouted. 'Can we get going now?'

They turned east, circling the basin as if following a single contour on one of Gerard's topographic maps. It took them down into streamless gullies and over the small regular ridges that ran from the foot of the escarpment above them down to the valley below. They passed through stands of enormous trees, their upper branches thick with epiphytes. Each one an apartment building for birds — she liked that description of his — alive with the scuttle of insects and lizards. They saw trees full of flying foxes, squealing and kicking inside the leather sleeping sacks of their wings. She wasn't feeling tired now but alert to the next thing. Her balance was better, her feet seemed to be finding their own way. They came over another small rise and, with almost no warning at all, found themselves in the baking heat, dazzled by sunlight.

Linda stared at the great orange gash in the hillside, at the mess of branches and tangled vines and walls of churned up soil. The bulldozer was still there, quite literally stopped in its tracks. She floundered over the piled-up dirt, her sandshoes breaking through the crusty ridges left by the caterpillar tread. The whole space seemed to throb and radiate heat like an infecting wound. She pushed past the fibrous roots of a fallen gum, and tiny clods of earth came raining down.

It was making her dizzy, the baking sun. She took a swig of water. She lifted her hair and trickled some more down the back of her neck. Through the loosened clay she could feel the stomp of Gerard's boots. The forensic click and burr of his camera made her think of murder.

'So what is your plan for this meeting?' she asked.

Gerard lowered the camera. 'Fucked if I know. You'll have to ask Phil. It's not my meeting and it wasn't my idea.'

'Why did he make it public? Why would you do that? You could get loggers coming, people from the mill.'

'That's what he wants. Community consultation, everything out on the table. I'll do my talk and slideshow and they'll all sit there dumbstruck, rethinking their shithouse attitudes to the natural world.'

Linda took off one of her sandshoes and shook the dirt out of it. 'So why did you agree to it, Gerard? You've been so cooperative. You've done all the posters and stuff.'

Gerard shook his head. 'Phil's the one in charge now. He runs the fucking commune, he's got all the friends. He reckons I'm too militant, that I'm just busting for a fight. Sees himself as the great peacemaker, you know what he's like.'

'You met with the Forestry Department too. You read all their reports.'

'Yeah, for two years I talked to them and look where that got me. There's a bloody great bulldozer sitting here. They removed forty trees just to build the road. And all this time, they've been sitting across the desk from me, on the other end of the phone, listening to my concerns. It's too late for talking, that's what I think, too late for sitting in circles. They could start work in a week or two while we're holding hands and chanting.'

'But you still need to rally support. You need to get more people involved, that's what Phil told Jane. He reckons there's plenty of folks out there who'd oppose it if they knew what was happening — straights, old-timers, all sorts. That's who he's hoping to reach.'

'That's bullshit.'

'No, it's true. There are people in Repentance who've never been out here. They see the logs coming into town, they don't know where they come from.'

'They don't care, Linda. I'm telling you, these people are morally bankrupt — Forestry, the sawmill, the good people of Repentance, that prick from the Council who owns the shop. Their whole world view is screwed — you can't talk sense to them and you certainly can't talk science. Money is all they think about. They call this harvesting. Sandy Mitchell from the mill: he seems like a smart enough guy, but he'll sit there and tell you, point blank, that the timber industry has been the saving grace of this forest and that cutting it down is essential to its survival.'

Linda looked into Gerard's glowering face and sweaty black ringlets. He was such a beautiful looking man, but he wasn't much of a leader. People found him off-putting, even scary. God knows, she did sometimes. He might have commitment and passion and a natural science degree, but it was the ebullient Phil de Beer and his Hummingbird guitar who was able to bring the people with him. He was an imposing figure, Phil, six foot four with the large ruddy face and crystalline green eyes. Loping along in his stripy pants, leaning into his bar chords, he drew people to him like the Pied Piper, like Mr Tambourine Man.

Next to him, Gerard appeared dark and dangerous. He'd become the harried conservationist doing battle with the system and with apathetic hippies who couldn't give a shit. His manner was combative, his language bellicose. His vibe was just too heavy, man, negative energy. Once Phil de Beer became involved, people began to take notice. The self-appointed guru of the Druidane Commune, he was everything Gerard was not — charismatic, conciliatory, charming. He was a folk singer and a songwriter, and women just adored him, especially the older women, who indulged him like a son. Gerard must have seen that he needed someone like him. He'd brought him on a walk like this, a wander in the woods that proved an epiphany for Phil. Six months later he was running the whole campaign, with Gerard as his shadowy wingman.

Linda looked around her, at the bulldozer, the muddy clearing, the smooth, milky trunks of the trees bursting from the bracken.

'Do you really think they'll start next week? I thought they were talking next year.'

'It's possible, that's all I'm saying. The only thing that's stopping them now is that one wonky bridge. And they're working on that, don't worry. They're nearly ready to go. We should be talking tactics now, discussing a plan of action, not meeting with the enemy and trying to win them over. You don't want a public show of support at this stage of the game, you lose the element of surprise. They think it's only me and Phil who care about this thing. The crazy bloke and the gormless one, no need for them to worry.'

He turned around and kicked the side of the bulldozer.

'This thing's been here for more than a month with nobody guarding it. They can't move it till they've fixed the bridge, so they leave it sitting here. And that's perfect, that's what we want. We don't want them on high alert, we want to catch them off guard. And you've got to be prepared to play dirty 'cause that's what they're going to do. The moment we stand up to them, you'll see the gloves come off. So what do we do then? Start singing a new song? Get a hundred people to dance around in front of a machine like this, or send one man with a bucket of sand, into the fuel tank, easy?'

'Have you done that?'

'What?'

'The fuel tank. Fuck off, you have not!'

Gerard laughed and shook his head. 'You want to see the bridge?'

She followed him down to where the road straddled a deep gully, full of tumbled rocks and fallen branches. The site was cordoned off with strips of orange plastic. By the time she got there, Gerard had ducked underneath them and disappeared from view.

Linda skittered down the embankment, her sandshoes slipping in the mud. The soil at the bottom was different, a mustard-coloured clay full of a sharp silica grit that felt crunchy underfoot. The gully was dry now, but you could feel its potential for flooding in the carved-out banks and tideline of muddy debris in the trees. Linda imagined the raging torrent rising out of nowhere and felt a dangerous thrill run through her body.

Gerard had crawled inside one of five large concrete pipes that lay side by side, anchored with chains, beneath the wooden bridge. She ducked her head and looked inside but didn't follow him in. It looked dank and cold in there, and mildly claustrophobic.

'This is what they had before,' he said. 'More like a causeway, but it didn't work, so they had to build a beam bridge on top.'

'What was wrong with it?'

'The driver said he felt it shift when he was bringing the dozer over. The engineers came out and said it had to be done again.'

'How do you know all this?' Linda asked. 'Do you have a mole at the mill?'

Gerard's laugh rang hollow inside the concrete pipe. 'I spend a lot of time up here. I keep an eye on things. And I like bridges, I always have. I find them interesting.'

'Still the Boy Scout, hey, Gerard?'

'I was one.'

'I know, I remember. You used to wear your uniform to church.'

'I did not.'

'You did! The first time I met you. Your mother said you were going to a jamboree and my mum thought it was wrong to do things like that on Sunday.'

'You're kidding.'

'I'm not. You know what my mother was like.'

'I thought she was still alive.'

'Not to me, she isn't.'

Linda turned and walked a short way up the gully. In one afternoon she and Gerard had broached the two countries of their past, after months of avoiding any mention of either. Toona Bay and now Sandy Bay: the girl in the duffle coat. Another country, certainly, and a very different girl.

She felt a chill of perspiration. 'Gerard,' she called.

He had moved to the other end of the pipe and was looking down the gully.

'You've never told anyone, have you? You haven't told anyone here?'

'What about?'

'My mother, the picket line.'

'No, why would I do that?'

'And you wouldn't, would you? You promised me, remember? I'm serious, Gerard. Look at me! Not even Melanie knows.'

Gerard crawled back through the pipe. He appeared to be smiling, and then the smile faded and he was looking into her eyes. Linda felt her chest constrict. He was coming straight towards her. She braced herself, but he pushed right past and went over to the place where he'd left his bag. He sat down, opened his camera, and began to change the film. Linda felt foolish and exposed.

'I was going to say —'

He looked up.

'I was thinking that I could be your campaign assistant or something.'

'Campaign assistant? And what would that involve?'

'I could help with the meeting, with the setting up, like a stage manager.'

'Stage manager?'

'Stop repeating everything I say. I want to help, what's wrong with that? I can do office work, take care of the correspondence.'

His smile was gentle now. He liked it when she pleaded. But she was quite desperate to be involved, for him to think her useful. For the first time in a long time she could see a purpose for herself, a fate, the closing of a circle, a reason for her stopping here on her way to somewhere else.

'Are we taking the road back, then?'

'Yes.' Gerard shut the camera and stuffed the plastic canister into his pocket. 'You can help if you want to, Linda, but I'm not sure what you can do.'

He climbed up other side of the gully, turned, and offered her his hand. She took it and let him haul her up, her shoes scrabbling for traction. She felt strangely exhilarated and even gave a little skip as they set off down the road. That was girly too. She pulled herself into line, but at least they set off together this time and he didn't stride ahead.

Gurayir

The odd bird may have noticed them leave or perhaps the giant lace monitor that lurked near the entrance to the track where Gerard had parked the jeep. Apart from that, the space they occupied in the forest that day — the partings they made in the undergrowth, the webs they broke, the mosses and ferns they compressed underfoot — all of this would soon bounce back and close over.

They left and the forest continued on through the afternoon, a warm, still netherworld, a spectrum of insect noise from the erratic buzz of a single fly to the steady hum of bees, and all around the metallic screaming of cicadas, a tremulous curtain of sound rising and dissolving through the trees.

This hot, harsh time of the day belongs to the raucous birds, and the raptors that soar on the thermals above the range. They look down, eagle-eyed, on the woolly scrub that clings to its upper reaches and the billowing crowns of the broccoli forest below. Here and there a blazing flame tree, an incongruous hoop pine, the creamy trunk of a gigantic beech or brush box rising from the canopy like a pillar of marble.

The forest extends all the way to the border, over seventy rugged miles to the north. From above, it appears to spread and drape itself over the rim of the caldera like a giant starfish, its tentacle legs reaching down into the gullies and farming valleys on either side. But this is an illusion; there is no extension or spread. This is a shrinking vestige of Gondwanaland, an ancient organism in retreat.

It perseveres nonetheless, a mass and multitude, a relentless flow and cycle of running creeks and seeping swamps and dribbling rockfaces. Water swells and quivers on the ends of drip-tip leaves and drenches the spongey hearts of bird's nest ferns. It leeches through the thin red soils, soaking into the cottony mass of algae underground. It is drawn into the roots of trees and hauled up through the xylem, a charged line travelling all the way to their transpiring crowns a hundred feet or more above the ground. The climb to the top can take an hour, it can take a day, depending on the weather and the type of tree. But the movement is perpetual, the tension unbroken — the steady rise of nutrients, the slow descent of sugars — and time in a forest like this is a relative thing anyway. It turns like circles inside circles, running fast and slow. One long afternoon is less than a minute in the life of an ancient box but nearly half a lifetime for a birdwing butterfly. And the forest itself is said to be at least a million years old, making the passage of those spring days in 1976 little more than a flicker of shadow and light on the landscape.

For the birds, however, the end of that day was welcome and long-awaited. They grew vocal again as evening fell, as if only the cooler, gentler air could carry their liquid notes. The dee-dee-ah-wit of a golden whistler, the curling mewls of catbirds, the rattle of a Lewin's honeyeater ricocheting through the trees.

And so it goes on, day and night — the incessant burble of water, the dissolving of rocks, the scramble of vines, the chemical chatter and exchange of filaments in the soil. All of this continues, whether people are there or not, with or without the Latin labels and metaphors we apply. The forest houses no pantheon of spirits as we imagine them. It has no truck with vaulted ceilings, cathedrals, grand salons. It exists beyond all concepts of its worth and usefulness. It just is, day and night, circles within circles, regardless of how we think of it, or even if we do, and insensible to the frequency of picnics.

Chapter Five

The museum volunteer stepped in front of the shuffling class and held her arms out wide.

'Do we have any Mathesons in this group?' she called. 'Any Sneaths? Judds?'

She directed their attention to a dark oil painting hanging in the entrance hall of the Balbirnie Museum. Here was the land as the pioneers knew it: brown-green scrub, a whisper of smoke, an axe in the top of a tree stump, bearded men in soft white shirts drinking from pannikins. Joanne squinted at the tiny plaque screwed onto the ornate frame, identifying the figures in the foreground. *G. Matheson, P. Sneath, F. Judd, R. Gibson.* Her eyes travelled around the flushed and whiskery faces and then back into the murky shadows behind the trees. Did anyone else notice the Aborigine lurking there, his body and spear rendered with a few quick strokes of the brush?

The woman handed out worksheets snapped onto wooden clip-boards. Then off went the class, through the musty rooms of the old Victorian house, shoving their way past the mayoral portraits, the shelves of rusty kettles and flatirons, the wall-eyed dummies dressed in faded silks.

'What's the answer for number two?' they hissed to one another. 'Bullock teams.'

'Where's it say that?'

Joanne raised herself on tiptoes and looked around for Melanie. They were meant to be working on their dairy project after the general tour. She'd been there at the beginning. Joanne had seen her lingering at the back of the group as they arrived, looking bored and reluctant. Their eyes had met briefly as the teacher ran through the schedule for the afternoon. Joanne wished she'd been paired with someone else. Hippie kids didn't like all this local history stuff. They weren't from around here and it meant nothing to them. Melanie had told Joanne last week that she was born in Bali.

'What industries do they have there?' Joanne had asked, having not the faintest idea where Bali was.

'I don't know — rice. We moved to Melbourne when I was a baby. I don't remember anything. And then we went to stay with a friend of Mum's near Holbrook.'

'Where's that?'

'Down south. It took us two days to drive from there to here.'

The conversation had petered out at that point. Joanne had been to Sydney twice but couldn't think of anything to say. They had hardly exchanged a word since then. Their work on the project had been reduced to exchanged glances, pursed lips, and defensively folded arms. Joanne was coming to accept the fact that she was working alone.

Which was good — she preferred it that way. The museum was really interesting and she was relieved not to have to pretend otherwise. There was an entire room on the history of dairying, including an old separator and a reconstruction of a cream room, its table spread with hand churns and wooden butter paddles. Joanne was brimming with ideas. She made careful notes and sketches. The last hour flew by. The class was dismissed. Most kids from Balbirnie walked home, while those who had buses to catch dawdled back to the school.

The Catholic kids had done sport that afternoon. You could smell it going down the aisle of the bus, the humid stink of damp socks stuffed into vinyl bags. Joanne slung her port into the overhead rack and sat down five rows from the back. Five rows, always the same. In ten months of high school, no progress.

Repentance was only fourteen miles from Balbirnie via the main road, but the school bus, on its roundabout route, took an hour and a half each way. It was one of the longest bus runs, and theirs was the roughest bus. On a steamy afternoon like this, there was always going to be trouble.

Melanie was the last to get on at the bus bay outside the school. Brian the bus driver had already closed the door when she appeared at the bottom of the steps. He looked down and shook his head but pulled on the hydraulic lever. She climbed in and cast her eyes towards the back. Joanne glanced around at Mick Doherty. He was sitting, as he always did, in the middle of the back seat, his feet planted wide in the aisle. On either side of him sat his favoured ones, his sidekicks and admirers, and Libby Bartlet with her almond eyes and shiny, red-tanned legs.

In front of them, within easy reach, sat the second-form boys. They were the ones that got jumped on and dakked whenever things got boring. They grinned, these boys, no matter what was being done to them, even as their nuts were being cracked around the chrome bars of the seats. Their eyes would water and their throats constrict but their mouths would remain a rictus of grim determination, as if this were a price they were all too willing to pay.

Next came the cheer squad of slim, pretty girls like Tracy Willis and Rhonda McKay. They were almost always up on their knees, facing the back and watching for trouble, squealing in half-hearted protest when a rumble was underway. 'You guys are such bastards!' they'd chime in high voices, taking care never to sound too upset or censorious. But even they could sometimes come to grief, losing the buttons off their blouses or having their bra straps snapped against their skin. Everyone knew how things worked down the back, so what was with Melanie, then? Joanne watched, appalled, as she walked coolly down the aisle and attempted to squeeze into the seat next to Libby Bartlet.

The kids' heads turned and their mouths opened as if pulled by a single string. Mick Doherty was on his feet, his dark eyes glittering with menace.

'Hey!' he barked, hauling on Melanie's arm. 'What the fuck do you think you're doing?'

She wrenched herself free. She looked so slight and small in her oversized uniform, like a tiny clapper inside a voluminous bell.

'You can't tell me where to sit,' she said.

'Fucking right, I can. Back you go, go on, back ... back!' He flicked his hands at her, bringing shrieks of laughter from the kick-pleat chorus of girls.

'Okay,' he shouted, holding out his hands for silence. 'Who wants this stinking hippie chick to sit down here with us?'

He held his nose — phew! The laughter shrank to a nervous titter. Libby Bartlet recrossed her legs and stroked the corners of her mouth.

'See? No one does. So fuck off back where you came from.'

'You're a dumb shit,' Melanie sputtered.

'And you're a fucking bush pig,' Mick Doherty replied with a charming smile.

Surely now she'd make her retreat. There was nowhere to go from here. Five rows down, Joanne moved towards the window to indicate that the seat next to her was free. Melanie turned and looked at her. She seemed to be weighing her options, but she hesitated just that little too long.

They jumped her. They had her on the floor and pinned.

'Unzip the tent!' Mick ordered above the squeals of the girls. The zipper of her uniform was tugged down to her waist revealing her pale torso. 'Ha ha, no bra!' They flicked and fingered her nipples. Melanie struggled and kicked, and they seized her legs as well.

'Let's see if she's got any pants on?'

Melanie made a desperate grab for the hem of her dress. There was a loud rip of fabric. Casting around, Joanne caught Brian's eye in the rear-vision mirror. The bus pulled over, the engine stopped, and the boys let Melanie go. She got to her feet, clutching her torn uniform and made her way unsteadily to the seat beside Joanne. There was a hush as Brian hauled himself upright and came lumbering down the back.

The chorus girls snickered. Over the years Brian's body had swelled and sagged into the driver's seat to the point where he now seemed to be built only for bus-driving. On his feet he looked ridiculous, like Kermit the Frog standing up, and his rare excursions down the aisle always caused an uproar. There was the time one of the Sneaths fell through the emergency exit, leaving a cartoonish jagged hole in the Perspex. Then there was his brief crackdown on smoking after a doctor had driven behind them and written to the local paper about the disgraceful fug of smoke hanging over the back seats. Most of the time, however, Brian remained aloof and indifferent to the goings-on down the back, and all the screaming, all the little boys' yelps of pain, all the cigarette smoke in the world wasn't enough to budge him.

Now he stood awkwardly in the aisle, looking into their faces, one at a time. He frowned at Mick Doherty and glanced under his elbow at Melanie. She sat hunched in the seat, white-faced and unblinking, sucking what looked like a small cut on her lip.

'Keep the noise down, will you? Or I'll have to put youse all off.'

He turned and walked heavily down the aisle, gripping the metal corners of the seats as he went.

'He's not allowed to do that,' hissed Libby Bartlet. 'It's illegal.'

Joanne glanced at the girl in the seat beside her. Melanie's breathing was short and sharp and caught in her throat now and then, but she didn't cry. She continued to stare at her lap, her hand holding the flap of her torn uniform across her chest like a brunch coat. Only when the bus began the steep climb up Lancasters Hill did she raised her head and catch one of Joanne's glances.

'What did you expect?' Joanne whispered.

Melanie's lips parted.

'Why do you want to sit down there?'

'I don't! It's wrong, that's all, the way he bullies people. Who is he anyway, just some stupid pig farmer's son!'

Joanne felt a twinge of discomfort.

'He doesn't even go to school anymore, did you know that? He just goes into town and hangs around all day so he can play King Shit on the bus.'

Joanne had heard this rumour from a kid at the Catholic school, but she wasn't sure if it was true.

'Your lip's bleeding,' she said.

'I know.'

Joanne turned back to the window as the bus began its weary climb. This hill was always a challenge for it. Every change of gear was followed by a nervous silence. Then the engine would re-engage and pull once more, whining higher and higher as the river flats dropped away and the bus groped its way to the top like a dying mountaineer.

'Where did you get to today anyway?' Joanne asked Melanie. 'I couldn't find you.'

'I went to a cafe.'

'A cafe?'

'I was bored. It was nice. They had hummingbird cake.'

'We were meant to be doing our project.'

'I know.'

'They had a whole room on dairying. I had some good ideas.'

Melanie didn't answer. She stroked at the torn edges of her uniform with her thumb. The dress had been ripped right open, from the bottom of the zipper to the hem.

'I've got safety pins in my pencil case. Do you want them?'

'Yeah, thanks.'

Joanne clamoured over Melanie's knees and was reaching up to the rack when Melanie suddenly grabbed her around the hips and pulled her down.

'What are you doing?'

'You're bleeding too, on the back of your uniform.'

'Shit!'

'Have you got a tampon?'

'I haven't got my periods yet.'

'I think you've got them now.'

'No! How bad is it? Will they see it when I get off?'

Melanie pushed her off her lap. 'Have you got a jumper or something?'

'No.'

'You could carry your bag behind you.'

They were only a couple of miles from Repentance now. The bus had turned at the top of the ridge and was heading through a tunnel of trees shrouded in morning glory. From the bag at her feet, Melanie produced a mass of rainbow-coloured cloth.

'What's that?' asked Joanne.

'It's a scarf. You can tie it around your waist.'

'How come you've got that with you?'

'I like it. I wear it. Do you want it or not?'

Joanne took it reluctantly. It was a kind of scratchy muslin. 'What am I supposed to do with it?'

'Here, I'll help you.' Melanie passed the scarf around Joanne's waist and tied it in a knot at the front. She seemed pleased with the result, like it didn't look weird at all.

The bus stopped at the top of Main Street and a lot of the kids got off. Joanne and Melanie hung back until almost last and then shuffled down the aisle together, covering each other, front and back, from the watchful eyes of Mick Doherty and his mates. Once outside, they sat, dazed, on the steps of the cenotaph and waited until everyone had dispersed. Melanie held a tissue to the cut on her lip and Joanne stared down the street in front of them, imagining herself dripping blood all the way home.

'Mum picks me up from here,' Melanie said.

'Yeah. I know.'

'I'll be all right if you want to go.'

Joanne turned and looked up at the names on the marble plaque behind them: *Matheson, Sneath, Gibson, Judd* and the rest, some of them marked with a tiny cross.

'I used to think these people were buried under here,' she said.

'What, like a grave?'

'Yeah, when I was little. It looks a bit like a grave, don't you think?'

Melanie burst out laughing. 'You're a jerk, Joanne!'

Joanne grinned. It was the first time she had heard Melanie use her name. 'Do you want those safety pins now?' she asked.

'Yes, okay.'

'We sell sewing kits in the shop too, if you need one.'

'Nah, it's right. Someone at home has a sewing machine. I think it might be Jane's, and Gerard's got needles and cotton and stuff, I'm sure.'

'Gerard?' The clips on Joanne's school port snapped open one by one. 'You live with someone called Gerard?'

'Yeah, why?'

'Dark hair? Funny last name, starts with A?'

'Ansiewicz.'

'You live with Gerard Ansiewicz?'

'Yeah, well — we're staying there, just for a couple of months. We're actually on our way up north to this place called —'

'Melanie —' Joanne breathed. The fluoro tubes in her grandma's kitchen blinked and buzzed into life. Now it was Melanie creeping down that dark, wet path to the bathroom, past the spot where nine-year-old Barbara had once rucked up her nightie and, weak with laughter, pissed into a pot plant.

'The old place on the top of the hill, after Wayne Mackenzie's gates?'

'Yes.'

Joanne shook her head. This was just too weird. 'That's my grand-mother's house you're living in. My uncle owns it now.'

Back in her bedroom, Joanne untied the rainbow scarf from her waist. For a moment she hesitated, and then turned in front of the mirror. The bloodstain on her uniform was nowhere near as bad as she'd imagined. It was more like a brownish dribble, like Worcester sauce or something, except that it was at the back where you didn't spill sauce on yourself. Now she had to deal with it without anyone seeing, sneak her uniform out to laundry and soak it in a bucket, or bundle it into the washing machine with a load of other stuff.

She resolved not to tell Delia. She found her mother's enthusiasm for the whole horrible subject irksome. *Any sign of your period yet, Jo?* She was always checking, like someone looking up the tracks for a late-running train. These enquiries had assumed an urgency that Joanne found unnerving, as if Delia feared she might miss it altogether if it didn't arrive very soon. The dreaded sponge bag had been ready for over a year, stuffed with belts and pads and booklets on becoming a woman. Everything in it was pink or lilac and covered with butterflies. It had lain in wait all this time at the back of Joanne's top drawer. A few months back, she had smuggled a box of tampons out of the shop, curious to see why her mother didn't think they were a good idea. Mrs Phelps, who was also the girls' mistress at school, had recommended them once at a special girls' assembly. 'Girls!' she announced, holding a wrapped tampon in the air like a flaming torch. 'These things are the best invention since sliced bread!'

But pads it was for the moment. Awful, but easy, and, Joanne thought that night as she lay on the bed beside her mother watching television, there was something almost comforting in the soft thick-ness between her legs. So far, that was the only thing that felt any dif-ferent, and Delia seemed oblivious to the fact that it had happened, that the train had arrived, her daughter had crawled from the chrysalis. It felt like a guilty secret, but Joanne was resolute, unable to deal with the earnest conversation that would follow. They were watching a comedy. Delia was listless and hadn't eaten her tea. It was one of her favourite TV shows, but she was falling asleep, despite the sudden bursts of raucous laughter.

'Is that real people laughing or just a machine?' Joanne asked loudly, hoping to startle her mother awake.

Delia didn't answer. The blue light of the television danced on her skin. The bones of her face were obvious now, as if the flesh were sinking. For the first time Joanne could see, in the waxy plains and hollows of her cheeks, the young woman in the wedding photo on the lounge-room wall. Such a small mound in the bedclothes now. Getting smaller all the time. Joanne slipped out of the bed, accidentally pulling the top sheet with her. Delia's one remaining breast had fallen out of her nightie. All her clothes were so large on her now, the necklines too loose and low on her scarred and withered chest. The breast was much smaller than it once would have been. The nipple was brown and shrivelled like a piece of dried pear. Joanne froze at the sight it and clutched the hem of the sheet. For the briefest moment she saw herself as a baby, eyes shut and mouth searching and insistent. Something ached inside her — a faint contraction in the pit of her stomach. It might have been period pain, but it felt like — homesickness. Which was silly but exactly right. It was the same curling feeling she had felt back in third class when she'd gone to stay at Tracy Willis's place. It was only for two nights and just three streets away, but lying on the camp bed in Tracy's bedroom, she had suffered the same deep-seated longing for home.

She flung out the sheet and watched it settle over her mother. In her sleep Delia smiled and gathered it under her chin. Turning in the doorway, Joanne saw what looked like a fossil impression — a small shrivelled bird, all claws and beak and angular bones, lying almost flat under a fine sediment of cotton.

Chapter Six

The Mitchells' place was one of the few houses in Repentance that might be described as grand. It was not particularly large or imposing, but it had the look of a true Queenslander with its painted fretwork, wide verandas, and gleaming timber floors. Built of red mahogany, most of it, such a lovely timber. And then there were the grounds, a huge corner block with mature trees, rose borders, and expansive beds of cannas and spider lilies. Jean took great pride in her garden, but walking through it now on his way to the garage to fetch the meat for tomorrow's lunch, Sandy could see that she was struggling to contain the spring growth this year. The jasmine was running riot along the back fence, and the flowering vines on the pergola that ran down the side of the house had grown as thick as elbows, twisting and crushing the lattice.

Sandy had loved this yard as a boy. Crossing the lawn now, he recalled some of his favourite spots for hide and seek. He remembered the creepy feeling of squeezing behind the hibiscus. He could feel the ache in his calves and hear the sound of his breathing as he pressed his chin to his chest and waited to be found. When he was a bit older, maybe nine or ten, he'd had the genius idea of climbing into the trees. There he'd be, slung comfortably in the limbs of the leopard tree, looking down at the younger kids searching for him among the shrubs and fishbone fern. Great games they were, played with a crowd of cousins on Sunday afternoons. It had given him such a kick as a young father to watch James and Imogen discovering all his old hiding places, adopting his old tricks.

Soon, at last, there'd be another generation of children playing in the yard. In a few weeks' time James and his wife, Amanda, would be driving up from Sydney, she six months' pregnant with Sandy and Jean's first grandchild. They already knew she was having a girl. Amanda had had one of those ultrasound things done and had asked the radiologist what it was. Jean was appalled when James told them on the phone. It wasn't just that it spoiled the surprise. For her there was something almost immoral about knowing the baby's sex in advance. It was all a bit too Brave New World, she admitted to Sandy later. She had been doing her best ever since to blot out the information and was still stubbornly knitting with lemon wool.

Sandy, on the other hand, was quite pleased to be having a granddaughter, despite the jocular remarks at the mill about the line of succession. A boy was no guarantee anyway. Look at James with his fancy business degree, talking job opportunities in Sydney, in Singapore for God's sake! It was Amanda's influence. She wasn't a country girl. She spent Christmases here looking bored, scratching her hair, whingeing about the humidity and the distance from the coast. In five years she'd never once come down to the mill. James did, or used to anyway. Not so much these days. He used to like walking around the place with his hands in his pockets, joking with boys he hadn't seen since he was in primary school. But by the end of university, his interest had waned, and even though they'd never had the terrible conversation, Sandy understood that his son's heart wasn't in the future of the mill.

Amanda may not have been the only reason for this shift in his son, but she was certainly a factor. Sandy and Jean had visited her family home in Sydney, chocolate brick, split level, with a vast entertaining deck overlooking the Lane Cove River. Jean and Amanda's mother had found plenty to say to each other on the subject of camellias, but Sandy had remained detached that evening, observing the fiancée and her family with a growing sense of unease. Amanda had the polish and carriage of a well-groomed pony. She wore her smooth brown hair in a swinging ponytail, scraped back from her forehead with the confidence of a girl who knows that she is extremely pretty. It was hard to imagine her upping stakes and moving to a town like Repentance, regardless of the future offered by her boyfriend's family business. Amanda had her own family wealth, her own accounting degree and ambitions that went way beyond keeping the ledger at the mill.

Sandy kicked open the side door and blinked into the gloom. This garage hadn't housed a car in over twenty years. It was more of a garden shed these days, a jumble of tools and dusty pushbikes. And in the far corner, the deep freeze, his mission, the lamb cutlets. Dusky light slanted down from the strip of windows in the opposite wall. He picked his way through the clutter and opened the lid of the chest freezer, wincing as the cold air hit him in the face. Jean was mad keen on this thing. She read articles about it, ripped them out of the paper, and stuck them on the fridge. What could be frozen, how long would it keep, how to bag up half a vealer. He gritted his teeth and dug down into the splintery frost, where his hand closed around a cardboard packet. Sara Lee, an apple strudel. He stared at the box in surprise. A rosy-cheeked Fräulein beamed back at him, holding a strudel aloft. He'd never known his Jean to serve up a TV dinner, let alone a ready-made dessert. And apple strudel, good God! His mother used to make them but stopped during the war. There'll be no Jerry food served in this house, she had declared at the time. Now he studied the packet, the drawing of the girl in her puffy blouse, with lurid yellow plaits wrapped around her head. There was nothing in her polished cheeks that resembled the hitchhiker he'd picked up the week before. Just the fact that she was German, that was as far as it went, but here he was, thinking of that awful girl again. He pulled out the cutlets and slammed down the lid of the freezer.

Why did he stop for her? Sometimes you just do things, you don't even think. He saw her as he rounded a bend on the Balbirnie road, and felt he couldn't leave her to fate. She could have been hit by a car or molested by some psycho. Before he knew what he was doing, Sandy had applied the brakes and swung to the side of the road.

At first he didn't realise that she had a dog with her. She opened the door and in it flew, an ugly broad-headed bitser, all tongue and tail and flapping breath.

'Get that thing out of here!' he snapped. 'Put it on the back of the truck.'

'Have you got any rope?' she asked him.

Bloody hell, he thought, and opened his door with a sigh. When he saw her, illuminated in the red tail lights of his ute, he wondered what the hell he'd got himself into. She was wearing what looked like a petticoat with stocky walking boots, and had a grimy calico bag slung over her shoulder. There seemed to be bits of shell and feather tied into the ends of her hair as if she'd been rolling around in a chook pen. And she looked young — very. Imagine finding his Imogen flouncing along in the dark like that, half-undressed with her thumb stuck out, like she was anyone's — he'd kill her, he'd bloody well kill her. That was just asking for trouble, that was.

The girl climbed into the passenger seat and stared through the windscreen. There was something hostile about her, even then.

'So where are you headed?'

She turned to him, eyes narrowed, as though he had no business asking.

'So I can drop you off,' he prompted.

'Repentance.'

'No worries. I can take you all the way. That's where I'm going.'

They set off through the night, through the monotonous tunnel of trees. Sandy made a few attempts at conversation, but the girl's answers, when they came at all, were curt and wary. She had an accent: he picked that up. He thought it might be German. There were a lot of young Europeans coming up this way. Backpackers, they called themselves. A scungy-looking lot they were too, hard to distinguish from the hippies half the time. Where did these young people find the time and the money to travel? They were at it for months, years, some of them, with no income, paying God-knows-what for airline tickets, bus fares, accommodation. Such things weren't possible when he was young, unless you went to war. He stopped himself at that point. Just thinking of the war with a German in the car made him feel awkward.

They were deep inside the state forest by then, ploughing around the bends. The bone-white branches of the eucalypts flew overhead and a pale moonlight flickered inside the cabin. Sandy occasionally glanced at the girl. She turned once to check on the dog, but mostly she just sat there, hugging her calico bag, staring at the road ahead. The moonlight played on her face, on her skin. It reminded Sandy of a picture theatre somewhere in his past. He felt restless, annoyed that he'd bothered to pick her up. She was so frigging unfriendly, so ungrateful.

You could tell she came from a cold country. Those blonde eyelashes, that pale skin. She had lovely skin, sort of furzy looking, not shiny and tight like the skin on Australian women. The sun here seemed to scorch off that peachy fuzz. It caught the light and softened the edge of the girl's sharp profile. It grew in swirls on her forearms, soft on her unshaven legs.

Sandy grabbed the bag of meat. Jean was calling him. She was coming across the garden, she was at the garage door. Ray Parmenter had just rung, she said. Was he still going down there for a beer?

'I think it's important you go, Sandy. Ray needs his mates at the moment.'

'I intend to.'

'Well, you'd better go now or you'll be running into their dinner time. And make sure you pop in on Delia. She says people are avoiding her. I'm just cutting her some roses.' Jean brandished her secateurs. 'Hers haven't done any good this year, Ray's no good at pruning.'

Sandy set out for the Parmenters' place. It was downhill all the way. It meant a bit of a climb going home, but he felt like the exercise. So much of his work at the mill these days was sitting at a desk. He was less and less involved with the physical side of the business and didn't get out into the bush much anymore. The bush crews worked on contract now. They weren't his employees. They were still the same blokes, mind you, the same families of fellers and hauliers. He was still in close contact with many of them, but they didn't need him coming out on the job the way he used to.

He always enjoyed this walk down the hill, through the quiet residential streets. There were no footpaths but not much traffic either. You could choose to walk on the wide grassy verges or down the middle of the road itself. There was nothing self-consciously pretty about Repentance as a town. Any rural charm it had was mostly accidental and was only becoming apparent now, as other places changed. The harder and hotter and neater the brick and tile sprawl elsewhere, the more character there was to be found in Repentance's lack of curb and guttering, its backyard chook pens and mounds of vibrant bougainvillea spilling over its garages and garden sheds. There was an unkempt loveliness about it, and the huge camphor laurel trees, pests though they were, made a pleasant avenue down the side of the primary school.

Ray's neighbour Dawn Blainey was minding the shop. Sandy greeted her on his way through, holding the roses discreetly by his side. Dawn said Delia was probably asleep. Ray was waiting for him, though; he was out the back.

'Go through,' Dawn told him. 'You can leave those roses in the kitchen sink. I'll take care of them.'

Ray was sitting on the back porch with a longneck of beer and two glasses on the table in front of him. As Jean had intimated, he seemed very down in the dumps. He and Peg had decided that Delia should go back into palliative care. They couldn't manage her pain here, even with the nurse coming every day and doing most of her meds. The girls didn't know about the change of plan. Sandy mustn't say anything. It was going to upset them, knowing their mother's fervent wish to remain at home.

Joanne came out the back and Ray stopped talking.

'What?' she said, looking at him.

'Been watching telly, have you?'

'Mum fell asleep.'

'We got Delia a little TV,' Ray told Sandy. 'Just a small black-and-white one, not expensive. I never thought we'd be a two-telly household, but there you go.'

'What were you watching, Jo?' Sandy asked.

'*Are You Being Served?*'

'Hah! It's funny, that show. That bloke, what's his name, the pansy?'

Joanne sat on the floor and leant against the laundry wall. 'Mr Humphries,' she said.

'That's the one. *I'm free!*'

Above their heads, tiny moths bounced around the light. From inside the house came the low burble of the television.

'I should've turned it off,' Joanne said.

'Go and do it now, love, and while you're at it —' Ray nudged the empty beer bottle. 'Get us another of these and some nuts if you can find some. Grab a packet of Nobby's from the shop.'

Sandy smiled after her. 'How's she dealing with all this, Ray?'

'Not too bad.'

'Is she going to come and work for me, like her sister?'

'Nah, I don't think so. She's the brains of the family, that one. We reckon she'll go on to sixth form, become a teacher, something like that.'

'Your Barb's a good girl,' Sandy said. 'I'm very pleased with her. Gets on well with all the blokes, keeps us organised. She's getting a Christmas bonus, don't tell her, but she is.'

Ray sat back and crossed his ankles, his fingers folded neatly on the snap-down buckle of his belt. 'What about this community meeting, eh?'

Sandy snorted.

'Reckon they'll get many people?'

'I'm going.'

'You're not!'

'Bloody oath, I am. It's a community meeting. I want to hear what they've got to say. There's a few of us going from the mill. Want to come?'

'Nah.' Ray jerked his thumb at the house behind him. 'I can't make any commitments right now. I'm interested to hear how it goes, but. The girls have been taking their posters down. Jo got bawled out by that Gerard bloke the other day. You know where he's living, don't you?'

'Yeah, Barb told me.' Sandy took a gulp of beer. 'When's his lease up?'

'What difference does it make? There'll be some other greedy bastard happy to rent him a shed. Everyone's doing it — the Mulligans, Clarkey, you know that old stable of his? You should see what we're dealing with at Council, the by-laws they're breaking.'

Sandy leant forward in his chair and tapped his thumbs together. From out in the darkness came the swish and jigger of the neighbour's sprinkler.

'I gave one a lift the other day,' he said.

'One what?'

'A hippie, a German girl. Hitchhiking, can you believe, on her own, in the dark.'

'Where was she going?'

'That's the weird thing. She told me Repentance. So we're going along and everything's fine. She doesn't say much, but you know. We're going along and then, all of a sudden, she tells me she wants to get out. Just like that, in the middle of nowhere. About three miles from the turn-off, she yells at me to stop.'

'Did you?'

'Yeah, of course I did — as soon as I could, I did. You can't just pull over any old place. Anyway, out she gets and wanders off in the other direction, with her filthy dog and my bit of rope, mind you. No thank you, no nothing, just walks off like I've somehow offended her.'

'What was her problem?'

Sandy shrugged. 'Changed her mind, I s'pose.'

'Prob'ly on drugs.' Ray said. 'I reckon a lot of them are.'

A tiny praying mantis fell from the light above them and landed in the faded ginger hairs on Sandy's arm. He examined it absently and it stared back at him, its heart-shaped head tipped to one side.

'So when's she going back?' he asked Ray.

'Who?'

'Delia, to the hospital.'

'We're not sure yet. Maybe Friday. They're ringing me tomorrow.'

'Can she take the telly with her?'

Ray stiffened in his seat. Glancing behind him, Sandy saw Joanne through the screen door.

'Oh Jeez, Ray, I'm sorry,' he muttered. 'Do you reckon she heard?'

'It's okay, don't worry about it. I was going to have to tell them anyway.'

The praying mantis on Sandy's arm wrung its tiny hands. With excessive care, he carried it down the steps and placed it on the leaf of a begonia. When he thought it might be safe to look, he glanced up at the door again. The shadow of Joanne Parmenter was gone.

Chapter Seven

Gerard had done nothing but pick at her all afternoon, about everything, from how she took down his phone messages to the way she was packing the jeep. Where was the projector screen, why didn't it go in first? What was she doing smoking a joint less than two hours before the meeting?

'Because you're stressing me out!' Linda snapped as he pushed past her on the steps. She blew the smoke at his back and watched him lump another crate of stuff down to the gate.

'You're supposed to be helping,' he called over his shoulder.

'I have been. It's five o'clock, I'm allowed to take a break.'

'You'll be off your face.'

'I will not. It's that crappy leaf of yours.'

Poor old Gerard. She grinned and coughed. Why did everyone say that — poor old Gerard — like he was some frail old man? She looked at his muscled shoulders moving under his cotton singlet. Nothing could be further from the truth. Physically, he'd hardly changed since they were together, and he'd always felt things passionately: that was why he was such a good fuck. His gaze had always been intense, his grip firm and strong. But that mocking smile of his that she'd found so appealing in her early twenties was more like a grimace these days, and the passion dark and obsessive.

It wasn't that she didn't understand his feelings for the forest. She'd felt elated herself after their walk: in awe, incensed, alive. That was all very well, but she'd gone and offered to be his campaign assistant without having any real idea of what that might entail. And yes, it had been tricky. To begin with she did little more than stand in the corner of the kitchen while Gerard and Phil held their often-heated discussions, making cups of tea and agreeing with their ideas. Then as the meeting grew closer, Gerard began to throw a whole lot of work her way, random things like organising a screen for the overhead projector. That was hard for someone in her position, someone who was new to the district and didn't have local connections. When she finally managed to borrow one from the Repentance primary school, Gerard complained that it was too small for the size of the Braemar Hall.

Then he decided that he didn't like the poster she had designed. It was too Phil de Beer, he said of her whimsical border, not serious enough. The paper stock she'd chosen was too dark in colour, too expensive, too heavy, too hard to stick up.

On their own, none of these things were a big deal, but they churned up a dark cloud of feeling inside her, stuff she'd forgotten, subtle stuff about the way he used to make her feel. Those tiny needles of self-doubt that he was able to insert with the precision of an acupuncturist. He could make her feel like shit, like she didn't have a clue, when in fact she was quite smart and he could go fuck himself.

Gerard closed the flap on the back of the jeep. She took another toke on the joint. She hoped people would come to this meeting, but she wasn't confident. There was even a rumour that Phil wasn't going to be there. He and Gerard hadn't spoken since the previous Thursday, when Linda had come home to find them at loggerheads in the front yard.

'Listen to yourself!' Phil was ranting. 'Tactics, strategy, holding the ground — it's the language of fucking war, man.'

'And what are you planning for? A singsong, you and your flaky friends?'

Linda had coaxed Gerard inside, fearing they would come to blows. She made him sit down at the kitchen table and put the kettle on.

'I can't believe you're fighting about the principles of peaceful resistance.'

'He's changed his mind about the meeting,' Gerard said. 'One week out, can you believe that? We've got posters all over the district.'

'But you don't think it's a good idea.'

'We've got people travelling to get there. We're expecting — I don't know. I've paid for the hire of the hall. I've been out there, drumming up support. I've been all the way up to the border, to all the collectives out that way, to Braemar and the markets. We'll look stupid if we cancel now. You're collecting people's names. We'll do this thing and then decide where we go from there.'

'But no music.'

'No, no music. It's an information night. We've got to sound half serious, like we know what we're on about. There'll be plenty of people, don't worry. There's fifty coming just from Druidane.'

'Or not. If Phil doesn't come —'

'He'll come, of course he'll come. You couldn't keep him away. When he knows we're going ahead with it, he'll want to run the show.'

Linda almost regretted smoking that joint as she and Melanie pushed piles of chairs across the hall. She felt tired and anxious. Ever since she and Mel arrived at Gerard's place, she'd been taking constant barometer readings of his response to her. Cool, fair, detached, resentful, chance of a change. Today the needle had leapt to stormy: he was thoroughly pissed off with her.

'Go and ask him how many chairs he wants,' she told Melanie. 'Tell him they're metal, they weigh a ton.'

Gerard was at the front of the hall, setting up the overhead projector. The grimy white wall behind him was framed with drapes of claret velvet edged with a crumbling brocade. In the middle, below a very young portrait of the Queen, stood the portable slide screen she'd borrowed from the school. It did look rather small in this space and maybe a little bit wonky. She glanced at the clock. They had less than half an hour before people started to arrive and there was no sign of Phil.

Melanie came skittering back. 'He said about two hundred.'

'And people say he's a pessimist.'

'And he wants to know if you're doing the door, because there's people coming in already.'

Linda gave the chairs a sulky shove and went to fetch her clip-board from one of Gerard's overflowing boxes. She was to sit in the foyer and collect people's names, and a phone number if they had one, and ask if they were interested in joining the Action Group.

Cars were pulling in along the road outside. Ten, fifteen, twenty people — another seven in a Kombi. By seven o'clock, the foyer was filling nicely. Everyone seemed to know one another. It made Linda feel like a stranger, all these people hugging and waving across the room. She nodded at Jane, who arrived with a group of friends, including the lumpish Tess, the previous owner of Melanie's volumi-nous school uniforms. Andy wasn't with them. Linda glanced outside. Maybe he would come with Phil. They were quite close friends.

It was a muddy-looking crowd, she thought. Where were the rainbow bearers, the petticoat wearers, the flamboyant motley men? Where was the whirling Marguerite, in her yellow ruffled skirt, who turned up to dance at every market and music festival? This group looked more like a mash of dull-coloured vegetables, decked out in their boiled felts and home-dyed cottons. 'Good earth people', Jane would call them, as if that were some recognised subspecies of the genus *Hippie*. Flossy-haired children ran between the adults and raced into the hall, beckoned by its echoing expanses. They ran, jumped and bounced about, their shrieks leaping to the ceiling, their bare feet thumping on the floor.

Melanie juddered past with another pile of chairs. It would

have been nice to have some sort of music, Linda thought, even a tape recorder, anything to take the edge of this awful echoing din. Meanwhile she was doing a half-arsed job with the contact sheet. Whole groups of people seemed to be slipping past her. She felt awkward chasing after them or butting in on their conversations. Perhaps Gerard could say something and people could come and find her.

Then, as suddenly as it started, the stream of people dried up. No rainbow bus from the commune, no Children of God, but thankfully no horrible man from the shop or millworkers. Linda stared at the empty doorway and looked inside the hall. Once everybody had caught hold of their kids and pulled them onto their laps, the crowd in there too seemed to diminish, barely filling the first six rows.

She slipped into a chair by the door. Melanie came and sat beside her.

'All these empty seats,' Mel grumbled, 'and we've got to put them back!'

Gerard was already standing at the front, his eyes flicking from the darkened foyer to the clock on the wall. Linda hoped he wouldn't take out his frustration on the people who'd bothered to come. He didn't look frustrated, just nervous perhaps, and well he might be, having to run the entire meeting on his own.

He turned on the carousel and put up the first slide. It was a picture of the rainforest, out of focus. He jiggled with the projector. A young man darted forward to help him. They muttered between themselves and then pulled the screen aside and focused the square of light onto the grimy wall instead.

The first slide looked familiar to Linda. It looked like one that Gerard had taken on their walk together. That same wash of cool green light, a radiant tree fern, a blur of water rushing between lichen-mottled rocks. Gerard raised his eyes. The audience fell quiet.

Then someone made the sound of a whipbird, the long, drawn-out note and the sudden explosive cracking of the whip. *Choo choo*, came a female retort from the other side of the hall. There was

81

restive laughter, and then a whole chorus of birds: butcherbirds, warbling magpies, the pumping coo of a pigeon. The little kids loved it. There was no shutting them up now. A flock of tiny kookaburras flew to the back of the hall and resumed their boisterous play. Linda pressed her hand over her mouth and glanced at Gerard — please let him be laughing. He wasn't, but there was the faint trace of a smile, tight and controlled, like that of a teacher waiting for a naughty class to settle.

Next came a transparency on the overhead projector. It was a map, showing the different types of forest in shades of green. Over it, in thick black texta, Gerard had drawn the new access road and turning bay, the proposed log dumps marked with crosses and the snig tracks branching off.

Linda tried to concentrate, but his words became a drone. She found herself just watching him instead, the light of the projector playing on his face. She was thinking of the birth mark on the back of his neck, right up under his hair. It was thirteen years since she'd seen it, but it would still be there. His stork bite, he called it. She used to find that cute, the image of a stork carrying baby Gerard by the scruff of the neck. It would flare red in the afternoon heat in their shack at Toona Bay as they lay together in a sweaty twist of sheets. He kept his eyes open during sex. He whimpered like a puppy when he came. These were images she'd called on again and again in her periods of loneliness.

The projector light disappeared. A latecomer had ducked inside and was blocking Linda's view.

'Sorry!' whispered the girl.

Linda moved her bag off the empty seat beside her.

'Have I missed anything?' the girl asked. Her accent was foreign. 'The police are outside.'

'They are?' Linda peered into the darkened foyer.

The young girl fingered the white fluffy tip of her plait. 'In Germany they always come, to all the demonstrations,' she continued in a hoarse whisper. 'Last year at Hanau, they were in the forest, everywhere in the trees as we were marching, with their shields like this.'

She clutched her fist in front of her. In the half-light, her face was sharp and grim. Round eyes, pale skin, blonde lashes, thin lips: she reminded Linda of a piece of sun-bleached coral.

Gerard was comparing the local rates of deforestation with rainforest in other parts of the world. He put up two more transparencies, one overlaying the other, showing the entire region with its dark forest remnants shrinking away like puddles in the sun.

'This guy is really boring,' whispered the German girl.

Linda shot her a look.

'He's also very attractive. Do you know his name?'

She hesitated. 'Gerard Ansiewicz.'

'Really? That's him?'

'You've heard of him?'

'Oh yes. When I told the people in Sydney I was coming up here to help, this is the name they gave me.'

'He doesn't need any help,' said Linda, folding her arms and fixing her eyes to the front.

'He needs a new speechwriter,' hissed the girl.

There was a rumbling in the foyer, and into the hall marched a group of men in boots and skimpy work shorts. Old, young, fat, thin, a few with only bumfluff on their faces. They grinned around at the small audience as they made their way down the back. There were two policemen at the rear, but they didn't come into the hall. Linda felt Melanie's grip tighten on her arm.

'It's fine,' she whispered. 'We knew they'd come.' But she was rattled inside. How was Gerard going to run this thing? Did he have a plan in mind? And what the hell was with the police? What were they expecting?

The millworkers, foresters, whoever they were, none of the men sat down. They stood at the back, behind an empty row of chairs, feet apart, arms folded across their chests.

'You can take a seat, if you want,' Gerard said.

'Yeah,' scoffed one of the men. 'There's a couple of empty chairs.'

'Welcome to you too, officers,' Gerard called to the police in the foyer.

In the darkness behind her, Linda could hear the soft creak of their leathers.

'We were expecting you earlier. We're nearly finished here. Perhaps we could open the floor to questions. Would you be happy with that?' Gerard began a hammy act of packing up his papers, tapping the edges together on the table in front of him.

A big gingery man stepped forward. 'I thought this was a public meeting.'

The German girl touched Linda's arm. She batted her away.

'Sandy Mitchell, everyone,' Gerard said without looking up. 'Manager of the Repentance sawmill.'

'Proprietor,' Sandy said.

Gerard stood corrected. 'And yes, it's a public meeting. Like I said, we've been waiting for you. Everyone is keen to hear what you've got to say.'

The man turned a rabbit-felt hat in his hands, walking his blunt fingers around the battered brim. Linda wondered what he was doing, wearing a hat at night. Perhaps it was part of the uniform, like the rest of the men's King Gee shorts and work boots.

'I thought perhaps I could set you people straight on a couple of things,' he began, 'give you a few facts to work with.'

The 'you people' hit a bum note. There was muffled booing, but Gerard held up his hand and encouraged Sandy to continue. Linda didn't find this man particularly threatening. Not like the bulldog next to him, with his blue singlet stretched like a balloon over his gut. In comparison Sandy Mitchell appeared almost affable, like a giant teddy bear. His speckled bottom lip reminded her of the thick slugs that came into their bathroom, and his ears, nestled in the gingery grey splinters of his hair, looked like big dried apricots stuck to the sides of his head.

'What we're talking about here is a routine management operation.'

Shouts and boos and the drumming of feet on the wooden floor.

'There's no clear-felling happening here. That's a load of bull. It's the hardwood stands we're after, and they're way up the hill.' He ploughed on, through the din, launching into an explanation of 'selective logging', 'directional felling', all those terms Gerard hated. Then he started on about their rights under Section 8A of the New South Wales Forestry Act.

'Just hold it there, Mr Mitchell,' Gerard interrupted. 'I'm well acquainted with Section 8A *and* Regulation 56 (j).'

'Here we go,' Linda muttered. 'The battle of the by-laws.' She held her head as the two of them argued the point for a minute or two.

Suddenly Gerard ducked down and poked about in his boxes under the table. When he stood up, you could see he was holding something behind his back.

The two policemen stepped into the hall.

'Settle down, officers. It's not a gun.'

For that, Gerard scored his first laugh of the night, and he flushed with pleasure.

'Okay,' he continued, 'let's talk definitions, because I'm not sure that you and I speak the same language, Mr Mitchell.'

He paused for a moment, staring at the table in front of him. 'Sandy —' He raised his eyes to the men at the back of the room. 'What do you think of when I say the word "bread"?'

Sandy looked uncomfortable. 'What d'you mean?'

'A bit of word association, come on. A loaf of bread, what image springs to mind?'

'This is ridiculous,' Sandy said.

'Something like this, maybe?' From behind his back, Gerard produced a loaf of sandwich white. A murmur rippled through the hall.

'Yeah, I s'pose.'

'That's interesting, because if I were to ask someone else, a French person perhaps, they might think of something like this.' He held up a long baguette.

'What is that?' whispered Melanie.

'Shhh.'

'My point being —'

'Yes please!' Sandy Mitchell snapped.

Gerard switched on the projector and clicked through a couple of slides. He stopped at one of a massive tree lying on its side in the undergrowth. 'A red carabeen,' he said. 'One of yours, I believe, from the basin. Happened to be in the way of your new access road. You look at that and what do you see?'

Sandy shrugged. 'A carabeen.'

'A sawlog, yes? A nice one. What would you say the log volume was? Half a hoppus ton?'

'Could be.'

'What's that then? Roof frames? Floorboards?'

'It depends — on the defects, the grain.' The moment Sandy Mitchell offered this up, he seemed to regret it, as if he'd been goaded into playing.

'The point is,' Gerard said, 'I don't see that. I see a magnificent tree that was already a century old when Captain Cook sailed past here.' He pointed to the east. 'I see a tree that was home to maybe fifty species of birds, insects, fungi — shade for hundreds of small plants and mosses — a whole ecosystem — and it's dead now, Mr Mitchell, gone, butchered two weeks ago by you and your men.'

This met with clamorous applause. Sandy Mitchell wiped his fingers across his freckled lip.

'And when I see this,' Gerard continued. Up went another slide, this one of a track littered with broken branches. 'I don't see "uphill extraction", I see vandalism. It's vandalism, Mr Mitchell,' he said again, for effect. 'I see where a bloody great tree has been dragged along the forest floor, destroying every living thing in its path.'

Sandy Mitchell looked down at the hat in his hands and waited for the cheering to subside. When he eventually raised his head, his expression was thoughtful.

'Let me tell you something, young man,' he began. 'You don't know what you're talking about. Forestry is an ancient human activity. There's been laws regulating it for over a thousand years. It differs from other primary production because of the time spans involved. We understand that and we work with it. We aim for sustainable yield. This forest here is my workplace.' He wagged a finger at the slide. 'It was my father's workplace, and his father's before him, and I can tell you that nobody — *nobody* — knows or loves or cares about this forest the way me and my family do.'

Linda winced at the crack of emotion in his voice. She felt for Melanie's hand and pulled her under her arm.

'And you lot can blow in here and tell us what to do, and carry on up there, Mr Gerard whatever-your-name-is, like you're bloody Gregory Peck. You can paint us all as redneck bastards who wouldn't know their head from their arse —'

'You said it, mate!' yelled the young man sitting on Melanie's right.

'— and I don't care!' Sandy shouted over the top of the laughter. 'Because you'll all be gone tomorrow. You'll have screwed us over and done your dash with the local DSS and then — phtt — you'll all be gone, onto the next good thing.'

Linda would later remember this as the moment when everything froze. Just for an instant, as if caught in a flash, a portent of things to come: both sides in their positions, the police waiting in the wings, as they faced each other across the impasse of empty chairs.

Then someone hurled a shoe and brought the whole thing crashing down. It was nothing much, a rubber thong, and it missed Sandy Mitchell by miles, but it was enough to bring the police charging into the room. Scuffling feet, clattering chairs, the wailing cries of children. Gerard raised his voice above the fracas and declared the meeting closed. He had their contacts, he'd be in touch, thank you all for coming.

Linda thought of all the names and numbers she didn't manage to collect, and then, like a hammer blow, she remembered the clipboard. She'd left it in the foyer, out there with the police. Gerard would have a fucking fit! She grabbed Melanie by the arm and pulled her through the door, tripping over the bare legs of the German girl.

'Muum!'

'The clipboard!' She blinked in the darkness.

'It's here,' Melanie said, producing it from behind the wooden counter, its pen dangling on a string.

Linda snatched it from her and hugged it to her chest. Thank Christ for that! Thank God! She crept in behind the old ticket counter and gratefully sank to the floor.

'Come and sit with me, Mel. We're not going back in there. Let's just wait till everybody's gone.'

They sat on the floor, in the darkness, behind the high wooden bench, listening to the broken conversations of people shuffling out the door. The police left with the millworkers, sniping about the small turnout and that stupid thing with the bread. Soon there was nothing but the musty smell of the carpet and the sounds of people packing up inside.

'Stay here,' Linda said, getting stiffly to her feet and sticking her head around the door. Jane and her friends were stacking chairs on the far side of the hall. At the front stood Gerard and the young German girl, deep in conversation, coiling an extension cord between them.

'What's the matter, Mum?'

'Nothing,' Linda said, watching the slow looping of the cord.

'You're crying.'

She came back and sat down again, the clipboard on her knee. Melanie pulled a wad of tissue from her pocket, and she took it with a grateful nod.

'I'll be all right in a minute. I just — the police and all that. It makes me tense.' She was really crying. A tear ran down her cheek and splashed onto the list of names.

'But they've gone now,' said Melanie. 'It's just Jane and Gerard. We should go and help them with the chairs.'

'We should.' Linda went to move, but the tears overwhelmed her, and she sank back to the floor.

Melanie stared at her. 'What's the matter with you?'

'Nothing.' Everything. *The cold wind off the Derwent, her mother's brochures blowing down the street.* The clipboard slipped sideways; the pen fell on the floor. 'I'm just so fucking useless, that's all.'

Chapter Eight

A chunk of wood landed on the bonfire, collapsing the pile and sending orange sparks flying into the sky. Linda was pretty stoned by now. Things were getting on top of her. Deep Purple boomed from the speakers that Andy had dragged out onto the front veranda, and a handful of people she didn't know were dancing on the grass. A young man was juggling fire, his bare torso gleaming with sweat. The flaming clubs drew mesmerising squiggles in the air as his arms moved in and out of impossible knots. One of the dancing women squealed as his fire club zoomed past her. She flung her arms around her head and ran whimpering into the night.

Linda didn't think that the woman was in danger. Just off her face and freaking out, more like it. There was a lot of trippy stuff going down — and up, that too. People were toeing that dangerous line between magic and maniacal.

A cheer went up as yet another set of lights came over the horizon and tilted down the hill towards Wayne Mackenzie's dairy. He was going to have a fit about all these cars. Linda watched to see if they were shutting the gates behind them as they came through, but it was hard to tell in the darkness and who gave a shit anyway. It was a ute, this one. People were standing on the tray at the back, waving their arms and whooping as it bounced up the road. How did it happen, this impromptu party? How many more were coming? Linda wasn't in the mood. She was blue with exhaustion and couldn't see how the evening's events warranted such revelry.

But then most of these people hadn't been at the Braemar Hall. They were coming from Druidane, where, at the eleventh hour, Phil de Beer had organised a gathering of his own. 'Fucking brilliant,' was how he described it as he got out of his car. 'You guys were the perfect decoys, man. We got over a hundred people. It was fucking amazing, the energy in that room, the sense of resolve and common purpose. It was —' He shook his head, unable to find the word.

Linda looked at Gerard. He took a swig of his beer and slowly wiped his hand across his mouth.

'Anyway, the consensus was that you and I bury the hatchet, so we are,' said Phil with a flourish, opening his arms as if inviting a bear hug. 'Come on,' he cajoled. 'I love you, man, you know that. I've come to smoke a peace pipe, and look, I've brought one ready-packed.' He reached into the car and retrieved a small hash pipe. 'Let's go inside. Come on, we need to talk.'

Linda went to follow them, when all of a sudden a small pale creature came hurtling out of the darkness and bounded up the front steps. It was that bloody German girl — Bettina, her name was. From the garden, Linda watched Gerard introduce her to Phil. Bettina stood between the two men, ridiculously eager, her rapt gaze moving from one to the other. Gerard placed a guiding hand on the small of her back, and the three of them disappeared inside.

Bettina had come home with them after the meeting. This was presumably at Gerard's invitation and he didn't bother consulting anyone else. Neither did he explain that they'd be driving down to the creek below Repentance first to pick up some of her stuff. She was staying in one of the old teepees down there, where newcomers often spent a few days or weeks until they got themselves sorted.

'I couldn't stand to sleep in one of those things,' Linda said as they waited for her in the jeep.

'You didn't have to,' Gerard said.

That was true. She didn't.

Bettina emerged from the mildewed tent and walked towards them, along the dim beam of their headlights. She had what looked like a small duffle bag slung over her shoulder and a dog on a piece of rope.

'There's a dog? You didn't say that. Why does the dog have to come?'

It was some sort of cattle-dog bitser, fully grown but with the lankiness and oversized paws of a pup. It leapt into the back seat and over Melanie's legs, reducing her to squeals of excitement.

Linda turned around and glowered at her. 'Don't let it lick your face!'

'He's okay, he's friendly,' Bettina said, climbing into the back beside them.

Linda looked at Gerard. 'What about Donovan?'

'What about him?'

'He doesn't like other dogs, you know that.'

Gerard bent over the steering wheel. 'What's your problem, Linda?'

'I don't have a problem.'

'Good.'

Bettina and Melanie had chatted all the way home, about the dog, whose name was Wotan, and Germany, and the guy who threw the thong. They could have been sisters, Linda thought, with their slight builds and fair hair. There didn't appear to be much of an age difference either. She and Gerard were like Mum and Dad in the front of the family car, saying the bare minimum and exchanging hostile looks.

'Where did you get this bread from?' Melanie had pulled the baguette from the box under her feet.

'From town,' Gerard said. 'There's a baker there makes them.'

'That was funny, wasn't it, Mum?'

'It was,' Linda conceded. 'It was clever. Gregory Peck!'

'He didn't know what to say, that man, did he, Mum?'

'No, he didn't. None of them did. Semantics was a bit beyond them.'

'Yuuuck, it's stale!' Melanie squealed, her mouth full of bread.

'It's French bread,' Bettina said. 'It goes really dry. The bread in Germany is much better. Here, give it to Wotan.'

There was a commotion as the dog grabbed the baguette, wolfed it down, and began to clean up the crumbs with a slobbery tongue. Melanie was helpless with laughter. The dog was licking her foot. Then, in the chaos, it leapt at her head and licked her on the mouth.

'Stop it!' Linda shouted. 'Don't get it excited.'

'I didn't do anything.'

'You did. Shut up and sit still.' She sat rigidly in her seat, feeling the two girls smirking behind her back.

Sure enough, the dogs went for each other as soon as they got home. Poor little Donovan was dragged away and put on his chain out the back of the house while Wotan proceeded to sniff and piss all over his territory.

Now, alone by the fire, Linda decided to go and see Donovan, taking with her a bottle of vodka that someone had left in the grass. She took a mouthful as she made her way down the side of the house, enjoying the burn in her throat while telling herself not to drink too much. She hadn't eaten since midday.

Donovan was pleased to see her, poor little fella. He gave a squeaky yawn and stretched forward on the chain, his bum in the air and his tail wagging. Linda sat down on the septic tank and rubbed his velvety ears. She checked him over for signs of injury but couldn't see any blood.

'Is he okay?' Jane was standing on the back porch.

'I think so, yes. He's lucky. That dog's got those jaws, you know, those ones that lock and don't let go?'

'He's just a cattle dog, isn't he?'

'No, he's got something else in him too. He's got that broad head, like one of those vicious breeds. She shouldn't have brought him here. I told Gerard that.'

Jane came and sat with her. 'He's all right out here for a bit. How about you, Linda? Are you doing okay?'

'Yeah, why?'

'I'm really tired myself. I wish they'd all go home.'

'It was Andy who asked them to come.'

'I know.'

'What the fuck's with him? What was he doing at Phil's thing? Did you know he was going there?'

Jane slumped forward, her chin in her hand. 'He said his friends needed help setting up the band. He's good with all that stuff, you know, sound gear. And then he thought he'd make amends by bringing them all back here, and he's right, you know, Phil and Gerard have to work things out.'

An uncomfortable silence followed. Linda cast around for something else to say. 'How's your parsley going?'

'It died.'

'Oh, I'm sorry.'

For some reason, Jane found this funny. She threw back her head and laughed. Maybe she'd been smoking too. The dope was very strong. 'Hey,' she whispered to Linda, like a schoolgirl in a dorm. 'We didn't have dinner. Are you hungry?'

She went inside and returned a few minutes later with two pieces of cold vegetable quiche. She poked Donovan with her foot to get him to move aside, and handed Linda a floppy slice, rubbery with cheese.

They chewed. It was chewy. They raised their faces to the sky. A group of flying foxes came beating towards them and dived headlong into the mango tree. The bats squabbled and thrashed about in the foliage near the top. From the front yard came the steady throb of the bass guitar. Linda felt calmer, almost serene. She sensed that Jane was reaching out to her. She proffered the bottle of vodka, but Jane shook her head.

'You should go easy on that stuff.'

Oh God, here she was again. That caramel-coated voice, the reasonable smile like bloody, sappy Melanie Wilkes in *Gone with the Wind*.

'I don't drink much,' Linda said, taking a defiant swig. 'I found this lying in the grass. I don't know whose it is.'

'You're a bit upset tonight, that's all. The grog can make you maudlin.'

'I'm not upset, and this isn't *grog*, it's vodka.'

'I saw you crying earlier. I was a bit concerned.'

'Don't concern yourself with me, I'm fine.'

Linda expected Jane to leave and was surprised to find she was sorry. There was comfort to be found in the company of another woman. She thought about this for a moment and then apologised.

'You don't drink at all, do you?' she said.

'Not at the moment, no. We're trying to get pregnant, me and Andy. We've been trying for some time.'

Linda said nothing. She was pretty sure she was blind drunk at the moment of Melanie's conception, but she wasn't drunk enough now to say something tactless like that.

Instead she mumbled, 'You'd make a good mother. Not like me, I'm a hopeless mum.'

'You are not.'

'I know you think that.'

'Linda, I don't. I think you have a lovely relationship, you and Mel. You seem like — good friends. Are you close to your mom? Is she alive? You never mention her.'

Linda snorted. 'Neither have you. I know nothing about anyone's family here except Gerard's of course. He's lucky. His parents are really nice. I used to spend a lot of time at his place when I was young.'

'You two go back such a long way. Were you at school together?'

Linda shifted on her buttocks. She didn't want to be talking to Jane about this sort of stuff, but there was a tacit tit-for-tat in the swapping of confidences, and she could offer a few details without revealing too much.

'We went to the same school, but he was two years ahead of me. We didn't really get to know each other until uni. He was on the student council, and I used to help out in the office, and then we went up north together, up to Toona Bay.'

She would leave it there. No need to mention that his parents had belonged to the same church as hers. They had only stayed a year or so before they were scared off by crackpots like her mother. They were Presbyterian too, but soon came to realise that her mother's congregation was something else entirely.

Jane stood up and muttered something about having to soak the porridge oats for breakfast. She unclipped Donovan's chain and tucked him under her arm. Linda watched them go inside, Jane's ample bottom swaying inside her gathered skirt and Donovan's tail waving to and fro. Linda had no reason to remain on the septic tank. It was time to return to the party. She walked down the side of the house, under the mango tree. The fruit bats were still up there. Judas Priest was throbbing. There was something aggressive in the atmosphere of the night — a combination of the distorted guitar, the violent squeals of the bats, and the rancid smell of mangoes rotting on the ground.

Coming around the corner of the house, she saw Gerard and Phil sitting by the fire and that little on-heat bitch Bettina sitting between them.

'I told Gerard that. They were hopeless.' Bettina was raising her voice to be heard above the racket. 'That purple paper was too dark, you couldn't even read it. And that flowery border, what was that?

It looked like a party invitation.' She was talking to Phil on her left, but her body was ever so slightly inclined towards Gerard. Linda sat down on the other side of the flames and watched them through the smoke and wobbling heat. Phil packed a cone and handed the bong to Bettina, who shook her head and handed it to Gerard. Linda looked at their thighs. They were almost touching, Gerard's clad in jeans, Bettina's bare, except for a tiny pair of denim shorts.

'Linda did them,' Gerard said, without raising his eyes.

'You don't need pretty pictures,' Bettina continued, perhaps unaware of her presence. 'You want photographs — tree stumps, devastation — like that photo you showed at the meeting, clear-felling. I'll do them next time, if you like, if you need another poster. I did a lot of stuff like that in Germany. Lots of demonstrations. The Wyhl occupation, I worked on that, and Brokdorf too, last year. I've been going on marches since I was small. With my parents, I used to go. My first march was with my mother against the Shah of Iran.'

Linda couldn't help herself. She gave a honk of laughter. Gerard lifted his face from the bong, holding the smoke in his lungs. He blew it out the side of his mouth and said in a cold voice, 'Linda went to demonstrations with her mother too.'

For a moment she thought he was trying to include her in the conversation. Then the full horror of what he was saying hit her like icy water. The bastard; he'd promised. He'd said he'd never tell, and here he was, three weeks later, blurting it out in front of this little pleased-with-herself German tart.

'Demonstrations for what?' Bettina wanted to know.

'Nothing! I didn't. He's just teasing.'

You creep, she thought, holding his gaze. He finally relented.

'Yeah, that's right. It's just a joke between us.'

A joke, you fuckwit. Linda's head was starting to spin. It was then she noticed Gerard's hand around Bettina's waist, his finger stroking the pale skin between the hem of her cropped singlet and her little cunt-splitting shorts.

'Muuum?'

Melanie stood behind her, looking very young and rumpled in an oversized t-shirt. 'I can't sleep. There's too much noise.'

'Right. Okay. Are the windows closed?'

'It doesn't help. Can I use your earplugs?'

'Yes, do that.'

'Where are they?'

'Shit, Mel, I don't know!' She immediately regretted the irritation in her voice. She could feel Bettina watching her from across the fire. She could feel the circling stroke of Gerard's finger. 'Try the side pocket of my shoulder bag.'

'Can I stay out here instead?'

'I was just coming back inside.'

'No, don't. I want to stay out here with you.'

Linda felt caught in a time slip, in some bone-jolting correction. She was the mother now, not the child, not the girl in the jealous rage. Melanie nestled against her. Linda drew her close. 'They'll be going soon, sweetie,' she whispered into the girl's mussy hair.

A twig in the fire in front of them squealed and fizzed with sap. In the house the stereo had been switched off and replaced with the strum of guitars. Someone had a bongo drum. Everyone was going inside. Gerard pulled Bettina to her feet and they headed towards the veranda.

Soon only Linda and Melanie remained beside the fire. Mother and daughter huddled together under a starry sky. The flames purred and images flickered behind Linda's eyes, a cinefilm of mothers and daughters taking on the world. Mothers and daughters marching against the Shah of Iran. Mother and daughter standing on a bleak pavement in Hobart, their coats buttoned against the morning cold. Girl mothers running the gauntlet, their faces stricken with shame and their babies, their dirty secrets, hidden under their clothes. Babies glowing translucent with tadpole eyes and little bud arms and tiny fingers and toes. 'Think of the baby,' her mother would whisper as the girls jostled past them, and nine-year-old Linda would step out in front of them, holding the photographs.

Melanie stirred. 'Mum?'

'What?'

'You know Bettina?'

'What about her.'

'She looks like a Siamese cat.'

Linda smiled. 'Yes, she does.'

'A small one.'

'A kitten.'

'No, just a very small cat.'

'That's good. Well done.' She looked at the girl tucked under her arm, cheek against her breast, and thought for a moment that she'd gone back to sleep. Her eyes were closed, but her breathing wasn't entirely steady, and a tiny smile still lingered on her lips.

Monolepta

They swarmed just after lunch on the Saturday afternoon. It was a sudden attack on a mostly unsuspecting town, but like all these things, if you looked hard enough you could see it was a long time coming.

Poss Williams had found two of them on his avocado trees the week before: two tiny golden beetles in one of his jam-jar traps, floating on a scum of sugar syrup. He didn't think it warranted a call to the research station, but he did go to his shed that day and check on his stocks of Rogor. On the Tuesday night when Sandy Mitchell was closing up his office at the mill, he thought he saw some crawling on the outside light. He even muttered the word *monolepta*, but there was no one there to hear him, and when he went to take a closer look, they'd gone.

Who knows what called the beetles to descend on the town like that: the still days of sticky heat, the transit of the stars? Whatever it was, there were suddenly millions of them bouncing in the air, crawling thick on the ceilings of the verandas and raining down like bits of unpopped corn. By two o'clock, when Joanne Parmenter took the call from the hospital, they'd sucked the life out of half the leaves in town. By the time she stumbled up the street, crying her sister's name, the leaves on the neighbours' hibiscus bushes were hanging like crusty rags.

It was a disaster for Peg Parmenter too, on the following Thursday morning when she was doing the church flowers for Delia's funeral. She asked around for the usual contributions — hydrangeas, roses, Christmas bush, spider lilies at a pinch — but there wasn't a decent bloom to be found.

Chapter Nine

Afterwards Joanne and Barbara would laugh about poor Mrs Willis and her unfortunate remark at the cemetery. 'I wish she'd been cremated,' she'd said as the rain pelted down and people tramped towards their cars. 'We would've all been a lot warmer.' It was funny in retrospect, when a few weeks had passed and they were able to laugh about things like that — the woman's mortification as she saw the shock register on the faces around her, and then her equally unfortunate bluster about managing to dig herself into a deeper hole.

Neither of the girls had heard her say it; other people told them. In fact, Joanne's recall of the entire day was fragmented from the moment they left the house and walked up the road to the Anglican church. Some bits so vivid, others blank as if someone had pressed 'erase' on the memory cassette in her brain.

'No, that was your hippie friends later,' said Barb, when Joanne told her this. 'They must've slipped you something.'

Joanne managed to smile. It was the first reference Barb had made to what had happened out at Uncle Bill's. Joanne remembered that last part of the day very clearly, and the bit before, at the wake, with Aunty Peg in the kitchen. But there were decisions she had made that day, things she had done that she couldn't quite explain. The more she examined the events of that rain-sodden afternoon, the more the whole thing fell apart like tissue.

Thursday began much like every other day that week. For about five seconds after Joanne opened her eyes, everything was back in its old place. The bright split in the bedroom curtains, the neighbour's phlegmy cough, the distant clank and growl of the trucks heading out from the mill. But then, as she lay on her side, her curled hands under her cheek, the fact would return. *My mother is dead.* That awful, sickening jolt that drained the blood from her face and the colour from the room.

Barbara wasn't at work. There was too much noise in the kitchen. Joanne knew that when she went out there to make herself some breakfast, the food would turn thick and tasteless in her mouth, like Perkins Paste.

But today things were a little bit different again. Aunty Peg wasn't there, for one thing; she was busy at the church. And the shop would be shut all day for the first time since the weekend. Mrs Blainey had been keeping things going since then, opening up for a few hours each day, but no one was expecting to buy bread and milk on the morning of the funeral. Neither did people seem to be calling in, which was a relief. It was growing tiring, the endless procession of visitors, flowers, food. All those people trying to make themselves useful. Someone even came and gardened for them on Tuesday. That was Mrs Willis, Tracy's mum; she brought her own tools and everything. She cleaned up after the monoleptas, raking up the desiccated leaves from under the lemon tree. That sort of made sense, but then she pulled out all the nutgrass from under the sooty old rose bushes down the back. Nobody had touched those for years, and there didn't seem much point in tending them now.

Barbara had remarked on this the night before, looking at the freshly tilled soil under the roses. 'Do you remember that woman ever visiting Mum when she was sick? There are people who get off on this stuff.'

'What stuff,' Joanne asked.

'On death. All of a sudden everyone was Mum's best friend and they're here in the house trying to make themselves important.' She glanced around the yard that had been mowed by someone else. 'Some of them Mum didn't even like. She never liked Mrs Willis that much.'

The two girls had taken to sitting outside in the evenings after dark. Not on the porch but on the grass right down the back, where they could hardly see each other's faces and Barbara could sneak a cigarette. It was one of the new patterns they'd fallen into over the past five days as the normal rhythms of their lives gave way. Joanne liked this time with her sister: it made her feel grown-up. Out there in the darkness, they could giggle about stuff without feeling guilty, or talk about who was pissing them off without someone telling them not to be mean.

Last night, for the first time, Ray had come looking for them.

'Hello, girls,' he said.

Barb looked up, shading her eyes against the porch light blazing behind him.

'Hi, Dad. You want to join us?' The hand holding her cigarette hovered behind her back.

To Joanne's surprise, their father sat on the ground beside them. She looked at his good polyester shorts and found herself worrying about grass stains.

'We're just talking about Mrs Willis,' said Barb.

'Yeah?'

'About the gardening thing.'

'Oh yes.' He blinked stupidly at the piles of nutgrass. 'People are very kind.'

They hadn't seen a lot of him over the past few days, and the three of them had hardly been alone. In the darkness, he looked blue-grey and haggard. He'd missed a shave or two. They sat in awkward silence until Barbara finally gave up and took a drag. It wasn't like he didn't know she smoked. He just thought it was a filthy habit, and couldn't help telling her that.

The burning tip of Barb's cigarette glowed bright against her face.

'You got a spare one of those?' he asked.

'You want one?'

'Yeah. Hand 'em over.'

The girls watched, astonished, as he shook a cigarette from the box, lit it, and inhaled. Joanne wondered if he'd been drinking.

'Are you okay, Dad?'

'Yeah, I'm fine.'

He stared at the grass between his knees, his finger tapping nervously on the cigarette. Then his head jerked up. 'What about you two?'

'We're okay,' Barbara said. 'It's nice out here, isn't it? The smell is getting too much in there, those lilies.'

Ray peered around the yard and nodded. 'So you're both okay about the wake? About us holding it at Uncle Bill's?'

'Oh God, Dad! Not that again.'

'I just wanted to check. You seemed —'

'We don't care!'

'And it's not a wake, remember,' Joanne chimed in.

'Yeah, Dad, Catholics have wakes.'

'That's enough, you two. Give your Aunty Peg a break.'

The girls smirked at each other.

'To be honest,' said Barb, 'I couldn't see any problem with holding it here, but it doesn't matter. It just seems stupid, everyone having to get in their cars and drive all the way out there.'

'It's only ten minutes.'

'Yeah, okay. We're just sick of talking about it. No one ever mentions the actual funeral. That's the important thing.'

Ray stubbed out his cigarette. He'd barely taken a drag.

'Don't!' whined Barbara, looking for a moment like she was going to salvage it. 'What a waste.'

'I pay for them.'

'You do not! I put the money in the till, don't I, Jo?'

Ray got to his feet and brushed at the back of his shorts. 'It's a filthy bloody habit anyway,' he said and stalked back up to the house.

This morning here they were again, the three of them at the breakfast table. This was the shape of their family now, a triangle. They talked very little at first, until the discussion turned to practicalities like turns for the shower and clothes to be ironed. The doorbell rang only once, another lot of flowers. Joanne took delivery of them and brought them into the kitchen, a long galleon of red carnations and camellia leaves.

'They're nice,' said Barbara. 'Who are they from?'

Joanne frowned at the florist's handwriting. 'My school.' She was surprised by the sudden constriction in her throat, the strangled sound of the words. She hurried through to the lounge room and placed the arrangement among the others on the coffee table. Then she sank into a chair and stared at the flowers, picturing the women in the school office placing the order on the phone. It was like a message from another world, from the normal world where the school bus had gone every day that week. She'd been surprised by that feeling too, by the longing it invoked as she looked up the street and saw it pull away.

They left the house at one o'clock and walked up to the church. From that moment, the funeral directors took control, calmly steering them around to the back of the building to wait until everyone else had gone in. The window sills of the vestry were still covered with the decomposing husks of monolepta beetles. Joanne drew a 'J' in them with her finger and Aunty Peg warned her not to get dirty. Then Barb told their father that he had shaving cream on his neck. That was the last thing Joanne remembered anyone actually saying.

She did remember the stifling heat inside the wooden church and the slow flick of the ceiling fan turning in the rafters. Someone had tilted the tiny panes at the top of the stained-glass windows in a futile attempt to cool the place down. The zipper on her new dress was sticking into her side. She remembered the feeling of people's eyes drilling into her back during the service, and the murmur that ran through the congregation when the thunder rumbled outside. After all the fuss, Aunty Peg's flowers actually looked quite nice. She'd resorted to bunches of croton leaves, which the beetles didn't like, spiked with tough bromeliads, the common red and purple kind that grew under people's tank stands.

Beyond that, it was pretty much a blur — the wheedling organ, the hymns and prayers. Joanne had steeled herself for the first glimpse of the coffin as they entered the church, but even that didn't shake her up as she'd hoped it might. She sat in the front pew, just a few feet away from it, telling herself, again and again, that her mother was right there.

Chapter Ten

The storm front pushed across the sky. First came the wind, stirring through the avenue of pencil willows that ran the length of the cemetery, sending their leaves skittering along the narrow bitumen road. Thankfully the heaviest of the rain held off until the end of the committal. The small clutch of people who'd continued on to the burial rattled through the Lord's Prayer with a sense of urgency.

Joanne glanced behind her. Mrs Phelps, her history teacher, was there, and her uncles, Leo and Tony, her mum's younger brothers, who'd arrived that morning from Rockhampton. Sandy Mitchell and his wife, and Evelyn, her mum's best friend. Mr and Mrs Willis were at the back of the group, but Tracy wasn't with them now. Joanne had seen her earlier, standing with Rhonda outside the church. They must've both taken the day off school. Maybe they'd gone back already, or maybe they'd gone on to Uncle Bill's and she'd see them later.

The rain began to fall and everybody pressed a little closer. Women in heels stepped gingerly onto the AstroTurf that was spread like a blanket around the grave to cover the raw dirt. The edges draped over the sides of the hole, which was further obscured by the casket suspended on silver rails. *Our days are like the grass*, the minister said. Joanne studied the tiny blades of synthetic lawn at her feet. *We flourish like a flower of the field; when the wind goes over it, it is gone, and its place shall know it no more.* The prickle of rain increased on the canopy of umbrellas. Beneath it, people's faces were washed colourless and the air smelt warm and stuffy like a car boot. The coffin began its jerky descent. Quickly now, the quicker the better. *The quick and the dead,* he said. *Unto him that is able to keep us from falling, dominion and power, both now and forever.*

Then it bucketed down. People glanced at one another, wondering if they were free to go. The minister raced through the dismissal and they hurried for their cars, men holding their wives by the elbow as they stumbled across the uneven ground.

Ray and the girls waited a little longer by the grave under the sturdy black umbrellas provided by the funeral home.

'It's like those TV programs,' Barbara said.

Joanne looked up and, for the first time, noticed the backhoe waiting on the far side of the lawn. A man was standing beside it in a grey plastic poncho.

'The rain,' Barb said, 'the graveyard. Like those shows set in the olden days, those English ones, you know.'

'*Upstairs, Downstairs.*'

'Yeah, like that. It always rains at funerals in those things.'

They stood in silence while the two funeral directors packed up the folding chairs they'd provided for the elderly.

'Are we ready, then?' asked one of them.

Joanne hesitated. It felt too ordinary an action, to turn and walk away. Surely there was something more the three of them should do at this point. Then she saw the man across the way climb onto the digger. She gasped and hurried after Barb and her dad, towards the shiny funeral car that was waiting by the gate.

It took them back to the house, where they changed into their own car for the drive out to Uncle Bill's. The rain was falling in wind-driven sheets as they turned off the Balbirnie road and headed out along the river flats. By the time they reached Bill's turn-off, milky orange water was running down his drive. Great turds of mud lined the edges of the road where dozens of cars had already churned their way up the hill. Bill and Janine had gone straight home after the church service to be there for any early guests: those who didn't like burials or didn't want to get caught in the rain. That was most people, as it turned out. The paddock beside the house was already packed with cars, and the ground had been trampled to a quagmire. Someone had laid down planks of wood to get people to the front porch. Water puddled around the umbrellas leaning by the front door.

Once inside, Joanne felt like the late arrival at a party. With the new patio out of action, everyone was crammed into the lounge and living rooms. The windows had fogged over, and there was a loud and unrelenting burble of conversation.

Uncle Bill was staring through the patio doors at the rain bouncing off the pebblecrete.

'It's a damned shame,' he said, 'after all the good weather we've had.'

'Get yourselves a lemonade, girls,' Aunty Janine called. She was shouldering her way through the crowd, removing delicate ornaments and placing drink coasters on the polished rosewood surfaces. 'It's in the sink in the laundry. And help yourself to food. Look how much there is, we'll be eating cake for weeks.'

Aunty Peg and her Auxiliary friends were in the kitchen, fussing with the hot-water urn they'd borrowed from the church, and setting out trays of thick white china.

'There you are,' Peg said, raising her voice above the din. She bustled over and gave them both a kiss. 'Didn't they do well?' she said to the other women. 'Not an easy thing, particularly for a shy little mite like this one —' She squeezed Joanne's arm. 'Where's your dad, love, I'll get him a cuppa.'

'I think he's having a beer.'

'Oh,' said Peg. 'And what about you two? You must be starving. I'll bet you didn't eat before the service. If I'm not there to feed them, they hardly eat, these two.'

The women smiled.

'We did,' said Barb. 'We had Mum's soup. I found some in the freezer.'

'I thought you'd finished those.'

'There was just the one left. It was nice, wasn't it, Jo? Minestrone.'

'I hope you weren't wearing your good dresses, then. They stain like blazes, those soups of your mother's. Ruined a good blouse of mine once.'

Barbara's jaw set rigid.

'I'll have something,' Joanne blurted, picking up a cake plate.

'Good girl,' Peg said. 'That's the way. Off you go, then, both of you. And try my passionfruit sponge,' she called after them. 'It's the one I made for last year's show, but this one's better. Duck eggs!'

Every table top in the dining room was covered with food. Biscuits and slices, patty cakes, sponges filled with jam and cream, large platters of sandwiches garnished with sprigs of parsley. Mrs Phelps set down what looked like a plate of prunes wrapped in bacon. It was moved to the sideboard the moment she left the room.

Joanne took a piece of caramel slice and went to find Tracy and Rhonda. Someone had told her that they were in the television room, but she eventually found them in one of the guest bedrooms down the hall. They'd swapped dresses and were looking at themselves in the full-length mirror. They looked embarrassed when Joanne opened the door, and mumbled that they were sorry about her mother. She nodded, struggling to swallow a mouthful of caramel goo.

'So what do you think of this?' Tracy asked, turning in the mirror. She was wearing one of those Rio dresses, with the large flounce that pulled down off the shoulders.

'It's mine,' Rhonda told Joanne. 'It's from Hawaii Hut.'

'I want one,' Tracy said, 'but I'll need a smaller size. Do you want to try it on, Jo?'

Joanne wiped her mouth and shook her head. She knew the dress wouldn't fit her. In the mirror her round-necked, side-zipped *broderie anglaise* frock suddenly looked like something a little kid would wear. But even worse was her face. She looked different. 'Grief affects us physically, Jo,' Mrs Phelps had warned her. And here it was, grief. She could actually see it in the strange dry flatness of her eyes.

She wandered back down the hall, glancing into the rooms on either side. Ray had always described the new house as 'a lovely home', but her mum had never liked it. It was a brick and tile project home with roller doors and a carport, much like all the others that had sprung up in the new estates on the edge of Balbirnie. Her mother's objections had not been those of Aunty Peg: they had nothing to do with the Parmenter family heritage or Bill's decision to rent the old house out to hippies. Delia had simply felt that it didn't take advantage of the site, with its northerly aspect and views up the valley. It would be fine in town, she had said to Joanne one day on their way home, but she didn't like the low ceilings, and as for that cream carpet — what were they thinking? How on earth could anyone keep that clean in red-soil country like this?

Joanne slipped her plate and half-eaten slice onto a small hall table. She liked the cosy feeling of the house, particularly in the rain. It wasn't draughty like weatherboard houses were. The windows didn't rattle and the doors didn't slam. She liked the soft carpet, and the squidgy feel in the taps when you turned them off, without any hint of recoil in the walls. She like the kitchen benchtop with its moulded laminate, and the small, neat light switches that worked at the touch of a finger.

But full of people as it was today, it was stifling. She cleared a patch in the condensation on the dining-room window and felt sealed off from the rain-freshened world outside. You could hardly even hear the rain on the tiled roof. It didn't gurgle through the plastic pipes or gush into the water tanks, which were concrete and buried underground.

She found Ray in the lounge room talking with Delia's brothers about their sugar farms up north and the floods they'd had in May. Joanne like these uncles. She didn't see much of them. Even now, they were just staying the one night at Bill and Janine's.

'Why aren't you staying with us?' she asked. 'You're not even related to them.'

'Ah well, we thought, in the circumstances, you know —'

'Dad?'

'What?'

'Why aren't they staying with us?'

Ray muttered something about Bill having a guest room.

'But so have we.' It hit her the moment she said it. The spare room, the sick room, they didn't want to stay there. Even though her mum didn't die in there, even though people had come and collected most of the hospital stuff. How long would it be until someone was willing to sleep in that room again?

She looked around for Barbara. There was no sign of her, or of Michael Phelan, who'd arrived just after them, looking uncomfortable in a collared shirt and tie. Joanne went to look for them in the kitchen. Inside, Peg and two other women were washing and wiping up. They had their backs to the door and didn't see her.

'Will you be selling your place then, Peg?'

'Not at this stage, no. I could let it, but there's not much of a market. Not worth the hassle, really.'

'Unless you do a Bill, of course, and let it to some —'

'Phhh,' said Peg with a sideways punch of her elbow. There was stifled laughter.

Outside the kitchen, Joanne leant against the wall.

'Well, I have to say, it's very good of you. I wouldn't be taking on teenage girls at this time of my life.'

'It's not like I've got much choice.' That was Peg again. 'I'm there most evenings anyway, and Ray's not up to the task. Barbara's up to God-knows-what with that Phelan boy from the mill. I've told Ray, she'll get herself pregnant, you mark my words, she will. And Joanne,

she'll be getting her menses any tick of the clock. How's a man supposed to deal with things like that?'

Outside the door, Joanne winced.

'I always say —' Peg dropped her voice. 'Where is she, anyway?'

'Who?'

'Joanne.'

'In the TV room, isn't she, Marge? Janine sent all the kids down
there.'

'I always say,' Peg said again, 'that you can pick the girls without
mothers. They've got a look about them.'

'Oh.'

'With their personal hygiene.'

'Mmm.'

Joanne strained to hear, but Peg's voice had fallen to a whisper.
There was something about blackheads, about her weight and biting
her nails.

'They need a woman around the place,' someone offered kindly.

'They do,' said Peg. 'She's had no help for the last six months, that
little girl, and I'm sorry but it shows.'

Joanne's face was burning. The blood beat in her ears. She took
off through the house, casting about for Barbara. In the lounge room,
Ray was still sitting on the upright chair. He was holding a plate
of shortbread, as if he intended to hand it around but had lost his
train of thought. Bewildered. Not up to the task. Joanne felt her rage
subside. She opened the front door, stepped outside, and gulped the
cool, wet air.

Chapter Eleven

Outside the back gate, the path gave way to something more like a cow track that drew her around the crown of the hill and down through a patch of tobacco bush and camphor laurel saplings. It wasn't raining now, but the sky was still bleak and the leaves on the sapling trees continued to shudder and drip. Joanne's hair grew damp. The sharp wet grasses stung her legs, and her feet felt chilled and greasy in her sandals.

It was Aunty Janine's cat that had turned her in this direction. It shot out from under the house as she came down the steps, and ran with purpose, low to the ground, under the gate and away. Joanne simply kept going, resigned to the fact that the path would lead her to the dairy on the other side of the hill. That's why you walked it; that's where it went. For some time after they built the new house, Bill and Janine had continued to milk their cows on that side. They would come this way twice a day, in the early mornings and late afternoons, surrounded by the waving tails of dogs.

Bill said it didn't bother him, using the dairy after his mother died, and he laughed when Joanne told him she could never go back there, ever. She hadn't been inside it for almost four years, not since that long-ago afternoon, and she didn't think she'd have the courage now. The door would most likely be locked anyway, to keep the tenants out, but she could walk around the outside — that would be okay. There might still be mulberries on the tree in the yards. She felt an urge to stuff her mouth with mulberries wearing the white *broderie anglaise* dress that Peg had chosen for her.

There it was, the dairy, still distant, yet vivid against the heavy sky, crouched on the grassy spur below the old house. She'd been thinking about it a lot lately, since the museum excursion. She thought there might be old milking stuff in the cream room that she and Mel could use for their project. She hadn't mentioned this to Melanie. She didn't want her going down there and poking around on her own. She did, however, tell her that her grandmother had died in there, just to freak her out. And then she told her that her grandma had been born in Melanie's bedroom. This may or may not have been true — it could have been any room of the house — but she had been born at home. Joanne recalled what Delia had said on the day that her grandma died, as they waited up at the house for the ambulance to come. Her dad must have been there too by then — they'd rung him straightaway — but it was her mother's words that she remembered now. The two of them were sitting on the swinging chair out on the veranda, watching the cows disperse, unmilked and bellowing for their calves. Delia was hugging her when Joanne heard her say, 'Imagine dying just a few hundred yards from the house where you were born.'

As she made her way across the slope, the track became deeper, muddy and rocky, carved out over the decades by the daily plod of cattle. It was something she used to love watching from the house when she was little: how at four o'clock the cows would come trickling in from all over the farm to converge in the slippery quagmire of the holding paddock. When the air was still, you could hear the babble of a radio above the chug of the milking machine. Then, one by one, the doors at the back of the bails would fly open like flaps on a children's toy. From a distance it all looked like clockwork. It was hard to imagine that it was really her grandma and uncle down there, heaving those doors open with heavy wooden barge poles.

Joanne glanced up at the house. It looked like no one was home. There was no sign of Melanie's mother's car or that crazy Gerard guy's jeep. In her grandma's day, on a wet day like this, there'd be smoke coming out of the rusty pipe chimney above the kitchen. Splinters of wood were kept in buckets under the house and poked, piece by piece, into the kitchen stove. Not too much, you'll smother it. That's enough, Joanne! The flames burnt bright orange and made a particular noise, a thrilling flutter and purr. Her grandma would lean across and shut the oven door. 'You little pyromaniac,' she'd chuckle.

There was a fireplace in the lounge room too, but Joanne couldn't ever remember it being used. Nobody ever sat in there, except in the sweltering midday heat of Christmas Day when the Parmenter family gathered to do presents. She was gripped by a nagging curiosity to see inside the house now, full of hippies and their stuff. How would that feel? Would it look very different? Did they use the cavernous lounge room? Did Melanie hate going down to the bathroom in the dark?

It began to rain again, heavily, and Joanne quickened her pace, her feet slipping on the rocks. There was nothing for it now but to get to the dairy, to get in close under the eaves and wait for the squall to pass. She pushed through the gate, scratchy with lantana, and crouched against the wall. Rainwater chortled into the tank on the other side of the shed. It spattered in places along the path where the gutters had rusted through. She was drenched now and really cold. Her knees were mauve and goosey. As the wind whipped around, she leapt to her feet and pushed on the cream-room door.

It took a moment for her eyes to adjust to the darkness inside. She fumbled for the light switch, and behold, the light went on. But things inside were not how she expected them to be. Where the separator used to sit on its concrete block, there was a table smeared with mud. Or clay. There was a potter's wheel, and chunks of dried clay scattered about like bits of poo, and around the walls dozens of unglazed pots, as wonky and ugly as the ones kids made at school.

The table was the one from the laundry up at the house. The shabby vinyl chair she didn't recognise. She gave the potter's wheel a push and kicked the chair, angry with her Uncle Bill. He said he wouldn't let them come into the dairy. He promised. Or maybe it was Janine's fault, like Aunty Peg always said: it wasn't *her* family history being rented out to strangers, it wasn't *her* mother who'd collapsed and died on that dairy floor.

Joanne picked up a small pinch pot and broke it apart in her hands. She let the pieces fall to the ground, rubbed the dust between her fingers, and wiped her palms down the front of her dress. Then she turned and stepped across the oil-stained floor of the empty machine room next door, through to the bails on the other side. Open to the holding paddock, this space was loud with rain. It drummed on the iron roof and jumped like spittle on the concrete slope outside. This part of the dairy, she was pleased to see, showed no signs of occupation. You could still smell something of the cows, of old sacking and grain and the dust of manure pounded into the corners. Swallow shit from a nest in the eaves dripped down the wall like icing. They give you lice, those rotten birds, her grandma used to say. The chains at the end of the wooden stalls hung still, the links choked with cobweb. On the floor, right in the middle, was something only Joanne could see: the crumpled body of an old woman in gumboots, her cheek spattered with green manure. There was an upturned bucket. Whorls of soapy water soaked her thin white hair. Hooves clattered on the wet concrete, and all around, the air heaved with the steady munch of bran.

Joanne probed for some kind of feeling in herself, like searching around for a bruise under the skin. That was death, her grandma. When they wrenched the gumboots off her feet, her toes were cold white prunes. When they rolled her over, there was a sickening loll. Joanne remembered her mother lifting the hands, one by one, and placing them gently on her grandma's chest. The fingers were bent with arthritis, and a worn wedding band hung loose below one swollen joint. The skin on the back of the hands was shiny and thin, and underneath, the bones splayed like the claws of a bird.

That was what death looked like. But in her mother's case, there were no images like this. Everything that happened this week was unseen and unsaid. It was the empty space behind a square of hospital curtains where the bed and everything else had been quickly packed away. It was the small bag of her mum's belongings waiting for them at reception. It was the nightie that wasn't in the bag when they got it home, the one Joanne had given her for her birthday. It was words like 'funeral home' suggesting she'd been taken to a place that was warm and cosy. It was all a lie, but you weren't allowed to think it.

You weren't for one moment allowed to think of where she really was — in a fridge somewhere, in a box, in the ground. They'd ripped that nightie off her. They covered the dirt around the grave. Nobody mentioned the digger. And now her mum was out there, under the ground in the rain, and everyone was at Uncle Bill's, eating cake and talking.

Joanne bent forward, her arms wrapped around herself as if she'd been hit in the stomach. 'I'm thinking it,' she said out loud. The tears came, finally, and her breath in shuddering gulps. She crumpled, gave in to it, and wept.

Afterwards she sat there, hunched and still, knowing she should wipe her face but unable to do it. The cold lumpy concrete pressed into her shins. She shifted her weight and gradually steadied her breathing.

Then, with a flicker and a buzz, the light went on.

'Oh my, you startled me!'

A woman stood in the doorway, her hand pressed to her mouth. She wore a big gathered skirt and her hair in a low thick plait at the side of her head. Joanne looked at her, at the drowsy blue eyes. It was the woman who sold earrings on the street outside the shop.

'Did you get caught in the rain?'

The soft American accent. Joanne wiped her nose with the back of her hand.

'You're soaked through, look at you.' She leant down and stared into Joanne's face. 'Hey, wait, I know you. You're the girl from the general store. My spider-web earrings, right? I remember, and you didn't have pierced ears. Have you had 'em done yet?'

Joanne shook her head.

'So what are you doing in here in your good clothes, your pretty shoes? Why don't you come up to the house and get dry? What do you say? It's right here, just up the hill.'

'I know.'

'You know Melanie, don't you?'

Joanne swallowed.

'She lives here, did you know that? Were you coming to see her?'

'No.'

'She's home. She can lend you some clothes. Come on, come with me. I'm Jane, by the way.' The woman extended her big hand. Joanne looked at it, then took it and struggled to her feet. 'That's the girl. Now wait a moment. I came down here to get something. I won't be a tick.'

Joanne felt a pang of guilt watching Jane go into the cream room, but if she noticed the broken pot on the floor, she didn't let on.

'My flashlight!' was all she said as she came out the door. 'I'm always leaving it down here. And an umbrella for you, here you go.'

And that was how Joanne ended up having a bath in her grandmother's house on the day of her own mother's funeral, and why nobody quite understood how it came to be.

The bath was as sharp-clawed and deep as she remembered. It had the same brown stain under the taps that Barbara always used to say was poo. She'd tease Joanne about it when their grandma left the room, leaving the two of them in the bath together. You're sitting on the poo, Barb would squeal, and Joanne would lunge towards her, sending water slopping onto the floor.

Now she sat in the tepid depths, her legs stretched forward, the sloping wall of the cast-iron bath cold behind her back. The bathroom roof was the same — just rafters under the tin. The rain was as loud as the gas flames in the scary hot-water heater that stood, chimney-like, at the other end of the bath.

There was a soft knock.

'How are we doing?' It was Jane again, with a towel this time and a fat green candle.

Joanne sat forward and wrapped her arms around her knees.

'I thought I'd light this for you. It's nice in here with candles.' Jane pulled across a wooden stool — Joanne's grandad's shaving stool — and set the candle on it.

'It's scented. Do you like patchouli?'

Jane held the candle under Joanne's nose. She flinched at first, then nodded. It did smell nice. Jane lit the wick; it fizzed a bit, but then the flame grew steady and long.

'Melanie's finding you some clothes. She told us about your mom. So you've come from your Uncle Bill's place, yeah? We saw the cars earlier. You're going to have to call them, honey. They'll be worried about you. Is that water hot enough? You can turn up the gas. Just push this little handle here, see?'

'I know. This was my grandma's house.'

'Of course. Jeez —' Jane shook her head. 'That's kind of weird.'

'Yes.'

'So you know it real well, and the dairy too, I guess.'

Jane crouched next to the bath, that strange unsupported crouch she used selling earrings in the street. 'I love this old washhouse, don't you?' she said. 'This old bath, the atmosphere, it's so old-fashioned. I always imagine the farmers' wives boiling up that copper. Bill told us your grandma was born in here. Did you know that?'

'In the bathroom?'

'That's what he said. I guess they needed the hot water.'

Joanne wondered if Bill had also mentioned her dying in the dairy.

'There's your towel, okay? I'll send Melanie down with your clothes. Then you're going to make that call, okay?'

'Yes.'

'Good girl.'

At the door, Jane turned again. 'Do you know Mel's mother — Linda?'

'Just from the shop.'

'She said you two had *history*. What did she mean by that?'

Joanne hugged her knees more tightly.

'And you know Gerard also?'

'I know who he is. From his mail.'

Jane ran a thoughtful hand down the side of her face. 'Linda doesn't think he'll be pleased to see you here. Do you have *history* with him as well?'

Joanne shook her head.

'Hmm, okay. Don't forget to blow out that candle when you come.'

Joanne lay back in the bath and willed her feet to float. So far, Linda hadn't said a word to her directly. She'd been on the veranda when they arrived, just as Joanne had feared. She watched the two of them toil up the hill, and gave Jane a quizzical look as they came up the steps.

'I'll tell you in a minute,' Jane said. 'She's cold, she needs a bath.'

Joanne diverted her eyes as she walked past the woman. She felt Linda turn and stare as they entered the house. As she stood in the lounge room, only half-listening to Jane's drawling instructions, she was aware of Linda standing in the doorway. She didn't look as fierce as Joanne remembered. Her hair seemed less wild, more auburn than blazing red. 'I'll get Mel,' was the only thing she said before she left the room.

Joanne let herself sink deeper into the lukewarm water, felt it bulge around her jaw and fill her ears. Staring up at the rafters, she listened to the soft roar of her breath, in and out. Under the water she could hear the clank of the pipes in the walls, the inner machinations of the house. For a moment she could see herself from above, her fuzzy brown hair floating out, the soft pudge of her breasts and stomach breaking the surface. In and out. For the umpteenth time that week she wondered if her mother could see her, if all the dead were looking down from above. Did she really believe that? Did she want it to be true? She sat up with a rush. No. It was starting to get dark. She wanted to get out. Where was Melanie with her clothes? The candle flame threw wobbling shadows around the raw wooden walls of the room — the washhouse, Jane had called it. Bill told us your grandma was born in here. Did you know that? By the cold copper, Joanne could see a tangle of bloodied sheets. In the tree outside, a catbird mewled like a newborn baby.

Chapter Twelve

It was weirder than weird, this Parmenter girl in the bath. Gerard was going to hit the fucking roof.

Linda held out a flannelette shirt. 'What about that? That'd fit her.'

Melanie whipped it out of her hands. 'None of my jeans will, but. She's a little bit fat.'

'She is *not*. Here, undies.' Linda threw them on the pile.

'Yuck!'

'You don't have to get them back if you don't want to.'

'She could wear a sarong.'

Linda raised her brows. 'A sarong and a flannette shirt!'

'Well, I don't know. What else have I got?'

'Yeah, okay.' Linda opened another drawer of the old wooden wardrobe and pulled out one of her sarongs. 'She can have this one. It'll get her home, I guess.'

'Are we driving her back to Bill's place?'

'We could. She hasn't rung them yet. Her dad might want to come and get her.' Linda flumped down on the bed. 'Ray Parmenter, here, in Gerard's house. How fucking good is that?'

Melanie took the clothes out to Joanne, and Linda returned to the lounge room. She looked at the table, covered in Gerard's stuff. The piles had grown even taller. Timber-industry reports, a topographic map, duplicated booklets on plants and birds. There was his little red typewriter, and her clipboard from the meeting with the incomplete list of names. She covered up what she could with a page of the local newspaper he had saved for some reason. Letters to the Editor. Nearly all of them about the logging. She squinted in the dim light and read one at random.

> SIR. — I suggest that the Federal Department of Social Security look into these so-called conservationists complaining about the proposed logging in the Repentance Basin. Take away their entitlement to unemployment benefits and I guarantee they'd be out of this place in 24 hours.
>
> **THINKER**
> Balbirnie

Linda smirked. Thinker! Her gaze fell on a piece of folded butcher's paper in the pile. It was the drawing she'd been working on. She'd forgotten all about it. Now she pulled it out and spread it on the floor. It was large, a poster. Only about half of it had been coloured in. The rest was sketched in pencil. It wasn't bad. She rolled a cigarette and stood, smoking absently, her eyes fixed on the unfinished drawing. From the midst of the swirling mandalas, planets, and shooting stars came a line of script, unfurling like a ribbon: *the universe is unfolding as it should.*

She turned around. The girl, Joanne, was standing in the doorway wearing the flannelette shirt and sarong.

'Hello,' Linda said.

'Hello.' Joanne was looking at the packet of Drum sitting on the table. Linda snatched it up and pushed it into her pocket.

'Feeling better?'

Joanne nodded.

'Melanie's in our room. It's just through there. Second door.'

'I know.'

Joanne was looking around the lounge room. Up, down, to the corner, out through the double doors to the sunroom. Then she leant forward and peered down at the drawing on the floor.

'Do you like it?' asked Linda.

No reaction.

'It's not finished. I was thinking it could go up there, on that wall. Everything's so bare in here. It needs some decoration.'

'That's from *Desiderata*,' Joanne said.

Linda looked at her, astonished.

'I've got it on my bedroom wall at home.'

'You have?'

'I've learnt it off by heart,' the girl continued solemnly.

'Wow,' said Linda. 'That's quite impressive. You know it's bullshit that it was found in that old church.'

Joanne looked at her, dismayed.

'It's a poem. Some American dude wrote it in the twenties. But it's still nice, don't get upset. I don't know where that church rubbish came from.'

'Baltimore,' Joanne said.

Linda laughed. 'That's right!'

Then she stopped and turned her head. She thought she heard a car. 'You've got to call Bill,' she said to Joanne, more sharply than she intended. 'The phone's in the kitchen. I'll show you.'

Melanie came into the room. 'Sorry about the clothes.'

'They're okay. I like this.' Joanne touched the sarong. 'I like batik.'

'That's Mum's, that one.'

'Take her down to the kitchen, Mel. She's got to call her father.'

'She knows the way. She used to live here, didn't you, Jo?'

'My grandma did.'

'See?'

'Just go with her. And Joanne, tell them we'll drop you over. You can't walk back in the dark.'

Linda felt her pocket for her car keys. Then she noticed the tilting ash on the end of her cigarette.

'Shit!' she breathed, swinging around in panic. The ash dropped, fair and square, between the ribbon spools of Gerard's typewriter.

It was like reining in a runaway pony. Linda gripped the wheel and ploughed her way through the gears as the car fishtailed on the bend halfway down the hill. She hit the brakes. Dumb move! The car swung up onto the shoulder of the road and the tyres spun on the grass. For a moment she just sat there in the tilting car, staring through the flapping wipers at the silver spears of rain.

'I can't believe this fucking weather. It's hardly stopped all day.'

'This is nothing.'

Linda looked up at the solemn face in the rear-vision mirror. Joanne was sitting upright in the middle of the back seat, her wet dress and sandals in a plastic shopping bag on her lap. It was still surprising when she spoke, when she offered something more than a mousey 'yes' or 'no'.

'It rains heaps here in the summer,' she said.

'Oh God, does it? Like bloody Toona Bay.' Linda turned the key and leant on the accelerator. 'Come on, come on.' The car resisted like a horse refusing to jump and then slowly, finally, rolled back onto the gravel.

'Okay, girls, here we go. Hold on to your hats!'

Little by little, they scrunched their way down the hill. Linda felt her shoulders fall and her body gradually relax. 'I hope we can get back up again. Jeez, I hope we can, or we'll have to sleep at your Uncle Bill's. He's got a spare room, hasn't he?'

'No,' said Joanne. 'My uncles are staying there.'

'We could take her back to town,' Melanie piped in. 'We could stay the night at Felicity's place. I like staying there.'

'Okay, come on, don't overreact. We're a hundred yards down the hill. And we're past the worst of it, we should be right from here. Wind down your window, Melanie, we're fogging up.'

'Muuum!'

'Fuck!' She hit the brakes again and they skidded to a stop.

In front of them the causeway was a sliding sheet of water.

'The river's up,' said Joanne.

Linda dropped her chin to her chest.

'We'll have to go back,' said Melanie.

'If we can. We pretty much slid down the hill.'

'Mum, we can't stay here. It might get higher. We'll get washed away.'

Joanne said this was unlikely. They turned and looked at her.

'How deep do you reckon it is?'

She shrugged.

'Where else does it cut the road? Does Bill's driveway go under?'

No, she assured them with sudden authority. This little creek didn't cross his road. When the big creek flooded, everyone out here got cut off. But that wasn't going to happen. This wasn't flood rain.

Linda's arms were still braced on the steering wheel. She closed her eyes and thought longingly of sleep. Then, slowly, she straightened and pulled the gear stick down and across. Someone had once told her that you get better traction in reverse. She stepped hard on the accelerator and got fifty yards up the hill. But the water was coursing across the road, washing the gravel thin and leaving a shining slick of clay. The tyres spun and the car began to slide backwards. Linda gave up and let it roll back towards the creek.

'Gerard could get us across in his jeep.' That was Melanie again. Another of her bright ideas.

'And Gerard is where, exactly?'

'Okay. No need to bitch at me, Mum. He might be home soon.'

Linda threw back her head and stared at the tiny stars on the vinyl roof of the car. Behind her she could hear Joanne's quiet mouth-breathing. She could feel the girl hanging on their every word, her round rodent marsupial eyes agog.

'And won't he be pleased to find you here, Joanne Parmenter.'

Melanie turned in her seat. 'Don't worry, Joanne. He's nice. Don't listen to her.'

'She could be stuck here for days,' Linda said, watching the raindrops swell and trickle down the windscreen. Funerals, flooded rivers, girls in wet, muddy dresses traipsing across the fields. The sister would turn up next. Joanne would come down with a fever. Jane would minister to them both, carrying towels and steaming mustard baths to the bedroom. And there, glowering in the shadows, would be their very own Mister Darcy, his mouth set and his eyes dark with anger.

'No, I won't,' came Joanne's earnest voice from the back seat. 'The causeway goes down really fast once it stops raining.'

They left the car at the bottom of the hill and laboured up the slope, the two girls huddled under Jane's umbrella, and Linda walking behind them with the torch. She turned once and shone the beam down at the old white Holden.

'They'll think we've drowned,' she said, still feeling the melodrama of the thing. 'We should have left a little pile of clothes down near the water. Gerard and Bettina would feel sorry and be so relieved to find us alive, they'd forget to be angry.'

'Who's Bettina?' asked Joanne.

Melanie glanced over her shoulder. 'I'll tell you later.'

'What will you tell her?' Linda snapped.

'Nothing! Bettina lives here. She's only new, she comes from Germany.'

'Who else lives here?'

'That's all, and Jane's partner, Andy. You saw him, didn't you? I think he's home. He's probably in their bedroom.'

'So ... six people.'

'Yeah, Mum and I share a room. That's where you'll be sleeping.'

'Bettina's got a big room all to herself, but she never sleeps in it,' said Linda. She saw Melanie throw Joanne another look. 'What?'

'Nothing.'

Melanie smiled knowingly, and Joanne felt the thrill of being taken into a confidence, even though she could barely grasp who these people were. She moved closer under the umbrella as they climbed towards the house, aware of the sound of her breathing, the squelch of her bare feet, and the dark ooze of mud between her toes.

Jane cooked for the five of them. Nothing special, just another of her slightly tasteless veggie pies. Hunza pie, she called this one, which led to a conversation between Jane and the girls about who the Hunza people were, and how, on account of their diet, they all live to be over a hundred and twenty.

'Except the ones that die of typhus,' Linda chipped in, 'or in childbirth, or of measles when they're two.'

Andy grinned at that. He was sitting at the end of the kitchen table plucking on his guitar. He never played anything right through, just a whole lot of bits and pieces. Little flourishes of picking and then a sudden strum. Sometimes he'd sit and play one chord, over and over again, a look of intense concentration on his hangdog face.

The two girls helped wash up and then went into the lounge room, where someone had the bright idea of trying to light the fire. They'd got it started with wood chips from the basket in the kitchen, and then Joanne told them about the wood that was stored underneath the house. She and Melanie took the torch and returned ten minutes later with two big buckets of firewood, perfectly dry and neatly chopped by some long-ago axe.

The rain droned on. Linda retrieved her coloured pencils from under Gerard's stuff on the desk and settled with the girls on cushions around the big, low coffee table to work on the *Desiderata* drawing. She ticked Melanie off for drawing a stupid flower on it. It was supposed to be celestial, this picture. Joanne, on the other hand, did some remarkably good colour blending, filling in the rainbow that Linda had sketched for her. She seemed very taken with Linda's box of pencils. Kept rolling her finger across them all. How many were there, she wanted to know. Look at all the different greens. It was true, they were good pencils. They'd cost Linda a lot of money in an art shop in Albury on the way up. Joanne said they sold coloured pencils in the shop, but only sets of six, and they were really cheap.

Linda left the girls to their colouring in and went out to the veranda to smoke a joint. She sat on the swing seat and pushed it gently with one foot. In front of her, water fell from the gutters in a bright beaded curtain. There was no sign of Gerard and Bettina. God only knew where they'd got to. They'd been out a lot these last few weeks, into Balbirnie again and again, out to Druidane, up to visit communes and collectives on the other side of the range.

Bettina was proving indispensable to Gerard, fearless and experienced in all things militant. Just nineteen years old and she'd been arrested — Linda had watched her count on her fingers — maybe seven times? Not quite arrested, as it turned out, mostly apprehended. Only twice held overnight, only one court hearing. That was Frankfurt, the plutonium works, where the charges were dismissed. So many causes, so many things the girl was opposed to — nuclear power, battery chickens, the World Bank, acid rain. She'd faced off with neo-Nazis in Munich and marched for Palestine, her head swathed in a black and white keffiyeh. It seemed to Linda that some of these causes negated one another, but Bettina saw no such contradiction. For her it was all one and the same, summed up in a single word — *das Widerstand*, she called it, resistance.

And now here she was, travelling Australia with her grimy duffle bag and her mongrel dog on a string, sniffing around for trouble to be part of. Someone in Sydney had given her Gerard's name and address. How the hell had that come about? What question did she have to ask — does anyone know where dissent is brewing, where a girl might be of help? It was only three weeks since she'd walked into that meeting and sat herself down next to Linda. Three weeks! That was hard to believe. Three weeks since she'd wormed her way into their house and into Gerard's bed. Well, there you go. Linda put the joint between her lips and inhaled sharply. No wonder the girl had achieved so much by the tender age of nineteen.

The dope was stronger than she'd anticipated, and she realised she was quite stoned. Settling back into the cushions, she began to check herself, reciting snippets of poetry as a test of straightness.

My heart aches, and a drowsy numbness pains
My sense, as though of hemlock I had drunk ...

Fuck it! She knew perfectly well that she could recite the entire thing while completely off her face. She also knew that she couldn't go back inside feeling like this. Imagine Joanne relating that to her family in the morning. The ropes on the swing seat creaked as she leant forward and stubbed out the joint on the floor. She retrieved the roach and popped it in with her tobacco. Then she went to the bathroom and put a drop of Visine in each eye. Brushed her fingers through her hair, took a deep breath, and slapped her thighs. Right, she breathed, okay then — in we go.

But when she returned to the lounge room, no one was there. She met Melanie in the hall. Joanne was really tired. Melanie had pulled out the spare mattress and made up a bed for her.

'That's good,' Linda heard herself say. 'Thank you, sweetie. Goodnight.'

The bedroom door shut and she felt a tingle of relief. If Gerard did come home now, he wouldn't know Joanne was in the house. If they could get up early enough and get her back into town, he'd never even know that she'd been there.

Linda knelt down at the coffee table and began to put the coloured pencils away, carefully, in order, appreciating all over again the beautiful spectrum they made. She looked at the drawing. It was nearly finished now. The universe was indeed unfolding as it should. Fancy Joanne knowing that, memorising the whole thing. What a funny kid she was, full of surprises. Linda regretted biting her head off in the shop. It was, as Melanie said at the time, most likely her father's fault. She pulled the Drum from her pocket and considered smoking the roach, but tiredness overcame her and she went to bed herself.

Gerard and Bettina did eventually come home. Linda lay in the dark and listened: Bettina's high, reedy voice, Gerard's muffled responses. They were out in the kitchen. The bang of cupboard doors. Bettina's light steps in the hallway, his following close behind. And then the sound of his bedroom door, closing.

Chapter Thirteen

It was still early when Linda dropped Joanne home. Main Street was pretty much deserted. Melanie waved from the front seat as they did a U-turn and drove off. Joanne stood on the side of the road, opposite the shop, looking for signs of movement inside. Someone had opened up; she couldn't see who. The fly tapes hung motionless in the dark doorway. She could see herself reflected in the front window, faint between the bright transfers for Streets ice cream and Tip Top bread. She appeared squat and wonky in the glass, in the flannelette shirt and sarong, clutching a plastic shopping bag like a dero.

Jane had given her funeral dress a quick rinse before bed and hung it up on the veranda overnight, but the air was too damp and it wasn't dry by morning. It still had mud stains on it anyway, on the skirt at the back. She would go straight through to the laundry now and put it in some bleach.

An empty cattle truck went past. She shut her eyes against the hot, dusty stink of petrol fumes and manure. Then she was across the road and striding through the shop, bare feet quick on the lino. Mrs Blainey was stacking the bread rack. She raised her head, a bag of buns dangling from one hand. Joanne carried on, her eyes averted — comics, custard, cake mix — past the buzzing fridges and out through the door at the back.

The house had the shadowy feel of nobody home. The blinds were drawn, leaving the kitchen bathed in sullen light. Water plinked into a milky cereal bowl in the sink. Tupperware containers were stacked along the bench: other people's containers full of biscuits, slices, and slabs of cake. Joanne held her breath and listened. Was that footsteps?

'Hello?'

She checked the hall. Nobody. In front of her, the glass doors of the lounge room were firmly closed. She opened them to the smell of lilies and faintly rancid water. Silver and white sympathy cards stood in a row on the dresser. On the glass coffee table, the floral arrangements were clustered like boats on a pond. It seemed so long since she'd been here. She felt like a stranger. Again, in her chest, that contracted feeling of wanting to be home but not finding that sense of comfort in the place where it used to be. It was only yesterday, yesterday morning, that she'd sat in this room, looking at the flowers from her school. There they were on the table, the red carnations. Next to them stood the tatty lilies from Mrs Mitchell's garden, delivered with apologies for the damage wrought by beetles. They'd been among the first offerings to arrive on that long-ago Sunday morning and were now beginning to drop their petals and pollen on the glass.

Joanne filled a bucket in the laundry sink and poured in a measure of bleach. She pulled the dress from the shopping bag and punched it under the water. Give it a good soak, she heard her mother say. The water fizzed through the tiny holes of the *broderie anglaise*.

'Well, look who's here.'

Barbara leant in the doorway, her hand on her hip.

'Hello,' said Joanne. She turned back to the bucket and rubbed furiously at the dress.

'What are you doing?'

'Washing my dress.'

'What are you wearing? What the hell *is* that? You look ridiculous.'

Joanne glanced down at the checked flannel shirt. The fumes from the bleach stung her eyes and throat. 'Where's Dad?' she gulped.

'In town. He's got an early meeting.'

Joanne searched her sister's face for information. Was he really angry? Did she have to be scared?

'What the hell were you thinking, Joanne, running off like that?'

'I was looking for you.'

They glared at each other.

'I couldn't find you.'

Barbara fiddled with the gold chain around her neck.

'Aunty Peg's moving in,' Joanne blurted.

'I know.'

'Well?'

'Well what? Perhaps you shouldn't go running away, acting like an idiot. It's you she's worried about.'

'It is *not*!'

Joanne tried to push past her, but Barbara had her by the arm and pulled her back into the room.

'It's you!' Joanne screamed. 'She says you're going to get *pregnant*!' The word was a weapon. It caught Barbara off guard. Joanne broke away from her and bolted out of the house.

The back porch was still in shadow. It would stay that way for hours. Beyond it, the paling fence was an unbroken barrier, running tall and silver grey from one side of the yard to the other. Joanne felt a jolting, aching sadness, as though she'd fallen from a height and landed somewhere hard.

The day had begun so brightly up there in the house on the hill. She was the first person to wake up and had lain on her mattress for a while, dazzled by the light coming through the frosted louvres. The sun was out. The rain had stopped. She reached for the sarong and, keeping beneath the sheet, struggled to tie it on the way Melanie had shown her. Then quietly, carefully, she had picked her way across the jumble of clothes and blankets on the floor and slipped out of the room.

The entire house was heaving with sleep as she made her way down the darkened corridor, beckoned by a square of light — the glass window in her grandma's front door. It opened to a sunny morning and the gurgling of birds. Everything in the house paddock, all the way down to the dairy, sharp and clear and green and bright. Sparks of sunlight leapt from the wet kikuyu. The dairy squatted on the spur below like a lighthouse keeper's cottage above a roiling sea of mist. Joanne stood for ages on the corner of the veranda, her eyes aching from the brightness, her vision webbed and blurred. Down the saddle, across the creek, Mr Mackenzie was milking. The odd bark and shout and clang of metal carried on the air.

The screen door opened, hissed and closed. Barbara sat down beside her. She took Joanne's hand and placed it on her knee, covering it with her own.

'So what was Grandma's house like?'

Joanne shrugged. 'A bit empty. They don't have much furniture.'

'What did you have for dinner?'

'It was nice. Hunza pie. People who eat it live to be a hundred and twenty.'

'Jeez!'

'And we drew a big poster with coloured pencils — they had really, really good pencils. There was a line in it from *Desiderata* and I recognised it.'

Barb picked at her painted toenail.

'And we lit the fire in the lounge room. I showed them where the woodpile was under the house. They didn't know it was there.'

'What about bitch woman. Was she nice to you?'

'Yes.'

'And that bloke, what's his name, the nutter?'

'Gerard. He wasn't there.'

Barbara nodded. 'Did they say anything about the logging?

About what happened at the meeting?'

'No, nothing. This poster was really nice, Barb. We should do one for our room. It was really fun.'

'Colouring in?'

Joanne winced. It seemed childish all of a sudden. She looked sideways at her sister and felt overwhelmed by the need to explain how it all was. How people sat around the table playing music, and the talk and teasing and laughter over dinner. She wanted to tell her about the candle in the bathroom and how dazzling and bright it was this morning when she went outside. She kept thinking of the wind chime she'd found hanging on the veranda. It was made of tiny shards of glass, brilliantly coloured: ruby red and emerald green and blue. They were hung from a piece of wood, a twig, stripped and smooth, and made the loveliest tinkling noise when you ran your finger through them. Melanie had never even noticed the chimes. She shrugged when Joanne mentioned it, and said that someone probably bought them at the Braemar markets. It was so pretty. Joanne wanted one, that and a batik sarong. She leant forward and hugged her knees. She wanted to go to those markets.

Chapter Fourteen

Sandy had been jumpy all morning, knowing that James and Amanda were coming down to the mill. He was anxious to show the place off at its best and found himself doing ridiculous things like picking up the empty soft-drink cans that were lying around in the log yard. Barb Parmenter even caught him in the office, wiping down his desk. That was a world first, she said, him doing the cleaning. He'd ticked her off for being cheeky and sent her up to the shop to get some decent cream biscuits for afternoon tea. Amanda would be seeing the place for the first time, and even James hadn't been there for well over a year. His last few visits home had been fleeting and during the Christmas period, when there wasn't a lot happening at the mill. He hadn't even seen the new Canadian in action. That would impress him for sure. It was one of the best head saws you could get and had cost them a bomb. Sandy had arranged for some extra big logs to go through that afternoon, to show his son what it was capable of. Then, if they had time, he thought they could do a quick run out to the forest to see the new section being opened up for harvest. Of course Amanda might not be up for that in her condition. There'd be a bit of walking involved. They'd had a problem with subsidence just near the turning bay, but you could park on the other side and walk from there.

The young couple arrived just after two o'clock in their new

Honda Civic. Sandy went out to the landing and waved his arms like a traffic cop, directing them to park right here, in the shade beside the office. James got out of the car straightaway. Amanda took a little longer to lever her heavy body out of the bucket seat. She stood by the car for a moment, gazing around the yard, her hands moving absently over her pregnant belly. She already looked hot and bothered, and Sandy felt compelled to offer her a glass of water even though they'd only come a mile down the hill.

'No thanks, I'm fine,' she said, raising her voice as if to make herself heard about the din. It wasn't loud; the saws weren't even going. There was the usual clatter of timber, and shouts from the stackers out the back. Someone was welding inside the shed — maybe that was it.

'Fletch is on the bench,' Sandy told James. 'He'll be pleased to see you. You can leave your purse in the office, Amanda. Barb's in there. Hey, have you two met? Barb, come out say hello.'

The screen door opened.

'Hello, James.'

For the first time Sandy noticed the pallor in Barbara's face, the flatness in her smile. She had only just come back to work, and seemed pretty much her old self, but now he realised that she'd lost some weight and a bit of her usual spark. He wished he'd reminded James to say something about her mother. It was too late now. He could hardly bring it up in front of her.

'This is Amanda ... and Fred.' He pointed to Amanda's belly.

Barbara narrowed her eyes. 'I thought you were having a girl.'

'Shhh — we don't know about that.' Sandy winked at his daughter-in-law, and Amanda cuffed him playfully with her elbow.

'It is a girl,' she told Barbara, 'and no, we're not calling her Fred.'

'I was just going to take them around the place, Barb. If you could put the kettle on in, I dunno, half an hour?'

They entered the shed just as a large ironbark log collided with the Canadian. *That* was loud. Sandy looked at Amanda. She was laughing, her eyes wide, her hands clamped over her ears.

'You can have some muffs if you want,' he shouted.

She mouthed the words 'can't hear you'. The log travelled through and out the other end, and the splintering, jagging scream of the saw sank beneath the ambient throb of the surrounding machines. James nodded his approval and moved in to talk to the sawyer, Peter Fletcher. The boy was asking all the right questions. Sandy was chuffed and gave him an affectionate pat on the shoulder. He beckoned to Amanda and she came forward, proffering her small white hand to Peter Fletcher's large oil-stained grip. She glanced down at the man's short Stubbies and quickly looked away. Sandy chuckled to himself. He'd tease her about that later. He left her where she was and led James across to the men working on the far side of the shed. There were handshakes all round and some good-natured ribbing about how young Jim had wasted no time getting his wife in the family way.

'Has she been very crook?' someone asked him.

'She was —'

'She sure was,' Sandy said. 'Threw up every morning for weeks, didn't she, son?'

'Yes, she did,' James said. He looked mildly embarrassed. Perhaps it was all the pregnancy talk or maybe he felt ill at ease, standing here in his neat moleskins and open-necked shirt among these stocky, sweaty blokes in their singlets, shorts, and work boots. Sandy tried to remember how these moments had felt for him when he was young. He too had gone away to school, but he'd come straight back into the business after matriculation. No fancy business courses then. His place at the mill had been a given — it had been a gift. He couldn't remember considering any other life for himself. And, of course, Jean was a local girl, and that had made a difference. There'd been no dividing their time or loyalties between their respective families beyond decisions of where they'd be going for Sunday lunch. Their parents were well acquainted, and Jean had known exactly what it was she was marrying into. Sandy's dad had built up the business by then to the point where owning the mill was a matter of some prestige. It hadn't always been that way. His great-grandfather had been little more than an axeman clearing the scrub for farmland. There was none of the romance of the cedar-getter about him. It was all ringbarking and stump burning back then, with a few logs milled for fencing. It was heartbreaking now to think of all that quality timber gone to waste, but you couldn't go blaming the old folks. Life was different then. People did what they could to survive and, in the process, opened up some of the finest dairying country in New South Wales.

It was Sandy's grandfather Edwin who was the first to establish a mill. It was a modest bush mill, just a simple shed of rough-sawn poles beside a creek in the scrub. When Sandy was a boy, he and his father had followed the creek right up to see if they could find it, or what was left of it. They hacked away at the lantana for a whole Sunday afternoon to uncover a broken concrete slab, a few sheets of crumbling roofing iron and some bits of rusty machinery. Sandy wasn't all that impressed at the time, but his dad was very excited, particularly when they unearthed the remnants of the old skids under the dirt. Sandy had always intended to take James up there. It was too late this trip, they were leaving tomorrow, but maybe they could do it next time he was home. It was important for him to know what the business had grown from, to understand the hard yakka, over three generations, that had gone into making it the fine operation it was today. He wanted his son to get a feeling for that, before it was too late.

The Canadian started up again, and he turned to look for Amanda. He spotted her, slumped in a folding chair down the side of the machine room, hugging her belly and gazing up at the roof. For the first time in years Sandy looked up at the rafters and saw the swathes of cobweb, thick with sawdust. Those needed cleaning up, he thought. He'd get someone onto that. But then again, she may have found them interesting, these great dust-coated webs. He used to as a boy, used to marvel at them. It always intrigued him how they appeared but you never saw the spiders.

'How are you going there, sweetheart?' he called as they made their way towards her.

She stood up, dusted the back of her smock and smiled that inscrutable smile of hers. They went out to the log yard and around the kiln, the teepee burner, the stacks. They met young Michael Phelan there and stopped to have a chat.

'He's a nice kid,' Sandy said as they walked back to the office. 'He's a bit sweet on our Barb. I was going to move him onto the benches, but he wants to go back to hauling with his dad. You remember Pat and Marcie? I was just helping them out. The work's been a bit thin for them, so I put young Michael on here for a bit, until things improved. Now I'm sorry to lose him. Some of these young ones aren't worth two bob, but he's a real hard worker. Ah well, I guess we'll still be seeing him when he brings the jinker in.'

Barbara had the electric jug on and the biscuits out on a plate.

'How did you find that?' she asked Amanda.

'Good.'

'Stinks down there, doesn't it? Diesel. I can't stand it.'

Sandy laughed a little too loudly. 'Must be a girl thing, that. Every man I know loves that smell.'

'The dust too,' Barb continued. 'It gets into everything. You've got to keep everything covered in here, like the letterhead and stuff.'

There was a tinge of despair in her voice. Sandy was surprised. She sat slumped at her desk, her chin in the palm of her hand. She'd told him once, laughingly, about the lessons in deportment and make-up that were part of her secretarial course at Tech. Wasted on you lot, she'd said ruefully. It came back to him now, looking at her wan face and rounded shoulders. She'd given up wearing make-up to work somewhere along the line. Instead she kept a bottle of astringent on her desk. Her paper bin was always full of cotton balls smeared with grime.

Amanda took her mug of coffee. Sandy saw her glance at the label on the jar.

'Every time that big saw went off, the baby started kicking,' she said.

'See?' he chuckled. 'She knows her stuff, this baby girl. Born to it, I reckon. She'll be running the place one day, you watch, with all this women's lib.'

Amanda raised her chin and looked James in the eye. It was a direct and steady gaze, like a charged rod between them. It was 'Are you going to tell him or will I?' James shifted on his chair and Sandy saw the whole damn thing. He saw it clear as day.

But she would enjoy the forest, he was sure of that. It would be ten degrees cooler out there, for one thing. He put her in the front seat beside him, in case she got car sick, and told her to keep an eye out for koalas. She kept her head cocked out the window after that, until they hit the dirt road and the dust required that all the windows be closed. Sandy talked to James as they went along, describing the stumpage they'd paid for in the newly opened section and the problems they were having with subsidence up near the turning bay.

'Mum said you were having trouble with some of the locals too.'

'Locals!' Sandy snorted. 'I don't have any trouble with the locals.'

'Hippies, I mean.'

'Huh. They had this community meeting, did she tell you about that? Not many people came in the end, hardly anyone. It's all been whipped up by a couple of troublemakers. There's one chap who's off with the fairies. He's friendly enough, pretty harmless, and the other one has a science degree and talks all this Latin at you, like that makes him some expert on forestry.'

'What's his name?'

'Gerard someone, I can never remember. I'll tell you where he lives, but. Out on the old Parmenter place, he's renting the house off Bill.' Sandy shook his head and drummed his fingers on the wheel. 'He started writing to me a while back, asking what was going on, what our plans were for the basin. I got back to him, no problem, sent him some information and fobbed him off to Forestry. Next thing I know he's handing out leaflets at that bloody market they have out at Braemar, telling people there are trees on that slope that are more than a thousand years old and we're about to chop the whole lot down. So,' he shrugged, 'I went along to their meeting. It got a bit rowdy, you know, they've got this mob mentality. But I can't see there's any real interest there. They set up for two hundred people and got about fifty, even less if you don't count me and the other blokes from work.'

'Mum told me you came home upset,' James said.

'Naah!'

'She said they let your tyres down.'

'Yeah, well — they did. Someone did. Just the one, on the driver's side, and I had the spare. Fletch helped me change it over.'

'Where were you parked?' James asked.

'On the side of the road outside the hall, a little way along. We were a bit late getting there. We had to wait for the cops.'

Now Amanda turned and looked at him. 'How did they know which car was yours?'

Sandy laughed. 'Have you seen the bombs they drive? Mine's not a rust bucket, and I've paid my registration.'

They hit a pothole in the road. Sandy changed down. 'Are you okay there, love?' he asked Amanda. 'Hold on tight, it gets pretty rough from here.'

'I'm surprised the trucks can get around these bends,' she said.

'It's a bit hairy in places, but they're used to it. We'll take it nice and easy, don't worry. I don't want to make you sick.'

'Or send me into labour.'

'God no, we don't want that!'

Amanda threw him a teasing smile. 'It's possible. Speed bumps. They told us that at antenatal classes, didn't they, James?'

'You doing those classes too, Jim-boy?'

'Yes, Dad, of course I am.'

'You're not going to be at the birth, though?'

'Yes, I am.'

'Jeez, son, sooner you than me.'

'All fathers do it these days,' Amanda said.

'Do they have to?'

'No, they want to,' she laughed. 'Some grandparents come too.'

'No — you want a room full of people?'

'No, not me!'

'Thank God for that!' They hit another pot hole. 'Jeesuz!'

The three of them erupted into laughter. It felt good — nice and easy. Sandy swiped at the tears in his eyes and struggled to pull his attention back to the driving. The bends were growing tighter now. The sunlight strobed through the boughs of the gums above them. He hauled the Range Rover up and down the shoulders of the road, avoiding the worst of the tumbled rocks and washaway. Amanda wound down her window again, admitting a cool blast of air and the shrilling of cicadas.

'Aah, that's nice,' she breathed.

Sandy winked at James in his rear-vision mirror. The causeway was running just an inch or two deep that afternoon, just enough to send the water fanning from their tyres as they crossed.

Amanda looked upstream and gasped. 'Can we stop?'

Sandy pulled up on the other side and tugged hard on the hand-brake. Together the three of them walked down to the water's edge. Vines hung over the deep pool beside the road, and bright red and yellow leaves turned on its inky surface. Further upstream, cascades tumbled over the rocks, splashing brightly in the afternoon sun.

'That's so pretty,' Amanda breathed. She tucked her arm into James's. 'It looks like —' She paused and laughed. 'Like the champagne fountain at our wedding.'

Sandy was pleased with her response. This was one of his favourite moments on the drive into the forest. It was here that the palms began, that the rocks grew mossy and the light became tinged with green. 'There's a walking track starts near here, a little bit further along. It goes all the way up to a kind of hanging valley. There's a lovely swimming hole up there with a proper waterfall. We haven't been up there for years. Not since young James here got a big fat leech on his dick.'

Amanda turned to her husband, her hand on her mouth.

'Thanks for that, Dad.'

'Right on the scrotum, wasn't it, mate? He scratched like a dog for a week.'

James rolled his eyes. 'I was like six.'

'Can you swim here?'

'Yeah, of course you can. It's cold, but. You feel it.'

Amanda crouched down and dabbled her fingers in the water. Then she tipped her head back and looked up at the patch of sky above them. 'I love these palms,' she said. 'It's like a jungle, a tropical island. I didn't expect the forest to look like this.'

'What did you expect?'

'I don't know — gum trees — boring, like all those miles of bush on the way up from Sydney.'

'It's subtropical,' Sandy said. 'You get this sort of wet forest at the bottom of the gullies. We're going further up the hill, so come on, back in the car.'

Chapter Fifteen

It had become something of a running joke. Throughout the week that James and Amanda were staying with them, Jean had been working her way through the international food section of her cookbook. Every night, another country. Sandy had found it interesting, a bit of fun, and the young ones seemed quite impressed by Jean's adventurousness. They'd had cannelloni one night, and chicken and almonds from China. Sandy hadn't been so keen on the Scandinavian lamb dish she served up on Wednesday — too much cabbage for his liking — but Amanda had asked for the recipe, so Jean saw that as a winner. While she'd never admit it, she was constantly seeking the girl's approval. It was to Amanda that her eyes flitted during every meal.

Sandy sat at the head of the large dining-room table, his shower-damp hair combed over his scalp like the tails of sardines.

'Where are we off to this time, love?'

'Hawaii,' Jean said.

It was ham steaks with pineapple. It smelt very good.

'You marinate them first in pineapple juice,' Jean told Amanda. She'd gone to extra lengths with the table setting that evening too, it being the kids' last one. She'd picked hibiscus flowers from the garden and arranged them as a centrepiece around the candlesticks. 'Next time you come, we'll have the highchair out,' she said brightly. 'It's still out in the shed. You'd better get cracking and paint it, Sandy, and the cot.'

'Can it wait until after the birth or do I have to paint them lemon?'

'Stop it!' she said, slapping at his hand. 'Everyone's sick of that joke.'

Sandy poured them all a glass of good claret, and they drank to the baby's health. They discussed their plans to go down to Sydney when Amanda was home from hospital.

'James is going to be at the birth,' Sandy said. 'Did he tell you that?'

'Of course he is,' Jean twinkled. 'All the young dads help out these days.'

'Help out?' Sandy took a gulp of wine and wiped his mouth with his napkin. 'You didn't want me around, did you?'

'I wouldn't have minded a bit of support. I think it's only fair. Not that he would've been much help,' she said to Amanda. 'He faints at the sight of blood.'

'Only my own,' Sandy protested.

'That's so funny,' Amanda said. 'James does too.'

'That's right!' Sandy pointed at his son with his fork. 'He fainted after that leech bite. I was just telling Amanda about that today, about that leech he got when he was little, on his willy, remember?'

'Don't go telling her things like that. The poor boy,' said Jean. She stabbed her fork into a pineapple ring and sawed through the meat beneath it. 'I can't believe you took Amanda out to the forest today. It's too rough underfoot for someone in her condition. She's lucky she didn't slip and fall.'

'She was all right, weren't you, love? She only got out at the causeway. She stayed in the car up the top.'

'No, I didn't,' Amanda said. 'You were gone for ages. I got out and walked around.'

Jean chewed and swallowed. 'And how did you find the mill?'

'It was fine.'

'Busy place, isn't it? Very noisy.'

'It wasn't too bad. The forest was amazing.'

'Was it?'

'Some of those trees, they're so tall. You look up and think that's the top, but it's just a branch or some ferns, and the trunk keeps going after that, and then again.'

'It is very pretty in parts,' said Jean. 'We should go there again, Sandy. I haven't been out that way for years. And you went up the new road, how was that?'

Sandy refilled his glass. 'It was fine, as far as it goes, which isn't quite far enough, but never mind.' He began to tell her about the engineer's report that Forestry had forwarded to him. There was a lot of stabilisation that had to be done before the roadwork could proceed.

'I think it's really sad,' Amanda said.

'What's that?'

'That you're cutting down those trees. I can't see how that's okay.'

There was an awful silence. James looked at Sandy, and Jean pinched nervously at her lips.

'I'm sorry.' Amanda's voice trembled with distress. 'They're just so beautiful, that's all.'

'Which trees are you talking about?' Sandy said at last. 'Not the palms, you know, not the rainforest. We're not touching the bit you liked.'

'I'm talking about the trees up the top. You call it the buffer zone, like it's some kind of no-man's-land, but it's beautiful, it's virgin forest full of birds and animals.'

'You're talking like a hippie there, love.'

'I don't care. I think they've got a point.'

'Oh come on!' Sandy thumped the table, and Jean grabbed for the stem of his glass. He held his head as if it hurt and slowly scratched his temples. When he looked up again, his face had assumed an expression of weary patience. 'Nobody's knocking the forest down. Why would we do that? It's those bullshit pictures the hippies put around, those smoking hillsides. It's nothing like that, what we're doing up there. Nothing!'

Sandy saw James lay his hand over Amanda's, his wedding band shining golden in the candlelight. He murmured something into her hair, and Amanda bit her lip. The clock on the mantelpiece chimed the half-hour.

'Time for sweets,' Jean announced, pushing back her chair. 'Who's for apple strudel?'

'Excellent, love,' Sandy said without enthusiasm.

James nodded without raising his eyes, and Sandy felt a flame of annoyance. Why wasn't his son defending him here? Look at him holding her hand. He knew the difference between a tree and a forest. He knew that it wasn't old growth on that side of the creek, that the whole damned slope had been logged before, back in his grandfather's day. You take out one big crown and ten trees take its place. It was all about good management. James knew all this stuff, yet he sat there and did nothing to set the silly girl straight.

Tick, tick, tick. The clock counted the beats of silence. Sandy considered going out to help Jean in the kitchen. He wished Amanda would go instead. That would relieve the tension. Jean was good in these situations: she would smooth things over and turn the conversation to recipes and stuff. He lifted the hem of the tablecloth and rubbed his thick fingers over the gleaming surface beneath.

'Red bloodwood, that is,' he muttered. 'That's a rainforest species.'

'Dad!'

'And so's that lovely deck of her father's, overlooking the river. That's merbau from Queensland. Comes from a forest like this. His builder bought it direct from the mill and trucked it down to Sydney.'

Amanda's eyes were huge, her mouth small and set. And suddenly Sandy couldn't stand to sit there a moment longer. He bumped the table as he got up, and the candle flames jiggered. 'Tell your mother I've gone outside for some air.'

The gloaming, his mother used to call this time of day. There was a song she used to sing in her thin soprano voice, evoking the soft purple hours of an English twilight. Here the gloaming lasted only a matter of minutes before a heavy darkness fell, filling the valleys and rising to engulf the tops of the hills. Sandy stood on the veranda and watched the colour drain from the garden, leaving only the white spider lilies and iceberg roses. He crossed the lawn to the garage with no real intent or plan of action. Stacked against the far wall was a clutter of old furniture, children's bikes, suitcases, a totem-tennis pole. Sandy began to pull things aside to reach the pieces of the cot at the back. The highchair he couldn't see. It must have been under something. He pulled a hanky from his pocket, wiped the seat of an old kitchen chair, and sat down.

> In the gloaming, oh my darling, when the lights are soft
> and low ...

It was more like breathing than singing. The rest of the words wouldn't come. He screwed up the hanky as he groped for the next line. It was the same frustration he had felt at that stupid meeting, like those dreams you have where you're drowning and you can't make yourself heard. Yes, he was upset that night, upset and angry. He'd had a lot of trouble getting to sleep. Eventually Jean got up, made him a hot Milo, and perched on the arm of the lounge-room chair while he drank it in the dark. 'I'm not a bad person,' he said to her then. He'd repeated it over and over, consumed by a furious indignation. A good father, a good boss, his business was the lifeblood of this town. But when pressed, he couldn't find the words to justify himself, and why did he need to anyway — and now again, with Amanda?

Jean tapped on the door jamb. 'Are you coming to have sweets?'

He laid his hand on the cot. 'I couldn't find the highchair.'

'I didn't mean look for it now, Sandy.'

He shook his head.

'Come on, it's on the table. We're all waiting for you.'

They walked together towards the yellow lights of the house. Jean's fluffy white cat came running and smooched around their legs.

'Virgin forest,' he muttered.

'Sandy, let it drop.'

'No such thing as a virgin round here. I should've told her that.'

'Really?' Jean sighed, bending down and scooping up the cat. 'That's another tired old joke that's had its day.'

Chapter Sixteen

Brian was finally doing it. He was putting them off the bus. All the kids who sat up the back, everyone in the last five rows, were to be dumped by the side of the road. He ignored their howls of protest and refused to make any exceptions. At first, no one had believed him. He'd made threats like this before — you just had to sit them out — but this time he was serious. He stood at the front of the bus on his Kermit legs, waiting for them to move. One by one, the kids stood up and retrieved their bags from the rack; the girls first, then the younger boys, and eventually Mick Doherty and his mates from the back seat. Some objected, others smirked, but most of them said nothing as they shuffled along the aisle, down the steps, and onto the stony shoulder of the road. There they remained in a huddle, hushed and disbelieving, as the door shut and the bus pulled away. They half-expected him to stop a few yards up the road, to hear the remorseful gasp of the pneumatic door. Instead Brian put his foot down and the bus accelerated and disappeared behind the trees on a distant bend in the road. Then erupted the babble of indignation — how fucking dangerous, how dare he, they weren't even being that bad. How far was Repentance? How long would it take? How were they going to get home?

Joanne walked over to Melanie, who was standing apart from the rest of the kids, hugging her canvas shoulder bag to her chest.

'That is so unfair,' she spat. 'We weren't doing anything, you and me. Why do we get thrown off?'

'Let's get going,' Joanne said.

'We're not going to walk —'

'We have to.'

'How far is it?'

'I dunno — four, five miles?'

They'd been left on the river flats, not far from the intersection at the bottom of Lancasters Hill. It was a landscape that made you feel stranded and alone. Unlike the country above them — the lush pasture, tumbling creeks, and tucked-away valleys — the farmland here was flat and dull, the grass the colour of straw, burnt by the occasional frost and bedraggled by floodwaters. The railway line ran across the plain on a raised mound of dirt and scattered gravel. Even the cattle on this stretch looked scrawnier somehow, a crossbred mottle of beasts scavenging for food among the thistles and bog rushes.

The other kids were still standing around and arguing. They were trying to hatch some kind of plan to go to the nearest farmhouse and phone someone's parents to come and get them.

Melanie whispered in Joanne's ear. 'Come on, let's hitchhike.'

'Isn't that dangerous?'

'Not as dangerous as walking along this road, and then there's the hill. They're all blind corners there. We'll get hit by a car.'

They stopped and let the others dawdle past. They needed to be at the back of the group to get the first lift from town.

'I'm s'posed to be working in the shop today,' Joanne said, gazing down the empty road.

'From when?'

'Five o'clock.'

'We'll get a lift by then.'

'Dad'll be angry.'

'Why would he be?'

'Because there was trouble on the bus. That makes him really mad. And Aunty Peg knows Brian's wife, so she'll be pissed off too.'

'It wasn't your fault.'

'Doesn't matter.'

'Won't they believe you? Linda will. She knows how much I hate that fucking bus.'

They squinted into the low, burning afternoon sun. A dog barked in a distant yard. A lone bull grumbled and wheezed in the paddock beside them. And then — they stopped and turned — the faint whine of a vehicle. They fixed their eyes on the road. Finally, as if they'd conjured it up by the sheer effort of staring, came the tiny silver wink of a car.

Melanie stuck her thumb out.

'They mightn't be going up the hill,' Joanne said.

'Doesn't matter. They might feel sorry for us and take us home anyway.'

They strained to get a clearer look at the car coming towards them. It was silver — no, it was white.

'It's yellow,' Melanie said.

Joanne felt a stab of dismay.

It was indeed yellow, a bright yellow Corolla, the very car that Joanne had washed the previous term as part of a school fundraiser. It hurtled towards them dragging a parachute of dust. Behind the wheel was the ample form of Mrs Marjorie Phelps.

Mrs Phelps had an uncanny knack for turning up at times like this. It was as if she had a teacher's nose for trouble. Slap, slap, slap, she'd come across the school quadrangle to sort out all the squabbling girls, the teasers and the bullies, and dole out her particular brand of wisdom and advice. She wore those horrible tent dresses — kaftans, they were called — bold and totemic on some days, earthy and home-spun on others. Today it was a calico one that she'd potato-printed herself. Pushed out in front by her breasts, and floundering at the back over her heavy hips and bottom, the dresses hid most of Mrs

Phelps, but they also revealed quite a lot, including the odd glimpse of an unshaven armpit, slightly dewy with her sweat. Her voice was loud and her jewellery chunky and knuckle-busting. She was the only fat woman Joanne knew who wasn't ashamed of the fact. That in itself was unforgivable in the eyes of the kids she taught.

She passed them in the car and immediately pulled over to the side of the road.

Melanie didn't miss a beat. 'The driver let us off because I was feeling sick.'

'He left you here? Are you kidding me? Bus drivers, I don't know! All right, then, in you get. She leant over the seat and pushed at a pile of school books that slid onto the floor. It was only then that Joanne noticed the two little Aboriginal boys sitting in the back seat.

'What's wrong with them?'

'Nothing. *Their* bus didn't stop for them at all. It happens sometimes, doesn't it, William?' she said, raising her face to the rear-vision mirror. 'Their principal calls me and I go and pick them up. So I won't be taking you girls straight home. We've got to go out to Bindjira.'

'Bindjira?'

'Ever been there?'

Joanne shook her head.

'Well, come on, jump in. You get in the front with me, Melanie, if you've been feeling sick. Here you go —' She pulled the key from the ignition. 'You can put your bags in the back.'

Behind the car, the girls exchanged looks of dismay.

'What'll we do?' Melanie whispered.

Joanne shrugged.

'We could say you're in a hurry and wait for another lift.'

They turned and looked down the road. Not another car in sight.

'Hurry up, girls,' called Mrs Phelps.

Joanne shoved her port in the boot. 'I'm going to be so late.'

They passed the intersection at the bottom of Lancasters Hill. There was no sign of the other kids from the bus. The turn-off to Bindjira was another two miles along the flats. They passed under the railway line through an arch of silvered timbers, and headed into the low, straggly brush on the other side. The road grew rougher as they went along, and the clay turned an infertile shade of yellow. Mrs Phelps gripped the wheel and cursed under her breath as they bounced over a gutter and hit the sump on a rock. Apart from that, nobody spoke. The two little boys sat hunched inside their ill-fitting seatbelts, breathing through their mouths and staring at Joanne, their eyes like huge polished stones. They looked young, she thought, maybe six or seven. The grey socks hanging lose around their ankles bore the blue and yellow stripes of the Catholic school.

'How does their bus get down here?' Melanie asked Mrs Phelps.

'It doesn't,' she said. 'They normally walk this bit, don't you, boys?'

The one called William gave a tiny nod. Joanne wondered why Mrs Phelps was driving them all the way home now.

'How much further is it?' she asked.

'Not far. How are you feeling, Melanie? Let me know if you need to stop.'

'I'm okay,' Melanie said. She turned her head ever so slightly and snuck a look at Joanne, who pressed her hand over her mouth and looked out the window.

The scrubland eventually opened into a small grassy paddock containing a rusty bathtub trough and a scruffy pinto pony. On the other side of the clearing was a cluster of fibro cottages, small and squat and linked together by loops of electric wire. Two dogs came running towards the car, followed by a gangly man in a grey singlet, smiling and waving with one arm.

'They been naughty, teacher?'

'No!' Mrs Phelps laughed, getting out of the car. She leant her hands on the top of the door and shook her head at Joanne. 'They always presume their kids are in trouble. I'll go in. You stay here, girls.

I won't be a sec. Come on, boys. Get your things together.'

Two more dogs came bounding out, a small brown kelpie and one that looked something like a border-collie cross. A woman with a baby on her hip appeared in the doorway of the nearest cottage. Mrs Phelps walked towards her, holding the little boys by the hand. Even with the car windows open, the air was heavy and still. A fly buzzed in confusion in the corner of the windscreen, and Joanne's thighs grew slippery on the vinyl seat.

'Is this like a reserve?' Melanie whispered.

'What are you whispering for?'

Joanne opened the car door to the green-eyed kelpie. It ducked away from her reaching hand and pissed on the back tyre.

'We didn't have any Aborigines at my school in Holbrook,' Melanie said.

'None?'

'Not that I can remember.'

'There's not that many live around here. The ones at school are mostly from the other side of town. Dad says there weren't any near Repentance when he was a kid. They've all come in from somewhere else, he reckons.' Joanne hesitated, remembering the painting in the museum, the Aborigine standing in its deep lacquered shadows. 'There might have been some in the olden days,' she added feebly.

The two little boys came running out of the house and took off across the paddock. They were lively now, calling to each other in high voices. Mrs Phelps emerged soon after, smiling to herself. She sat heavily in the driver's seat and punched at her calico dress, which had puffed up around her like a soufflé.

'Okay, girls, your turn,' she said. 'I'm like a taxi driver today.'

'Do they have to live here?' Melanie asked.

Joanne threw her a warning look.

'The Robertsons?' Mrs Phelps glanced once more towards the cottages. 'It depends what you mean by "have to".'

Here we go, thought Joanne. It was a bad idea to go pressing Mrs

Phelps on stuff like this. She didn't even like the word 'Aborigine'; they weren't allowed to use it in class. *Koori* was the correct term, she said — *Koori* kids, *Koori* culture. She was the same about the hippies. *Alternats* was her word for them, as in *the alternative society*. She was similarly protective of the hippie kids at school. You could see it in the way she spoke to Melanie, tolerating her most smartypants opinions and shrugging off her long bouts of absenteeism. Mrs Phelps had once triggered an explosion of snickering in class, describing the arrival of the *alternats* in their region as being 'a breath of fresh air'.

But that afternoon, to Joanne's surprise, there was no further talk of Kooris or hippies or social injustice. She didn't mention the Aboriginal kids again. Instead the conversation turned to the girls' history assignment, which was due in two weeks' time.

'So how's it coming along, girls?'

Joanne felt a prickle of panic.

'We haven't even started,' Melanie said languidly. She turned to Joanne and smiled, twisting her hair around her finger.

'You'd better get cracking. It's fifty per cent of your mark this term. You two need to get together and make a start on it.'

In the back seat, Joanne slumped over her folded arms.

'We could do it this weekend,' Melanie said. 'I'll ask Linda. You could stay Saturday night.'

'That sounds like a plan,' said Mrs Phelps.

That was no plan at all as far as Joanne was concerned. Her father would never allow it. She couldn't even imagine herself having the courage to ask. And how come Melanie was so enthusiastic all of a sudden? She hadn't lasted two rooms of the museum before sneaking off to eat some weirdo cake in a cafe. And what about all the work Joanne had done already? She'd been to the library, she'd interviewed Aunty Peg. She'd come to presume that she was working on the project alone.

'Her dad says we're hippies. He might not let her come.'

'Do you need me to talk to him, Joanne?' asked Mrs Phelps.

'No, thanks.'

'I could write a note if you need me to, or perhaps Melanie could come and stay with you.'

'But we want to visit her Uncle Bill,' Melanie said. 'He lives next door to me. He's got all this old milking equipment, hand churns and stuff. Joanne was going to ask him for a lend.'

'A loan,' corrected Mrs Phelps. 'That all sounds good to me. What about you, Joanne? Do you think you'd be able to go?'

'Yes, of course,' Joanne snapped.

Who was Melanie to say what her father would or wouldn't allow her to do? She pushed her finger along the stitching on the vinyl seat and thought through the pros and cons of various alibis. Tracy Willis, Rhonda McKay — there were so many things to consider, like which families might come into the shop or be at church with Aunty Peg on Sunday. Her mind wandered to clothes, to the embroidered cheese-cloth top she'd bought with her birthday money. Rosellas flew like arrows across the road in front of them. Rocks flew up and thumped beneath her feet. Perhaps she could secretly borrow Barb's macramé belt. What else did they have in their wardrobe that might possibly pass as hippie?

Chapter Seventeen

Joel Spender locked his gate and watched the jeep drive off, the dust pricking his eyes and the weeping membranes in his nose. He would make himself another cuppa — tea this time, not coffee like the German girl had asked for. He was hopeless at making coffee. He should have just told her that instead of grinding away at the powder hardened in the jar. He had heated the milk on the stove, thinking that might improve the situation, but she hardly touched it and he laughed at himself for trying to impress her. It was the first time they'd met and he liked her immediately. She was so interested in everything, in the skins he was tanning and his collection of old tools. Her father was raised in Solingen and she knew her knives and blades. She was astonished that he'd heard of the place, but then of course he had. Working as a saw doctor for nearly forty years, he knew of all the world's famous knifemaking towns.

The chap, Gerard, he'd met before, through Phil de Beer. He was nowhere near as likeable as his girlfriend. There was something closed off, bottled up inside that young man. According to Phil, Gerard had been the driving force behind this protest they were planning. You had to admire him for that, and he certainly knew his trees — that was impressive. Once or twice that morning, as he showed the two of them around, Joel had recognised aspects of himself in the younger man. He could imagine Gerard living alone on a farm like this one day, passively feuding with his neighbours, agisting most of his land and spending a good part of his time wandering in the bush.

From his kitchen window, Joel looked down on the paddock in question. It was good flat land for camping with the creek at the bottom and the track cutting through, leading up to the ridge. The path was already used by people going to swim at the falls. He didn't mind as long as they came in through the fence and didn't touch any of his stuff. His real concern was for his trees, for the dozens of tiny saplings that had sprung up in the grass. He had sold most of his Herefords just over a year before and decided not to agist this paddock with the rest of his land. That was all it took: you kept the cattle out, and back came the forest — lilly pilly, cudgerie, sandpaper fig — springing up through crumbly red soil. It was marvellous to watch, and he'd become a bit obsessed with it. Gerard had shown an interest too and had helped to identify some of the saplings as they walked around that morning. There could be a hundred people, he'd said. That was a lot of trampling feet. Joel stood at his kitchen sink and wondered what he'd got himself into, putting his hand up to help at that meeting out at the commune.

He finished his cup of tea at the kitchen table and then walked, a little stiffly, down the long back steps to his shed, where he turned Bettina's bandicoot pelt in its salt solution. How funny that she should ask him for a hat. Most hippie girls flinched at the thought of his skins and hides. He'd taken a stall once at the Braemar market, selling cowhide rugs, rabbit skins, and a fox fur. He copped so much flak about his slaughter of animals that he hadn't bothered to go back again.

Bettina, however, had arrived with her own dead animal in a bag, a bandicoot that she had found dead on the side of the road.

'I wanted to skin it myself,' she told him, unwrapping the lump of bloodied flesh and fur, 'but Gerard said you could do it for me. What do you think? I'd like a cap. Do you sew the skins as well?'

He inspected the bandicoot. For a small piece of roadkill, it wasn't in bad shape. All the same, there was only enough fur on it to make something like a bandeau.

'That's good,' she said, her eyes shining. 'Look at all these skins. Is that a fox?'

He had ten skins and a hide pinned out on frames around the shed, and another soaking. Gerard shuddered visibly and left them to it.

'He's squeamish,' Bettina laughed. 'He didn't want to stop to pick up the bandicoot. He said it would have maggots, but I think it's very fresh.' She pointed to Joel's rack of knives and scrapers. 'These are amazing. Do you hunt?'

'They're mostly just for skinning. Take a look if you like.'

That was when he noticed how expertly she handled the blades, wetting her finger, running it forward, turning them on the flat of her hand. They talked about Solingen and the beauty of folding knives.

'You used to work with chainsaws,' she said.

'Chainsaws, bandsaws, circular saws. I was a saw doctor.'

She laughed. 'So I heard. That's a funny name. Do saws get sick?'

'No, but they do need constant care. It's a specialised job. I had to train for five years, nearly as long as a real doctor. It was good work. I liked it.'

'So why did you stop?'

Joel smiled and lifted the hem of his shirt to reveal the ropey scar of his flesh wound.

'Oh!' Bettina gasped. 'How did that happen?'

'It's a long story, but I decided it was time to retire. What do you know about bandicoots?'

'Nothing,' she said. She leant forward and looked into the glassy eye of the animal on the bench.

'They're rather sweet,' Joel said, poking at its snout, 'but people round here don't like them much. They say they spread TB.'

'Do they?'

'Possibly.' He raised his knife. 'Are you prepared to die?'

'For your bandeau? Of course. Cut away, saw doctor.'

He gently pulled the skin from the flesh and began to scrape at the fat and membranes on the underside. 'It's got to soak now, in salt and alum. That'll take about three days. Then you tack it up and stretch it out while it dries.'

'How long will that take?'

'About a week.'

Gerard was back, and she turned and smiled at him. 'That's perfect, isn't it? I want it for the blockade. We think it could start in about a week. That's what we're planning for.'

Joel bundled the skinned carcass into the bag she'd brought it in. She wanted to take it home, she said. Gerard rolled his eyes. She wanted to put it out in the field, where the crows would pick it clean.

Funny little thing. As they made their way back to the jeep, Joel saw her stoop and pick up a chook feather. It was just a boring wing feather from one of his white leghorns, but she thrust it through the little topknot on the left side of her head. He watched, amused, as she marched behind Gerard with the bandicoot bag in her arms and all the fierce dignity of a little Indian squaw.

A hundred people in about a week. Joel stirred the bucket of solution. He wondered again why he'd agreed to let them onto his land. It was that charming Phil de Beer: he had a way of talking you around. Joel hadn't exactly got cold feet, but he had phoned Phil after the meeting to lay down a few ground rules for the camp.

He was happy for them to run a power cord from his shed, but they couldn't use his rainwater tank or toilet. And they'd have to keep an eye on the kids and keep them away from the house. He had a lot of stuff lying around — old machinery, the bodies of two cars. He didn't want them treated like bits of play equipment. Most importantly, he would stay out of the action. He wouldn't join the blockade. He was getting himself into enough strife as it was, and he knew half the blokes in the bush crews. No matter what they thought of him these days, of his reclusive lifestyle, he didn't want them spotting him up there on the frontline. He would stay inside and guard the gate, keep an eye on who came in. Gerard had suggested a padlock with a code.

Chapter Eighteen

Joanne would remember the peppery odour of the warm basalt beneath her cheek. She wasn't sure if it was the rock itself she could smell or the dribbles of river water evaporating around her. She lay on her stomach, her eyes closed, her fingers cupped and curling on either side of her wet hair. Above the monotonous roar of the waterfall, she could hear the murmurs of the women sitting on the rock around her: Linda, Jane, Melanie, and the other carload of people who met them there unexpectedly but whom they seemed to know. There was a young woman called Aurora with an elfin face and long fair hair that fanned out around her as she floated naked on her back in the swimming hole below. Earlier, sitting on the rock, she had reminded Joanne of the little mermaid with her long hair cloaking her pale breasts and belly. Everyone was in the nude. The little kids were mucking about in the smaller cascades upstream, and the men were jumping over the falls. Every now and then came the thud of running feet and a splash as someone plummeted into the pool below. They called to each other across the water, their deep voices ringing hollow inside the sheer rock walls. Then, one by one, they made their way to the top again, hauling themselves up the steep mud path, worn smooth by the scramble of a thousand wet feet. Joanne shut her eyes more tightly as each man reached the top and strode across the rock platform in front of her. She couldn't let on for a moment, but she found the sight of their dicks hanging bald and pale in their nests of pubic hair deeply shocking. She'd never seen a naked man before, not the bottom bit. The closest she'd come were the drawings in her biology textbook, the drooping cutaway of the male penis and scrotum. Those diagrams were embarrassing enough but they didn't jiggle and flop about at the bottom of a hairy torso. They were hideous, she thought with a thump of guilt and fright. The bodies of the women were no way near as bad — she was more prepared for them — but she'd found whole skinny-dipping thing stressful from the outset.

'You don't need swimmers,' Melanie had told her in response to her first excuse. 'It's miles from anywhere, this place. No one cares.'

Melanie's mother, Linda, had come to her rescue.

'She can wear a pair of yours if she wants to, Mel. Where are your crocheted ones?'

'They'll be too small.'

'They're stretchy. Go and dig them out.'

Of course, they were too small. The stringy cords cut into her, her breasts spilled out the sides, but they were swimmers, they'd have to do, and there were sarongs and towels on hand once she was out of the water. She did, however, feel deeply uncool when everyone else stripped off. All of a sudden she stood out in a way she could hardly bear. Then came the separate terror of leaping over the falls. Once she'd done that and surfaced, it didn't seem that much of a stretch to slip out of her swimmers underneath the water and place them on a rock.

'See?' said Melanie. 'Doesn't it feel nice?'

It did. It felt amazing. The water caressed her skin with a fuzzy softness. She looked at Melanie and saw with relief that her own naked body would be nothing more than a pale pink squiggle beneath the surface. She swam across the pool, turned like a leaf, and breaststroked slowly under the thundering falls. A rainbow quivered in the spray above her, and she squealed as the water pounded down on her head and shoulders. It was wonderful but the tension returned when it was time to pull herself out of the pool and make her way up the cliff face. There was no redonning that tight, wet tangle of a bikini, and there wasn't much point anyway. It was a huge relief to lie face down with her elbows tucked in by her sides and know that the only thing visible was her bum, and somehow that was okay.

She could almost fall asleep. Maybe she did for a moment. Maybe she was sleeping now. Her breath was slow, her lips slack, her belly had spread and moulded to the warm rock underneath her. The wind stirred through the branches of the trees. Fragments of the women's conversation hung sharp and echoless in the air.

Surprise Rock, they called this place. They all knew it so well. Melanie couldn't believe that Joanne had never been there, when Andy and Jane announced their intention to go that afternoon.

'How come?' she asked.

How come indeed. How was it that she'd never heard of the place when she'd lived here all her life? How did the hippies know about it, how to get here without any road signs? How did they know where to park their cars on the stretch of unsealed road and duck through the barbed-wire fence with their towels tucked under their arms? This was obviously common knowledge: the bottom strands of fencing wire sagged in that one spot, and from there a clear track was worn across the paddock, over a small creek and up the hill on the other side. Towards the top, the path forked, leading left and right. They turned left and quickly descended into a hanging valley. And there it was: the hidden creek, the deep round swimming hole, the falls thundering over the big cantilevered rock that was a surprise to nobody but her. Even the Aborigines had known about this place. According to Jane, it had been a sacred meeting place and you could find traces of their ancient fires in the muddy banks of the creek.

'Which way is Repentance?' Joanne asked when they first arrived.

'It's just over there,' said Melanie with a careless wave of her hand. 'You know where they're going to log the forest? That's just over the hill. We've come in from the other side, that's all.'

Joanne struggled to process this. The winding road on the way out had caused her to lose her bearings.

'I'll show you on a map when we get home,' Melanie told her. 'It's really not that hard. If you look that way from the top of the ridge, you can see the smoke from the mill.'

The authority in her voice filled Joanne with resentment. Lying on the rock above the falls, she wondered if she'd ever seen a proper map of the district, not counting the simple tourist map outside the Council Chambers. Maybe they could use one in their project somewhere, showing the location of the milk co-ops, and the cheese factory that now sat derelict by the creek below Repentance.

The project. She raised her head and looked at Melanie sunbaking beside her. They were supposed to be working on it now. It was due on Thursday and they'd hardly done any work on the diorama. Again she felt the panic rising up inside her. She had risked so much to spend the weekend out at Melanie's place, but the whole plan seemed to be unravelling.

It looked like it was going to be so easy to begin with. After Mrs Phelps dropped her home, after the bus debacle, she had found Aunty Peg in the kitchen, in the throes of Christmas baking.

'I'm doing a couple of puddings and three cakes,' Peg announced. 'One cake using your mum's recipe and two using mine. I'll keep one of mine for the Balbirnie Show. I left it too late last year. There wasn't enough time to feed it.' Bang, bang, bang went the cake tins onto the bench, three enormous square ones and two round pudding basins. 'Where would I find a measuring jug?' Peg was looking flustered. 'It's hard cooking in someone else's kitchen.'

'I'm going to a friend's place this weekend. We're working on a project for history.'

'That's nice,' said Peg, thumping a roll of brown paper on the bench. 'Here, make yourself useful. You can line the cake tins for me. I'll find you some scissors, hold on.'

'They're in that drawer,' Joanne said. 'I'll be sleeping there Saturday night.'

'Mind you leave a good inch around the top. Fruit cakes rise up in the oven.'

No questions, no lies, no names required: Joanne couldn't believe her luck. If her dad asked, Peg would say she was staying with 'a little friend from school'. Even better, the scary Gerard and his girlfriend were going to be away. Joanne had arranged for Melanie's mum to pick her up at the war memorial and drop her back at the same place on Sunday afternoon. She'd bought four sheets of cardboard at the newsagent in town, along with some DAS modelling clay and a packet of plastic farm animals, which included four black and white cows, a cattle dog, and two horses.

She had arrived at Melanie's place that morning ready to get to work, but even before she'd carried her things into the house, there was talk of them going somewhere for a swim.

'We'll do it tomorrow,' Melanie said. 'It won't take all weekend. We can get the backdrop painted after dinner.'

Then Linda had breezed through the room saying things like 'go with the flow'. Joanne smiled to hide her anxiety as her bag of craft materials disappeared under the pile of clothes pulled from Melanie's wardrobe in the search for the crocheted bikini.

Neither did they go straight home after their swim. Andy wanted them all to come and see a tree. It wasn't far, he told them, just over the ridge. It was one of the biggest in the basin, really fucking huge. They retraced their steps to the fork in the path and went the other way. The track grew steep and rocky and sometimes disappeared completely among the prickly undergrowth and twisted, stunted gums. On the other side, however, the bush began to change. The jagged escarpment rose up on their right, casting a deep shadow, and the trees grew straight and tall between the slanting shafts of sunlight.

Joanne and Melanie walked behind Aurora, who was now wearing long tulle skirt like a ragged tutu.

'She always wears that,' Melanie said. 'Mum calls her the Airy Fairy.'

'She's really pretty.'

'Yeah, maybe, but she's also a little bit weird.'

They came upon a break in the trees, a wide cutting of churned-up mud with a bulldozer sitting in the middle.

'That's the turning bay for the trucks,' Joanne heard Linda say. 'The bulldozer isn't theirs. It belongs to the road crew. It's stuck here till the bridge gets fixed. It's been sitting there for weeks.'

Jane looked at Linda, astonished.

'I told you. I came here with Gerard.'

'Did he show you this big tree?'

'Maybe. There's a lot of them. I'm not sure which one Andy means.'

It was obvious the moment they glimpsed it through the trees. Joanne had imagined something knobbly and buttressed like a giant fig, but this was a brush box, thick and straight and solid. It rose abruptly from the undergrowth, as clean and startling as a mushroom bursting from a cow pat. A few feet up, the rough, grey basal bark cracked open to reveal a creamy smoothness, like newly exposed skin. Andy beckoned for them to move to the other side of the trunk, where, just above their heads, someone had painted a yellow cross and a small blue arrow. There was a metal tag too. Joanne strained to read it. It was stamped with the numbers 386/1 and the letters REP. The swimming party murmured quietly among themselves and then began to organise. They spread themselves around the tree, eight adults and six kids, not counting the little ones slung on hips and sitting up on shoulders. They stretched their arms around its girth, reaching for each other. Joanne moved in to join them, and Aurora grasped her hand. She closed her eyes and pressed her cheek against the bark. Someone said they could hear the lifeforce pulsing within.

Joanne held her breath and listened, the blood beating in her ears. She craned her neck to see the top of it, following the trunk up and up to where it divided into a crown of smooth pink branches, strung with ribbons of bark and feathery tufts of fern. And onward still, to a canopy of leaves that was faintly disappointing, looking too ragged and thin for the grandeur of the tree beneath. Aurora withdrew her hand and gave a breathy giggle as a young man grabbed her by the waist and lifted her into the air. She hung, suspended, her arms raised like a ballerina, her tulle skirt swallowing the head of the young man. He carefully manoeuvred her towards the yellow cross. She wrenched the tin tag from its nail and hurled it to the ground.

They got back to the house in the late afternoon, tired and sunburnt. There was talk of dinner and feeding the dogs and hanging towels on the line. Melanie was first for the bath. Left at a loose end, Joanne wandered into the kitchen and asked if she could help.

Jane looked surprised and pleased. 'You can clear the table for me.' She handed her a wooden chopping board. 'That's all Gerard's,' she said of the magazines and envelopes. 'Put them in the middle room with his other stuff.'

Joanne pushed open the lounge-room door. She hadn't been inside this room since the night of the funeral. The doors to the sunroom were closed, and the cold hearth smelt faintly of rank ashes. Records lay on the carpet next to the record player, most of them out of their covers. In the corner was Gerard's messy desk. Joanne felt like a trespasser as she crept towards it and placed the letters on top of one of the many stacks of papers. Poking out was the corner of a map, which she carefully extracted and unfolded on the floor. It was just like the one she'd imagined at the waterfall that day, a proper detailed map of the local district. It showed the contours of the land in shades of green and brown, with the town and villages as patches of flesh pink. Only some of Balbirnie was visible on the left-hand side, but the map extended well to the north and west. Repentance was a trickle of pink running down from the ridge in the middle, surrounded by pale-green farmland on the edge of the dark-green forest. It showed the outline of the showground, and tiny crosses indicating the churches and cemetery. Joanne traced the road from Repentance to this house with her finger, passing the gravel quarry and the dip yard on the corner. She leant across to find the forest basin and the road they'd driven earlier that day. Surprise Rock itself wasn't labelled on the map, but part of the paddock they'd walked through was crosshatched in red texta. Someone had drawn an arrow leading from there to the side of the map, where they'd scribbled the name *Joel Spender* and a phone number. Joanne sat back on her haunches. It was Joel Spender's farm. She didn't know him very well, but she knew who he was. He always bought *The Australian*, never the local rag. 'I wouldn't wipe my feet on that,' he'd said to her one day. She knew he used to work at the mill and he'd had an accident. He had become something of a hermit since, living in the house that he used to share with his elderly mother. Ray thought that he'd gone a bit funny, letting his hair grow long and wearing it in a straggly ponytail at the back. Joanne remembered that the farm itself had looked pretty messy this morning, with lots of old machinery rusting away in the grass. There were other lines on the map too, blue biro marks on the road near the causeway, and more, almost invisible, in the deep forest green.

All of a sudden the pile on the desk above her slumped and fell to the floor. Appalled, Joanne stared at the mess: manila folders, a road atlas, hundreds of pieces of paper, a bird book, and plastic bags full of dirt and leaves.

'What are you doing?' Melanie was standing in the doorway, wearing a red Chinese dressing-gown, her hair wrapped in a bath towel.

'They fell. I was just — I was clearing the kitchen table.'

'We're not allowed to touch this stuff.'

'I didn't.'

Melanie crouched down and began to pick things up. 'Were they in any order?'

'I don't know. What is this stuff, anyway?' Joanne held up a bag of scabby leaves.

Melanie snatched it from her. 'He's a botanist, I told you.'

Joanne grimaced. Was there such a thing? It sounded like the stuff of history books, of Joseph Banks and Edwardian ladies painting fruit and flowers.

'Is that his job?'

'Yes.'

'Who does he work for?'

'Himself.'

Joanne got down on her hands and knees and peered under the desk. Things had slid right underneath and it was difficult to reach them. Her fingers touched the edge of a photo, a large glossy one, black-and-white.

'Is that everything?' she heard Melanie ask.

'Yes, I think so.'

She pressed the photo to her chest and pulled herself upright as Melanie left the room. It was a strange picture, taken at an odd angle looking up through leaves. Three people were standing in front of a big white four-wheel drive. Sandy Mitchell was one of them. The other man looked much younger, but you couldn't see his face. The girl was the giveaway. She was hugely pregnant. It must have been James Mitchell and his wife. They appeared to be deep in conversation, at least James and his father were. The wife was looking the other way, almost at the camera.

A door slammed somewhere at the back of the house. Joanne was meant to be helping. Carefully she slipped the photo into the restored pile of papers on the desk and, with one last glance over her shoulder, went back to the kitchen.

The girls didn't sleep in the bedroom that night. Instead, at Jane's suggestion, they pulled their pillows and quilts onto the grass out the front. It was a moonless night with hundreds of stars. The Milky Way spread like a gaseous cloud across the sky. The Saucepan, the Southern Cross — Joanne and Melanie pointed out the familiar constellations to each other and recited all the usual, unsettling facts about space: that planets don't twinkle, that the sun was really a star, that the stars they were looking at might no longer exist. Melanie guided Joanne's gaze to the left of Orion, where, if you stared and narrowed your eyes, the tiny Pleaides revealed themselves like a sprinkle of glitter.

Jane came out to the veranda and tossed the dregs from a teapot into the shrubs.

'Come out here,' Melanie called. Jane knew where to find the signs of the Zodiac. 'What are you?' Melanie asked Joanne. 'I'm Pisces.'

'Virgo,' Joanne said. She always wished she weren't.

'Hah, you're a virgin.' Melanie laughed.

That was one reason why, that and the fact that Virgos were meant to be dull and boring. As it turned out, neither Virgo nor Pisces was visible at that time, only Taurus and Gemini. Jane came down and showed them where to look. Joanne was disappointed in Taurus. It didn't look like a bull, except maybe the horns, but she figured you could join any stars in the sky and see horns like that if you wanted. The Pleiades sat on the bull's shoulder like a cloud of buffalo flies. Joanne said this out loud. The other two looked at her blankly. They might know a lot about stars, she thought, but not very much about cattle.

'Look at you all, stargazing!'

Linda leant against the veranda post at the top of the steps.

'Come and see, Mum, there's heaps.'

'What's Linda's sign?' Jane asked.

'You're Aquarius, aren't you, Mum?'

'I am.'

The end of Linda's cigarette glowed orange in the darkness.

'What's your rising sign?' Jane asked.

'Fuck, I wouldn't know. My moon is in the seventh house. That's right, isn't it?'

'No!'

'*When the moooon is in the Seventh House, and Jupiter aligns with Mars ...*'

Joanne giggled. 'Your mum's so funny.'

Melanie rolled her eyes. 'Stoned, more like it. What's she doing now?'

Linda had gone back into the house and was now in the lounge room, just visible through the French doors. Suddenly they flung open and there she was, arms outstretched, head thrown back. From behind her came the crackle and hum of the record player and the opening strains of 'Aquarius'.

Linda undulated like a piece of seaweed, her hands turning at the wrist. 'Come on!' she cried, shimmying down the steps and across the yard towards them. She grabbed Jane by the arm and, ignoring her laughing protests, pulled her into the dance. Then she beckoned to the girls. Melanie jumped up and joined them. She was used to this sort of thing. She seemed to know the moves. In fact, all three of them appeared to be dancing in unison, circling their shoulders and swaying their hips, their rapturous faces turned towards the sky. Linda crossed her arms and in one swift movement pulled her singlet over her head. To Joanne's astonishment, Jane followed suit, tugging off her old t-shirt and tossing it aside. For the second time that day Joanne was staring at their bare bosoms, Jane's bouncing like melons and the firm brown peaks on Linda's chest hardly bouncing at all. The dingo pup came running, as if sensing the excitement. He dashed between them, yipping and snapping at their heels. Melanie didn't take her top off. Joanne was pleased about that. She was also relieved that the stripping off was limited to shirts, because she knew what the song was, that it came from the musical *Hair*. She knew that people in that show danced completely nude. There'd been a photo in an issue of *Newsweek* once. They sold it in the shop. For a whole week, kids kept coming in to look at it and snicker.

The song merged into 'Let the Sunshine In', and the dancers fell in a laughing heap.

'What a hoot!' Linda sighed contentedly, rolling onto her back. 'I feel like chocolate. Do we have any? Chocolate and a camomile tea.'

Melanie climbed back under the quilt.

'Can Donovan sleep with us?' she called after them.

'Yeah, sure,' Jane called back.

'Surrre,' the girls giggled, mimicking her accent. The puppy burrowed between them, its body soft and warm. Joanne thought she felt a flea bite her leg, but didn't say. Neither would she repeat what Ray always said about people keeping dingos as pets: that they became vicious when they grew up and a threat to cattle and sheep. So many of her thoughts and emotions had gone unspoken that day. She'd worn the same un-telling smile while she'd felt, at turns, enchanted, shocked, mortified, elated. The staggering beauty of the forest she had lived near all her life; the rainbows hovering in the mist above the plunging falls; the behaviour of the grown-ups, so different from the adults in her life. It was almost impossible to believe that Linda was only two years younger than Delia had been, and just four years younger than her Aunty Peg. Everything was fun here, and frank and magical. The smell of jasmine in the air, the tinkling of chimes. Under the pleasant mustiness of the feather quilt, Donovan yapped and twitched his feet in a happy puppy dream. Joanne reached down and circled her finger in the fuzz at the base of his ear. It was only Saturday. She had another whole day to go. But we have to do the project then, said the old Joanne, sitting like a sulky child in the corner of her mind. She felt a tingle of anxiety but it quickly faded behind the trilling, croaking noises of the night. She descended into sleep, her thoughts turning like chips of glass in a kaleidoscope, forming and fragmenting and expanding in a starburst. She was a child of the universe curled on a grassy hill, happy in the velvet folds of the unfolding night.

She woke, startled by a sudden pull on the quilt. Melanie was bolt upright and alert. Over the rim of the valley came the headlights of a car and the distant barking of dogs.

'Who is it?' Joanne whispered.

Melanie hushed her. 'I'm not sure. It could be Gerard and Bettina.'

'You said they were away.'

'They were. But don't worry, he won't see you. They'll go straight to bed. They have really noisy sex sometimes, it's gross. But we won't hear them from here, unless they come out and do it on the swing seat. I caught them at it once, did I tell you?'

Joanne felt a sudden weariness. She didn't want to know.

'Hah, look at you! You're all freaked out.'

'No, I'm not.'

The jeep pulled up in the paddock beside them, flooding the yard with light. Wotan leapt from the back seat and came running towards them, drawing the puppy out to play.

'Hello,' called a high female voice.

Melanie shaded her eyes against the dazzle of the lights, while Joanne pretended to sleep.

'What are you doing out here?' Bettina asked.

'Looking at the stars.'

'All on your own?'

'No. I've got a friend sleeping over.'

'Hello, friend!'

Joanne pulled her head further into her shoulders and squeezed her eyes shut.

'Where have you been?' Melanie asked.

Why did she have to ask questions? Next thing she'd be inviting them to come and sit down.

'Oh God, everywhere! We've been busy, haven't we, babe? I'm so tired.'

Through half-closed eyes, Joanne saw a slim and pale young woman walking across the yard, her arms wrapped around a cardboard carton.

'We went to Surprise Rock,' Melanie said.

'Hah! We were just near there this morning. We went to see Joel about the camp. It's all happening. Then we had to go into Balbirnie and gestetner all this stuff.' She looked down at the box in her arms. 'It's so hot, that place, I hate it.'

The headlights went out, leaving only a pale rhombus of light falling across the yard from the window of the house.

'You should've made a fire out here, you two. We could make one now.' Bettina turned to Gerard, who was following behind her. 'You want to, babe?'

'Nah,' he said, slipping his hand into the back pocket of her denim shorts. Under the quilt, Melanie poked Joanne with her toe. 'Leave them. Her friend's asleep. Let's just go inside.'

Joanne was just letting go of her breath and the tension in her body when Bettina's head jerked back and the box slipped in her arms.

'Fallende Sterne!' she squealed.

They all looked to the sky. Joanne sat up in time to see the final falling star streaking from the horns of Taurus all the way to the faint outline of the hills across the valley.

'Ohhhh!' They gasped in unison and laughed like little children.

'That was amazing!' Melanie cried. 'Did you make a wish, Joanne?'

Joanne was up on her elbows, her eyes fixed on the place where the last star had fizzled and died. She had never seen one that big or bright. How quickly it was gone. She felt her awareness return to earth and the excitement fade around her. There she was, like a rock exposed by a receding tide. She could feel him looking at her. There was nothing she could do but turn and meet the piercing gaze of Gerard Ansiewicz.

Chapter Nineteen

'Was he mad, Mum?'

Linda thumped a bottle of milk on the kitchen table and glanced at the clock on the wall.

'He was mad,' Melanie said to Joanne in a gleeful whisper.

'No, he wasn't. Come on, eat up, you two. I've got to get Joanne home.'

'We have to wait for the paint to dry.'

'How long's that going to take?'

Out on the back porch, the girls had made a feeble start on their project. Poor kids, they'd only got as far as painting the backdrop green. Linda looked at the sheets of cardboard buckling with moisture, the vinyl paint still streaky and congealing. Her eyes were smarting with tiredness; her nostrils felt swollen and sore. Crying like that really took it out of a person her age, she realised. It caused actual injury to your sinuses and membranes, and you didn't bounce back the way you did when you were young. And she had cried a lot. He'd torn strips off her. That was exactly how she felt, like something hanging from a hook, stripped of its skin and weeping.

'You're going to have to leave it with us, Joanne,' she said in a dull voice. She turned and saw the girl's alarmed expression. 'How about we finish the backdrop here, and you do the rest at home. You wouldn't want to carry this on the bus anyway. We'll take it to school in the car. When did you say it was due, Mel?'

'Thursday,' said Joanne, 'and we have to do the journal too and the writing for the timeline. I could do that on bits of paper and stick them on at school.'

'That sounds good, doesn't it, Mel?'

'And we have to do the presentation,' Joanne continued. 'We were going to look in the dairy for old butter churns and stuff.'

Linda clawed at the messy pile of hair at the back of her head.

'Yeah okay, Mel can do that too.'

The clock again. Twenty to nine. Gerard wanted the Parmenter girl out of there first thing, and then he wanted everyone else out at Druidane for some kind of preparatory workshop. He was being a bossy shit. He was still in a foul mood this morning and then his jeep wouldn't start. He and Bettina had gone with Andy on the motorbike, leaving Linda and Jane to bring all his boxes of stuff from the lounge room. That was all she knew. He wouldn't tell her anything else while the girl was in the house. As he'd shouted at her the previous night, slamming his bedroom door, her timing really couldn't have been worse.

There was no room in the paddock at the top of the hill that served as a car park for the Druidane commune. Instead they had to leave their car by the road and lug the boxes of pamphlets down a steep, muddy path through the orchards. Sunlight spilled through the drooping leaves of the pawpaw and avocado trees. In the branches somewhere, a bamboo wind chime knocked and paddled in the breeze. They passed along a terrace of raised veggie beds spilling their straw like overstuffed mattresses. Gourds hung from their sagging tripods over patches of nasturtium and serrated lettuce leaves.

'Mitsuba,' Jane said wistfully, casting an envious eye across the beds. 'I tried to grow it once. I should try again.'

'I've always thought that you and Andy should live here,' Linda said. 'The gardens, the kilns, the cooking. It seems like your kind of place.'

'You have to buy in.'

'Yes, I know.'

'It's quite expensive. And there's a lot of rules. Andy doesn't like that either.'

'I don't like the lily ponds,' Linda said, 'and this shadowy valley, all the shrubs. I find it claustrophobic.'

They came to the two ponds and walked across the narrow bank of earth that ran between them. A few water lilies were in bloom, their bright yellow stamens crawling with bees. Dragonflies hovered above the water. A dusky moorhen pumped her way to the reeds on the other side. They put down the heavy boxes they were carrying, and Linda pulled out her tobacco. The air smelt of honey and citrus blossom. It buzzed with a lazy sweetness, and the more you stared the further you could see below the mirrored surface of the pond, down to the motionless tangle of weeds and the twisted stems of the lilies.

Melanie crouched at the water's edge and dabbled her fingers. 'These ponds are pretty, Mum. How come you don't like them?'

'Water chestnuts,' murmured Jane, pointing to a submerged tub of radiating pond weed. With each plant she identified, each fruit and vegetable, she appeared to sink further beneath the weight of her own failures.

In her packet of Drum, Linda found the roach she'd salvaged from the night before. Tears and dope in the churning darkness of the bedroom. It had buffeted her for hours, like a storm at sea. When the sun finally came up, it was on a scene of devastation: a stinging crust of salt in her lashes, sheets on the floor, a flotsam of torn and ragged thoughts that no longer hung together. Hopeless, selfish, fucking pathetic, the bang of his bedroom door. In the silence that had followed, she was sure she'd heard Bettina laugh.

Melanie was constructing a dam in the shallows, using chunks of gravel from the path. Frogs tock-tocked, and time trickled its way through the pipe connecting the two ponds. Suddenly, from down the hill, came a burst of applause.

'We should go,' Jane said, squinting at the sun.

'What's up first?'

Jane pulled a pamphlet from her box. 'Non-violent resistance workshop.'

'Show me that.'

'Haven't you read it?'

Of course she hadn't read it. Gerard and Bettina had only brought them home the night before. She'd heard all about it, how they'd had spent the afternoon slaving over a hot duplicator while she was out there at the falls, swimming with the enemy. Why was it always her fault? Jane was swimming too. She was the one who found the Parmenter girl in the first place and put her in their bathtub.

Now she read through the leaflet, front and back. All the practical details were there: where they were camping, what to bring, the obligatory quote from Gandhi. She was astonished to see how the campaign had got away on her. Somehow she'd taken her eye off the ball and been left behind. Staring into the water, she tried to think what she'd been doing these past few weeks while all this frantic activity was taking place. She was meant to have found herself a tent and be packed and ready to go.

'I don't have a tent,' she muttered. 'Do you?'

'Andy got one from the army-disposal store. They might have some spare ones, they bought a stock lot, or you could stay in one of the teepees. They're moving them from the creek.'

'No! I'm not doing that. I'll organise something, don't worry.'

Melanie destroyed her dam, sending a cloud of silt billowing into the water. 'What is this workshop thing?' she asked.

'Non-violent resistance,' Linda said in a flat voice. '*Link arms, go slack, lock on, roll back.* I know the drill. I've done my time on the picket lines.'

Jane looked at her strangely.

'What?'

'Nothing.'

'In Melbourne — Vietnam. What did you think I meant?'

'Of course,' Jane said, perhaps a little too quickly. 'I'm told Phil was very involved with all that, that he lay in front of President Johnson's car.'

'That's bullshit,' Linda said. 'Or maybe. I don't know. Everyone claims to have done that. They can't all be telling the truth. I saw the footage. There were people lying on the road, but not *that* many.'

'What about you, Linda? What did you do?'

'For LBJ's visit?'

'Yeah.'

Linda bit her lip. She was still with Tom then. Melanie was about two, and Tom had carried her on his shoulders all the way down Bourke Street. They'd seen a bit of jostling but missed the paint being thrown at the motorcade. It was one of the few parenting memories Linda had of Tom. By the end of that year he was gone, but on that day, that one time, they'd been like a family on a family outing. Sure, they were marching for peace, for the children being bombed and sprayed with chemicals, but what she remembered was Tom's freckled hands wrapped around Mel's ankles as she bounced up and down and squealed at the sound of the sirens.

'Were you with Gerard?'

'Hell no. We were well and truly over by then. I'm not sure where he was.'

Again it struck Linda how little she knew of his movements during those years. She was in Bali, then Melbourne. She heard vague things about him from friends, that he'd been back to Hobart to see his folks, that he was living in Sydney. After that he seemed to disappear; no one had news of him. There was a rumour that he was travelling in Asia, and Linda pictured him sitting cross-legged in an ashram on a mountain peak like Larry in *The Razor's Edge*. That was the kind of wisdom she imagined he was seeking at the time. Then, about four years ago, he turned up at party in Fitzroy, at the house of their mutual friend Louise.

Jane's eyes narrowed. 'Someone told me he was arrested at a moratorium march. In Sydney, for arson.'

'Arson? Gerard? Oh, come on, that's not true. Who is the mysterious *someone* who's telling you all this shit?'

But Linda was unnerved nonetheless. She could almost imagine it now: the sweaty intensity of the man, the brooding Che Guevara. She remembered the blazing anger in his eyes the night before. For a fleeting moment she had thought that he was going to hit her. He hadn't, of course; he wouldn't. She knew him better than that. For all his ardent feelings, he was still the Gerard she knew: the gentle naturalist, pointing to small birds and stooping down to stroke the leaves of a delicate rock orchid. At uni he'd been little more than a wishy-washy socialist turned activist by the causes of the day. Perhaps he'd made up the arson charge to impress Bettina. Yes, of course — little Miss Molotov Cocktail — she would be very taken by a police record like that.

'Did he dodge the draft?' Jane asked.

'He wasn't called up — I used to listen for his birthday — but I think that's why he went travelling, to get away from all that. And what about you, Hanoi Jane? What were you doing back then?'

Jane hugged herself as if she were suddenly cold. 'I was at college in Cleveland. It was a crazy time. People talk about all the peace and love, but it was really ugly. The police were shooting people. I remember feeling so scared. I think that's what sent me to Oregon in the end, and later out here, with Andy. I lost a lot of respect for my country at that time. I couldn't shake this feeling of shame.'

Below the ponds, the muddy path turned to mossy brick, and the straggly permaculture to luxuriant plantings of palms and shrubs: crotons, hibiscus, a splash of crimson coleus, the odd frangipani tree glowing in a splash of sunlight. Ahead of them were the hobbit-like buildings of Druidane: the stone common house with its high peaked roof and large round window, and the smaller dwellings dotted through the trees, a hotchpotch of wooden shacks, yurts, and mud-brick cottages, the ground around them peppered with chooks and children's coloured gumboots. Linda stopped and looked around: the place was usually crawling with kids. She found them in the courtyard on the other side of the common house, where a group of women was helping them paint rainbows, trees, and birds on pieces of cardboard and calico.

Inside, people sat in a large circle on the floor. It opened to absorb Jane and Melanie, and hands reached out for Linda too, but she backed away. She positioned herself by a door, as her father used to do in church on account of his claustrophobia. It was conch-passing time at the meeting. One by one, people rose to their feet to talk about the wisdom of the tribe, the unbreakable resilience of the circle. 'That's our strength!' an older woman in a strange felt hat kept shouting. She was immediately recognisable as one of the Children of God, and her interjections were like a liturgical response. Linda looked around for Gerard. He'll be hating this, she thought. He'll be itching to get to the practical bits, the strategy and logistics. Sure enough, there he was, standing outside the circle on the far side of the room. He looked more resigned than restless. She could even detect the twitch of a smile playing under his lips. Perhaps he'd come to accept the fact that he and Phil were a coalition. He drummed his fingers lightly on the wall behind his back, his eyes raised to the beams of the vast octagonal ceiling.

It was singing time again. Phil had written five new songs about the forest, a couple of them composed from scratch and the rest adapted from old anti-war songs. There were not enough lyric sheets to go around; people were sharing them like hymn books. Phil stood in the middle of the room, strumming and plucking at his guitar in the careless manner of a rock star about to tell his audience a funny anecdote. Two young women stood with him, barefoot and waif-like in their gypsy skirts, one holding maracas, the other a tambourine. They began a reworked version of 'The Teddy Bear's Picnic'. This brought the smallest of the children charging into the room, holding their wet paintings above their heads like flags. The women absorbed the force of them and gathered them onto their laps, whispering calming words into their hair.

Linda was reminded of being released from Sunday School and running helter-skelter across the yard to join the grown-ups in church. There was a woman waiting for her too, standing at the door, a finger pressed sternly to her lips. She was not there to gather the children in but to hold them back like a dam wall. As the last child scampered into the back of the group, she would allow them to trickle through, one by one, and walk decorously down the aisle to join their parents for the final hymn and blessing.

For the first time Linda noticed the camping gear stacked against the mudbrick wall on the other side of the hall, murky-coloured army-disposal tents and tarpaulins. She was astonished by the level of organisation. Her walk in the forest with Gerard, her bad purple poster, the disastrous meeting that resulted in nothing at all — none of that seemed so long ago. It was only a matter of weeks. When she'd first arrived no one was willing to breathe the word 'blockade', and now here they were, packed and raring to go.

She glanced across at Gerard. Bang! He was looking straight at her. Something like a lightning bolt jumped through the air between them. She pressed her back against the wall, her heart pounding. Don't look again, she told herself. Were his eyes still on her? She left the pamphlets on the floor and quietly slipped outside.

She chose a path at random, but it quickly petered out, leaving her staring at the twirling flowers of a hanging hibiscus. She heard Gerard coming. She knew it was him. He'd ducked out the other door.

'Linda?'

'Yeah?'

'Are you okay? You looked a bit freaked out in there.'

'I just needed some air,' she said, and then screwed up her nose. 'Not that there's much fresh air round here. It always smells of toilets.'

'Ahh, Linda,' he sighed, smiling. 'You've never liked this place. Look, I went a bit too far last night.'

She waited for an apology, but there was just a pause.

'I didn't mean to call you pathetic.'

'Right. Just hopeless and selfish.'

'Yeah,' he grinned, trying to make light of it. He placed his hand on her shoulder. She shuddered and pulled away. 'I admit, I'm a bit paranoid. I was really tired. You know who her father is. I've been avoiding his shop for weeks. I'm using a post box in town.'

'We've never mentioned it in front her, Gerard, not once. She doesn't have a clue. She's a twelve-year-old kid, for heaven's sake. She's just lost her mother. And she loved that waterfall yesterday and the giant tree. I didn't agree with my parents when I was her age. Maybe you should give her some credit for having opinions of her own.'

In the hall behind them, the singing stopped.

'Gerard, you should go back in. Off you go, piss off, go on, I need a cigarette.'

She watched him disappear through the heavy wooden doors and wondered where his mind was at. The mention of arson had triggered a memory of something he'd said to her as they drove home from the forest that day after their walk. He was reading T.H. White at the time, *The Once and Future King*, and was struggling to sort out his own ideas on the subject of a 'just war'. She was surprised by this and a little disturbed. Despite the pleasure he got out of using his military language on Phil, she'd always assumed that, in his heart, he was a pacifist. When she told him, he shook his head and said something really strange: if a tree falls in a forest and doesn't make enough noise, then nobody is ever going to hear it.

Anoplognathus

As if on cue, the Christmas beetles crawled from their underground chambers and whirred on tiny clockwork wings into the gum saplings. Pink, green, and gold, they encrusted the tender shoots, mandibles sucking, carapaces gleaming like the frosted baubles hanging on a hundred Christmas trees in the lounge rooms, shops, and churches of Repentance. The most beautiful of scarabs and the most clumsy and stupid, they were forever bashing into walls and landing on their backs, their hooked legs clawing at the air. It was a bumper year for them. People blamed the heat. Every morning Ray Parmenter declared it another stinker as he snapped the day's headlines into their metal cages and leant them against the veranda posts out the front of the shop.

Inside, the tinsel spiders rustled under the ceiling fan. These were the only decorations to go up in the shop that year. Delia used to go the whole hog, spraying snow on the windows and draping swathes of plastic holly around the pigeonholes. Ray never liked the holly. It was a damned nuisance at this time of year, when there was so much mail to deal with. He packed most of the decorations back into their box and gave it to Barb to take to the mill. As she carried it down the road, Barb could hear the beetles scrabbling around inside, buzzing like overwound toys.

At Repentance Public School they held a special meeting to discuss the infestation of Christmas beetles in several playground trees. The worst affected was the spotted gum. It was looking pretty sick and could start dropping branches if they didn't act. In the end the P & C voted for removal. It was a shame, such a lovely old tree, but you couldn't go taking risks like that where children were concerned.

Chapter Twenty

The night descends more quickly up there at the edge of the range, as though the darkness of the forest bleeds into the fingers of cleared land that push between its ribs. The lights in the Phelans' house were already glowing as Sandy drove up the narrow valley and parked out the front. A dog came running, barking, wagging. Someone yelled at it. A screen door banged, and there was Marcie on the porch, rubbing her hands on a tea towel.

From the passenger seat beside him, Sandy took a small wrapped gift and the paper plate of shortbread that Jean had bundled into cellophane and tied with red curling ribbon. It was much the same every year, the pre-Christmas visit he paid to the Phelans' place. Every year he invited Pat and Marcie to the staff Christmas party, and every year Pat Phelan found some reason to decline. Then Sandy would drive out to the forest to deliver their gift from Santa and a plate of home-baked goodies from Jean. The three of them would sit in the comfy chairs on the Phelans' screened-in veranda and enjoy a glass of sherry. Then Sandy would drive home again with a plate of almost-identical baked goodies for Jean. It was a ritual he looked forward to. There was something deeply comforting in the predictable flow of the conversation and the atmosphere of the modest fibro house, filled with the smells of Christmas cooking and the anticipation of family coming for Christmas Day. Even if Sandy was struggling to feel the Christmas spirit, he would feel it then, just for that hour or two out at the Phelans' place, cradled in that warm still air between the dark hillsides.

Pat Phelan was a man of the forest, as his father had been before him. The Phelans had been hauling for the Mitchells for more than two generations. They had built three houses in that time along this narrow strip of land, gradually moving up the slope and accruing a few more comforts as they went. The first house, a boxy slab cottage built by Pat's grandparents, still stood in the paddock down by their bottom gate.

The second house, weatherboard, was struck by lightning and burnt to the ground when Sandy was a kid. You had to leave your car to find any trace of that house these days, and Sandy had actually done this once or twice. He still found it haunting, the laundry slab crumbling among the thistles, and the four concrete steps at the back that ran up and stopped in midair. A dog, a kelpie bitch, had perished in the fire, locked inside the laundry and unable to escape. As a ten-year-old, Sandy was horrified at the thought of the poor animal leaping at the windows as the flames ran along the ridge of her back and sucked the air from her lungs.

The image still came back to him all these years later whenever he drove past the spot on his way out to the Phelans'. For some reason, it remained more vivid and disturbing than any memory he had of the day that Pat's father, Jim, was killed. Sandy was in his mid-teens when that happened, but it was somehow harder to picture a man being crushed by his own timber jinker rolling back on him. He did remember the funeral. It was the first time he'd ever stepped inside a Catholic church. Pat would have been about Michael's age now, around nineteen or twenty, and he and his brothers had looked so stiff and unnatural in their suits. Like Michael in his shirt and tie at Delia Parmenter's funeral. Yes, the Phelans had had their share of tragedy all right, but then, who hadn't over the years? In other ways they'd been lucky, raising five healthy kids and having four of them living nearby and married with kids of their own.

And now, just as Pat's back was giving him grief, young Michael was leaving his job at the mill to join the family business. Sandy was sorry to see him go — he was a real good worker — but the arrangement had always been temporary. It had been a lean time for the bush crews, these past two years or so. With all the hold-ups and red tape, log volumes were down. For the past year Pat Phelan and his team had been working on private land and in two different working circles, travelling miles a day to worksites on the other side of the range. Pat had even gone back to camping in the bush some nights, something he hadn't had to do for years. So the family had welcomed Sandy's offer to employ young Michael at the mill, just for twelve months or so, until things picked up again. He'd got his truck licence in that time and a good grasp of the milling side of the business. Sandy had offered to keep him on, to move him onto the bench, but that was never going to happen. Not even his blossoming romance with Barb was going to keep him there. With the clearance on that bridge, they'd have six to eight months' steady work very close to home.

'Hello, stranger,' said Marcie, grinning broadly. 'What's she done for us this year, that lovely wife of yours?'

'Shortbread, I think.'

'Nice. Sorry we didn't make the party. Pat's been a bit crook with his back and all.'

'Where is he?'

'Down in the shed. Get out of it!' she yelled at the dog that was sniffing at Sandy's pockets. 'Here, let me take those things off you. Go down and tell him to come back up, and I'll put the kettle on. Unless you'd like something stronger, that is. Yeah, why not? It's Christmas!'

'I've got a present for him,' Sandy said, pulling a folded envelope from the pocket of his shirt.

'What's that?'

He held it towards her.

'The okay from the engineers?' Marcie's broad, shiny face broke into a smile. 'About time too!' She pushed the screen door with her elbow. 'Wait there, I'll come down with you, I want to see his face. He's gonna be tickled pink when he sees that.'

Pat Phelan emerged from the creosote gloom of the shed, ducking under the side mirror of the Mack that was parked at the front.

'Is this new?' Sandy asked, pointing to the truck.

'This is the one I was telling you about. Picked it up last week. Some poor bloke down near Wauchope went out of business, poor bastard.'

'Looks like new.'

'It pretty much is, but the price was bloody good. That's the jinker over there. I've been makin' a few adjustments to the stanchions, you know me, I like 'em a bit longer.'

Sandy could see where he'd been working in a dim pool of light. He sniffed the air. It was solder he could smell, that stink of sparking metal that got into the back of your throat.

'So this one's for Michael?'

'Well, yeah, that was the plan. Not that I've got much work for him right now.'

'What about now?' Sandy laid the letter down on the bench with a flourish.

Marcie chuckled in the darkness behind him. 'What about that then, eh?'

Pat scanned the letter. He seemed to be pleased, but he wasn't one to show a whole lot of emotion.

'You must be relieved too,' he said at last.

'Bloody oath. I was about to send the staff on holidays two weeks early. It's a good compartment.'

'I know, I've seen it. I was up there last week.'

Sandy scuffed at the dirt floor with his boot. 'Forestry was there yesterday. They've done the first lot of marking, so we're good to go whenever you are, you and the rest of the boys.'

'Before Christmas?'

Sandy shrugged. 'We could. We've got two weeks. You could beat the heat and get a few loads in before the holidays.'

Pat looked thoughtfully at the unfinished jinker.

'Your bloke could leave his dozer up there over Christmas, couldn't he?'

'Yeah, no worries. I'll need to get cracking on this thing, but. I wanted to have it ready for Michael. And I'll have to ring Reg Velucci. He's been pretty busy cutting brush.'

Sandy glanced around the shed. One, two, three cabins. 'How many rigs have you got in here? It looks like a car yard.'

'A graveyard, more like it,' said Pat in a steady voice.

'What's that one there?' asked Sandy pointing to a rusting cabin at the back. It looked like a museum piece, with its rounded lines and snubby nose.

'That was my dad's.'

Sandy felt his chest constrict. In his peripheral vision, Marcie crossed herself.

'Jesus, mate, you kept it?'

'His mum did,' Marcie said. 'Wouldn't let anyone touch it, would she, love? Just the cabin, that's all. She always said it wasn't the cabin that killed him.'

'You've never used it.'

'God, no. I've stripped a few parts out here and there.' Pat glanced up at the roof as if worried his mother might hear him.

Sandy frowned at the rusting hulk, at the faded red upholstery through the dusty glass. For the second time that day he tried to remember where he was when he heard the news about Jim Phelan. If he was fourteen, what year did that make it? There were a lot of accidents back in those days, but even so, he could remember his own father's reaction, how deeply shocked he was that that such a thing could happen to a haulier as experienced as Jim. That was the extent of Sandy's memory, that and the funeral and the Phelan boys in their stiff-looking suits, and the mournful faces of the statues in the church.

They settled into the comfy chairs on the Phelans' side veranda and talked through the practicalities of the job. There were some bloody big crowns to come down on a thirty-five-degree slope. Pat didn't seem too worried about that. There was nothing he didn't know about bringing down a tree, and he had two excellent blokes working with him at the moment. They could be tricky, these rainforest trees, much harder work than bringing down gums in the more open bushland. The crowns were more likely to get tangled with each other, and the vines up there in the canopy could bring things down, branches and stuff, in unexpected ways. Pat said that was half the fun of it; he would enjoy the challenge. It just took a bit more time, and you had to use your brains. The main issue would be the size of the logs, but he didn't do the snigging these days and his man had a good strong dozer. With young Michael there to help him with the loading of the truck, and the site being so close to the mill, he reckoned they could pull out maybe ten crowns a day.

Marcie set a plate of gingerbread biscuits on the table between the two men. 'Are you expecting any trouble up there, Sandy?'

'What kind of trouble?'

'Hippie trouble. That man that held the meeting.'

'Nah, he's gone all quiet on us. Haven't heard a peep out him for weeks. Forestry says the same. I'm not even sure he's still around. I must ask Ray about that.'

'Oh, he's here,' said Marcie. 'Pat saw him, didn't you, love?'

Pat swallowed a mouthful of biscuit. 'Yeah, I did, last week. I was going to tell you before. When I went out to look at the road, he was there. He had a young woman with him.'

'What were they doing?'

'I dunno. I couldn't see them all that well, but I'm pretty sure it was him.'

'So he knows they've done the marking?'

'Maybe — yeah, I guess.'

'And the woman, did she have red hair?'

'Nah, blonde. Skinny little thing. I reckon they don't eat enough, they all look half-starved to me. No, her hair was really blonde, like almost white, you know? I think that's why I spotted them. It stood out.'

Sandy narrowed his eyes and took a sip of sherry. 'Did they see you?'

'I reckon so. I was right there, on the road.'

'And where were they?'

'In the bush, just below the bay.'

Marcie sat down heavily and reached for her glass of sherry. 'There's that waterhole they all swim in. They could've been going there.'

'Is there a back way in, over the ridge? I was talking to the road crew. They haven't seen any of these people coming or going.'

'Not that I know of,' Pat said. 'But the bush is pretty thin up top. You could easily beat your way through. It's slippery, but. There's a lot of rocks. It's not a walk I'd do.'

'Anyhow,' Marcie said, 'it was just the two of them, and they hadn't touched anything, had they love?'

'Not that I could see. I had a good look at the dozer. I couldn't see any damage.'

'So there you go!' Marcie lifted her glass in the air. 'Cheers! Merry Christmas, and here's to better things in 1977.'

The talk turned to Amanda's pregnancy, to the unexpected pleasures of grandchildren, to Ray Parmenter and his poor little girls. How were they coping with Christmas this year? Was Peg still living with them? Sandy thought he detected a sharpness in Marcie's voice when she spoke about Peg. He reflected on this as he drove back down the valley, past the spectre of the flaming dog and the stoic slab hut by the gate. He was puzzled by the way the Phelans spoke of the Parmenter girls, like they knew nothing about the goings on between Barbara and Michael. The 'poor little girls', Marcie had said, as if they were in infants school, not snogging her son out the back of the staff Christmas party.

He thought of the Virgin Mary looking down at him as he sipped his sherry on the Phelans' veranda. They had pictures like that all over the house — there was even one in the toilet — the holy family and various saints, their skin an unhealthy shade of mauve, their heads ringed in a sickly yellow light. Was that why Michael was keeping the Barb thing under wraps? Was it a Catholic thing? Sandy hoped not. He was fond of those two and liked to think he'd played a part in bringing them together: two nice local kids finding enough in each other to satisfy their hopes and dreams and settle down and stay.

Turning onto the tar at the bottom of the hill, he saw a tawny frogmouth sitting on the road, unmoving in the sudden sweep of his headlights. He crunched to a stop and switched to low beam, watching the bird watching him with its cranky yellow eyes. He knew it would flap away if he continued forward, so he sat there instead, playing a kind of mind game with the bird. Your move or mine, mate. The frogmouth didn't blink. Sandy leant on the steering wheel and tapped his thumbs together. The yellow eyes suddenly vanished into the broad scruffy head and the bird tilted and craned forward in a ridiculous imitation of a dead tree branch sprouting from the middle of the bitumen. Sandy chuckled. Silly old bird. 'Come on, get out of my way!' He blasted his horn and the frogmouth made an untidy dash to a fencepost.

Chapter Twenty-one

It was not a day to be standing in a car park. The morning bell had only just rung, but already heat was radiating from the asphalt, tainting the air with its tarry smell. *Joanne Parmenter.* They'd be marking the roll inside. Her maths teacher would be saying her name and glancing around the room. Joanne had come prepared; there was a late note in her port that Barb had written for her. As soon as Melanie arrived, she would drop it in at the office and the two of them would go down to the library and set to work. History was second period, a double. They'd have it all done by then. Joanne's text boxes would be glued to the back of the diorama; the model horse, dray, and journal would be Blu Tacked to the base. The shoebox would be assembled inside it as an old working dairy, looking down from above with the plastic cows parked inside its bales. Melanie was making a detachable roof for it, using the corrugated cardboard Joanne had saved from a fruit box, and painting it dark red. They would have to decide who was doing what for their presentation, and then carry the many components upstairs to the classroom, setting them up between the displays on timber and macadamia nuts, an industry Joanne considered to be a lazy choice for this project, having almost no history at all.

That was how it was meant to happen. Joanne had thought it through. She had phoned Melanie's house the night before to tell her to get a late note too, but there had been no answer. And now there was no sign of Mel or the diorama or butter churn and the time was ticking by. Surely she couldn't be away today. She said she'd finished all the painting. And Joanne knew that Uncle Bill had found an old glass hand churn and dropped it over to Mel. He'd even gone to the trouble of cleaning it up so that the handle would turn. This was going to be a highlight of their presentation. Joanne had a bottle of milk from the shop, unhomogenised. One of them would churn it while the other one was talking, until the curds separated from the whey and landed as a buttery lump between the metal blades.

Melanie missed a lot of school. A lot of the hippie kids did. Someone once said that their parents didn't believe in waking them up: that if their children didn't wake naturally in time to catch the bus, they didn't have to go to school that day. Joanne stared down the driveway and imagined Melanie fast asleep in the stifling heat of her room. A class on the lower sports field was doing PE, jogging in a straggly line around its perimeter. A car turned into the gate but it was only a teacher's aide, the one who helped with remedial reading. She parked, and dragged a heavy bag of books from the seat beside her.

'Are you waiting for someone?'

'Yes,' Joanne said.

The teacher's aide slung the book bag over her shoulder and said that it was too hot out here, and she should go and wait in the shade.

Joanne glanced at the woman's wristwatch. It was twenty-five past nine. Another five minutes and she'd give up and take her note to the office. She could still do her part of the talk. She had the models with her. She could set them out and explain that the rest was coming.

Her mood changed throughout the day, from anxious to angry to self-pitying. By the afternoon the bottle of milk in her bag had curdled, and she threw the soft yoghurt chunks behind a bush in the girls' quadrangle. She endured the humiliation of Tracy and Rhonda on the bus, skiting about the mark they got for their presentation. They'd done the timber industry. Their display was nothing special. They'd interviewed Sandy Mitchell, who had given them some brochures, and all they'd done was cut them up and glue them on a poster. Joanne was sure she heard them snicker as she set her plastic farm animals on the desk.

Even more painful were the things she imagined Linda and Melanie saying to each other over breakfast that morning while deciding whether Melanie needed to go to school. Joanne and her obsession with this childish project: boring, straight Balbirnie kids and their boring, white-bread history. The pain this caused her was almost physical. She stared at her hands all the way home and didn't speak to anyone.

Later she would wonder what she saw as she got off the bus. Did she think that the pub was unusually crowded for that time of the day? Not really, although, in retrospect, she could see a few people standing outside on the footpath, and recall the loud burble of voices coming from the front bar. The first thing that struck her as odd was the fact that the shop was shut: not 'Back in 5 Minutes' closed, but lights out and locked up with the little red CLOSED sign flipped over inside the door. Their end of the street seemed ghostly quiet. She glanced down to the mill. A plume of smoke was rising from the incinerator, but there was no clank and bang, no whining of the saw. Maybe someone important had died, like the Queen or someone. She found the key under its flowerpot and let herself in the side door.

There was a note from her father on the kitchen table. *Gone to town*, it said. He asked if she could open up for the busy time after five. The phone rang in the hallway, shattering the silence. She thought for a moment it might be Melanie.

'Is Dad back yet?' It was Barb. It sounded like she was at a party.

'The shop's shut.'

'Yeah, I know. Have you heard what's happened? The hippies

have blocked the forest road. The bush crew went out this morning and they couldn't get through. They reckon there's nearly a hundred people standing on the road.'

'So where are you?'

'We're at the pub. Sandy gave us an early mark. He and Dad have gone into town to talk to the police. They think the hippies are staying out there, that they've set up some kind of camp.'

Joanne twisted the telephone cord around her finger. Images flickered in front of her: the photographs of Sandy standing beside his car; the map with its texta lines and hatchings. Joel Spender. Bettina. *It's all happening.* That moment at the waterfall when someone said something and Linda pressed a finger to her lips and surreptitiously pointed towards Joanne.

'I'm having tea up here,' Barb said. 'Can you tell Aunty Peg?'

'She's not here either. I've got to go. I've got to open up.'

Joanne remained sitting at the telephone table after hanging up, revisiting the events of the weekend and Melanie's absence from school. She was at this blockade thing. They must all be there: Linda, Jane, Andy, Bettina, Aurora, and the rest. And what about the project? Had they known this all along? Did Melanie know she wouldn't be at school and just didn't care? She could have rung and told her — why didn't she do that? She could have dropped her stuff at the shop if she wasn't going to be there. But no, she didn't give a shit. She'd been like that from the start. Joanne remembered the hummingbird cake, and tears rose in her throat. The whole weekend, the time before, the colouring in, the swimming. The sense of belonging she'd felt out there, that feeling of finding herself. All that trying to look the part and striving for acceptance: the macramé belt, the paisley scarf, all of it for nothing. She would never be cool in their eyes. She would always be straight and fat. The girl in the shop, looking out at them. An outsider, looking in.

She stared at the handle on the door across the hall. The sick room. In her head she still called it that, as though it would never recover. Aunty Peg was sleeping in there now, but Joanne didn't think of it as hers. She hadn't even been in there been since they'd cleared away her mum's things, washed the walls, and replaced the bed.

She felt a thrill of trespass as she opened the door and went in. The room smelt completely different, of Peg's violet talc. There was a standing mirror on the chest of drawers and a clutter of creams and hairpins. The three-quarter bed was Peg's own. They'd brought it across from her place. She was fussy about beds, she said. She liked hers high and bouncy. The old base went to Vinnies, along with Delia's clothes.

There'd been some discussion about this, about whether they should use the St Vincent de Paul shop in Balbirnie or go somewhere further afield. Barbara was worried she'd pass someone wearing her mother's clothes in the street, but Peg thought this was unlikely.

'Most of it's plain jumpers and skirts and things. You wouldn't even notice.'

'What about this?' Barbara said, pulling the orange maxi dress from the top of one of the bags.

'Perhaps you could wear it,' Peg suggested. 'It's too small for me.'

Barb rubbed the floaty material between her finger and thumb and then, with a sigh, had put the dress back in the bag.

Joanne sat on Peg's high, bouncy bed. Her eyes tracked around the walls. 'It's hot in here,' she said, her voice loud and startling in the barely furnished room. It felt so long since her mother had been there, like another time and place. She'd been thinking a lot about time lately, about how it raced and slowed, how some things felt like yesterday and others months ago. On the floor was the ghostly phantom of a gladiolus flower. On the wall was a cross-stitch picture of Peg's, declaring the sweetness of home. Joanne stared at the brass balls of the mantel clock swinging back and forth. The glass dome was no longer dusty — Peg dusted everything — and the balls were spinning no faster or slower than before.

Chapter Twenty-two

Sandy arrived home that evening with a freshly cut pine tree strapped to the roof of his car. There was something vaguely absurd about this, given the day's events, but Jean had ordered the tree weeks before and he still hadn't picked it up. They were driving right past the turn-off to the Christmas-tree farm on their way home from Balbirnie, and Ray said he was happy to give him a hand. He needed the help as it turned out. God only knew why Jean had ordered such an enormous tree. It was ridiculous — Ray made some joke about needing a jinker to get it home. Neither of the kids was spending Christmas with them this year, and they weren't planning on doing much entertaining. But Jean was a great one for ritual. She kept doing these things the same way, year after year, even after the kids had grown up and moved away. Birthday breakfasts, presents in bed, Easter eggs laid around the house in little nests of grass clippings. It was a woman thing. Look at Ray. He wasn't bothering with any of the Christmas palaver now that Delia was gone. All the same, collecting the tree this afternoon had been a welcome distraction, something a bit festive and frivolous at the end of a difficult day.

Sandy parked the Range Rover on the driveway as he always did. He untied the ropes and dragged the pine tree from the roof rack. It flumped onto the gravel, its cut stump oozing resin.

'Finally!' Jean called from the front veranda.

'Yeah, yeah, all right.'

He pulled the tree across the lawn and dumped it at the bottom of the steps. 'I'm just going to put the car inside.'

'Why's that?'

He didn't answer. He looked around the garden and rubbed the treacly sap off his hands with a hanky.

'It was on the early news,' Jean said, 'on the ABC.'

'How did they hear about it?' Forestry hadn't mentioned seeing reporters up there.

'I thought perhaps you rang them.'

'Me? Nah. What did they say?'

'They talked to that man, the tall one, the one with the fair hair.'

'They talked to Philip de Beer? Are you kidding? Who else? Any of us?'

She shook her head and told him to come inside. He'd had a long day; she'd get him a drink. What did he feel like, a Scotch?

'Did they ring here?'

'They might have. I was out all afternoon. We had the Auxiliary luncheon down at the hall.'

'I'll ring Barb.'

'Sandy, don't. Wait for the main bulletin. It was only a snippet and I didn't see it all.'

Bloody Philip de Beer. Sandy stormed back to the car and drove it into the shed. He locked the doors from the inside and slammed the bolt across in a fit of temper. Perhaps he should go down to the mill and take a few precautions, as the cops in Balbirnie had advised. He didn't normally bother with the padlocks, didn't close the gates half the time. In all these years he'd never had any real reason to worry. One or two bits of graffiti, the work of a few silly kids, and now the police were telling him to hire a security guard.

Sandy leant against the dusty back door of the Range Rover and thought about the last time he'd spoken to Philip de Beer. It was some months ago now, before that ridiculous meeting in the Braemar Hall. He'd invited him into his office, Barb made them cups of tea, and the two of them had had quite a reasonable talk about resource management. Sandy had explained in some detail how the proposed logging operation was a kind of conservation. They weren't mugs, these Forestry blokes. They wouldn't shit in their own nests. You couldn't maintain production in an industry like timber without the careful management of your primary re-source. Parts of the basin had been logged before and you couldn't even tell. That Gerard bloke bleating on about a couple of twisted cedars — regrowth in both cases, he could almost guarantee. And that was the beauty of timber, it was a renewable resource, but talk until you were blue in the face, you wouldn't get through to these people.

He'd listened too, of course. He'd heard the young fellow out, even though what he said was all pretty silly in the end. He had this pie-in-the-sky idea about the future of forest tourism, of how it might well become one of the region's major industries, bringing in more money than all the mills combined and employing twice as many people. Sandy and the men had a laugh about that in the pub that afternoon, imagining Sandy leading tour groups with a furled umbrella, and Fletch prancing between cafe tables in a cap and frilly apron. But while Phil knew bugger-all about the local economy, he didn't come across as threatening in any way. He had mild manners, a broad, open face, a good, firm handshake. He smiled and nodded a little too much, it was vaguely condescending, but he didn't seem like the kind of bloke who would lead an angry mob. That was the thing about hippies, they were unpredictable, and from what Sandy had been told about the rabble out there this morning, Phil de Beer could be as stupid and stubborn as the rest of them.

Back in the lounge room, Jean handed him his drink and fiddled with the light switch and dimmer.

'You should tell Pat Phelan not to go out there tomorrow,' she said. 'Those people can't stand there forever. You should just wait until they get sick of it and go home.'

Sandy tinkled the ice in his glass. 'They've set up camp on the other side of the ridge. The cops sent a chopper over this afternoon. They reckon it's Joel Spender's place.'

'Joel the saw doctor?'

'I know, I find it hard to believe. He's an odd one, Joel, but underneath he's a man of the forest.'

'Maybe he's gone a bit funny, living on his own out there. You hardly ever see him in town.'

Jean left the room and returned with a metal bucket full of sand. 'Go and get the tree, Sandy, and we'll get this done. We've got half an hour before the news.'

He was happy for her to tell him what to do. She was good in these situations, good at distracting you with life's small pleasures. Together they lifted the tree, steadied it in the sand, and wound the strings of glass lights and tinsel inside its branches. The tiny lights were shaped like pine cones, acorns, and snowmen. They were as delicate as eggshell, and their frosted paint was scratched and worn with age. Sandy plugged them in and tested them. On ... off ... on ... off. That was a relief. There was nothing worse than hunting for the one globe that wasn't working.

'Now the fun bit,' Jean said, opening the box of single decorations. She lifted one by its metal hook, another by its golden string, expressions darting across her face as if she were greeting old friends. 'Next year we'll need a new one. BABY'S FIRST CHRISTMAS, remember those? They both had one.' She rummaged in the box to find Imogen's angel and James's lurid candy cane.

The local news was starting in the room next door.

'You go in,' Jean said. 'Call me when it comes on.'

He watched the bulletin right through. There was nothing about the blockade.

'Are you sure it was on the ABC, love?'

'It must've been,' Jean said, coming into the room. 'I don't watch the other channel.'

But the newsreader had moved on to local sports round-up, a young man with a microphone at a cricket match in Balbirnie.

Jean looked perplexed. 'It was on before, I'm sure of it. They must've decided it wasn't that important.'

The phone rang in the kitchen and she went to answer it. Sandy remained slumped in his chair as the national news came on. The US had performed a nuclear test in the desert in Nevada. Jim Cairns and Junie Morosi were appearing together at a Down To Earth festival near Canberra.

'He's as bad as the rest of them,' Sandy muttered. 'The whole bloody country's gone mad.'

He took a gulp of his Scotch and choked. His hand flew up to his mouth. There on the screen was the motley crowd of protesters with their bush hats and beards, carrying their droopy placards and half-naked kids. They were chanting and drumming. It looked like midafternoon. There was no sign of Pat or the bush crew, or the two cops from Repentance, or the Forestry guys who'd been up there first thing. It was the hippies on their own, in the middle of the bush, and all this carry-on was just for the camera.

He called out to Jean. He could hear her talking on the phone. Now he was looking at Phil de Beer, who was wearing a long cotton shirt and a string of wooden beads.

'Jean!' he called again. Who was she talking to?

The protesters were surging down the muddy road, whooping and clapping and having a wonderful time. Poor old Pat Phelan. He couldn't believe what was waiting for him when he got out there at dawn. He was fuming when he radioed the mill. Whatever you do, don't touch anyone, Sandy had warned him. Keep your distance, all of you. I'll call the police.

The news item had turned its attention to the forest. The camera lingered on a trembling leaf, on a bird, the bubbling creek at the bottom. It travelled slowly up the giant trunk of a strangler fig that no forester worth his salt would touch with a barge pole. Sandy burned with indignation. He thumped his fist on his knee. He could hardly bring himself to listen to what was being said. Then he saw her: the young German lass, the one he'd given a lift to. The girl who'd jumped out of his ute and run off with her dog. There she was at the edge of the screen, right at the front of the group, holding a painted placard: HANDS OFF OUR FOREST.

'*Our* forest!' he huffed. What a bloody joke. She was a foreigner, for crying out loud. She'd been in the country five minutes and now here she was, claiming to own the place. *Our forest.* He took another gulp of his drink. Was that why she got out of his car? Perhaps he'd said something that revealed who he was, but she couldn't have known all those weeks ago that this was going to happen. More likely she'd heard about it yesterday and rushed out there to jump on the bandwagon with the rest of them. She was young, that was the problem. They were all just a bunch of naive and rebellious kids. But now, looking at the people clustered behind Phil de Beer, Sandy saw that many of them weren't that young at all. There were quite a few grizzled old men, with deeply weathered faces. And women too, a few of them well into middle age. What the hell were they doing with their lives? What were they living on? What was the government doing paying people to live like this and bugger things up for all those trying to do an honest day's work?

'Look,' he said to Jean as she came in from the kitchen. 'It was on the national news, not the local. How the hell did they manage that?'

Jean glanced at the television, then turned and looked at him. He was startled to see that she was crying.

'That was James,' she whispered. 'Amanda's had the baby. Two pounds ten ounces. I'm going to have to go down.'

Chapter Twenty-three

Linda crawled from her tent into a bright morning mist. Cobwebs hung like gauzy handkerchiefs in the tussock grass, and a column of smoke was rising from the campfire across the way.

She had managed to score a four-person army tent in the end and had pitched it a short distance from the main cluster of tents, tarps, and Kombis, next to the barbed-wire fence that divided this paddock from the next. Sometimes at night she could hear the cows on the other side, their snuffling breath, their blunt teeth ripping at the grass. Melanie was sleeping in Bettina's little nylon pup tent, available now that its owner was ensconced in the captain's cabin. She had chosen to set herself up closer to the rest of the group, not liking the sound of the cows at night and maybe relishing having some distance from her mother for a change. That was fair enough; Linda felt the same. She didn't much like camping, but she was enjoying the privacy and vague possibilities of sleeping on her own again.

They were travelling back and forth anyway, she and Mel, sometimes staying at the house overnight when they went to feed the dogs. That was Linda's only real job so far, feeding the dogs and doing a run into town every couple of days to get supplies for the camp. A decision had been taken early on to get as many dogs as possible away from the campsite. They were proving too much of a hassle, fighting with one another and barking at the cows and horses next door. Then there was the problem of what to do with them when everyone was up in the forest. Not only was it wrong to take dogs into that environment, but there was also the possibility of the police bringing their own. In the end it was decided that people would make alternative arrangements for their pets — dogs, ferrets, goats, whatever they happened to be. Linda was even less of a dog person than she was a camper, but Mel was fond of Donovan and it was good for the two them to get away from the intensity of the protest camp every couple of days.

The shopping bit was easy. Many people had their own camp stoves and canned food, but pitched in to buy bulk supplies of vegetables, bread, and pulses. A couple of communal dishes were prepared each evening by a group of women that included Jane and the cooks from Druidane. They also maintained a central stock of groceries such as tea, cooking oil, porridge oats, soap, and citronella. The list was divvied up between a growing team of shoppers, whose petrol costs were covered by the kitty.

Linda had found herself a niche, purchasing 'contraband': alcohol, tobacco, and meat. Mel went around to collect people's orders, keeping a careful record of the names and cash supplied. The two of them bought cheap meat for themselves, mostly sausages, which could be moulded onto sticks and cooked over the flames. Thus they managed avoid the wrath of the vegetarians guarding the barbecue plates, if not their censorious glances.

It had been an extraordinary seven days: joyous and life-affirming. Even Linda had found herself marvelling at the camp's evolving complexity and cohesion. There had been only two confrontations up in the forest so far, and it seemed likely that the loggers would now delay their operations until after Christmas. There were some who wanted to strike camp until they returned, to conserve the group's energy and enthusiasm. But these ideas had been soundly quashed within the circle. The very fact of them being there was keeping the loggers at bay, Phil said, and the trucks would be back the moment they lowered their guard. Instead they kept their cockatoos posted on the ridge and along the Repentance road, using walkie-talkies to warn the group of any signs of movement. For the first few nights some committed folk chose to maintain a vigil in the forest, but they found it tough going — the fire ants, leeches, and mosquitoes, not to mention being pooped on by bats — and after a couple of days without any sign of action, they returned to the relative comforts of the camp. Phil and Gerard ran a drill to gauge the time it took people to get from their beds to the turning bay. Twenty-two minutes, maximum. That made everyone feel much better. If the call came through from the cockatoo stationed near the mill, they could have people up there blocking the road with five or ten minutes to spare.

This left them all plenty of time for play and home improvements. It left time for morning yoga and excursions to the falls. Then there was concern that people were becoming complacent. It was decided that everyone must rise before dawn every day and could only begin their chores and other activities once they received the all clear.

As well as the shopping and cooking, there were people responsible for child care, fetching water and firewood, and the maintenance of the pit toilets on the far side of the field. There was a first-aid tent and a massage post. Linda volunteered to do massage, but they didn't need her, having a full roster of people doing shiatsu and reiki, thanks all the same.

Meanwhile the camp had become a crucible for the creative arts of protest. New songs were being written; new words, new slogans were being painted on saggy strips of sheet. Then on the fourth day, the Arty Smarts arrived. They were a crazy bunch of guys who made giant puppets for parades and celebrations. Returning from a three-day harmonic-convergence event up the Queensland coast, they were now free to focus their energies on the Repentance blockade. A workshop was established under a large tarpaulin, and they soon had all the kids involved, making kites and rainbow flags and totems for the camp.

But before long the atmosphere grew tense again. There were

rumours that the loggers were gathering their forces and preparing for an all-out assault. Discussions on the Wednesday night were fraught and tedious. People remained committed to the circle, to its unbreakable psychic safety, but their ideas bounced around inside it like super balls in a bath, often puttering to a stop with little consequence. The meeting went into the night and became quite heated. There were accusations of bullying and dictatorship. Gerard stood accused on both counts by one of the Children of God, the shouty one in the tea cosy hat from the Druidane workshop.

'That's our strength!' Linda shrieked in a teasing falsetto as she passed him on her way back to her tent that night. 'You fucking fascist bastard, Ansiewicz!'

He grinned. He didn't seem too perturbed by his run-ins with these women, Phil's middle-aged acolytes and disciples. 'Consensus decision-making,' he groaned in mock despair. 'A lot of this stuff — the leadership's there, we're making the decisions. You've just got to sit there and listen, and then do what has to be done.'

Linda retrieved her sandshoes from under the flap of her tent. They were gritty and damp from the night before, but she pulled them on and made her way across the wet field. There was Gerard again, by the fire, cradling his cup of tea.

'Anything happening, Cap'n?' she asked, knowing full well that there wasn't or they'd all be off like a shot. She poured herself a tea as well and flicked ants out of the sugar.

'I've got the feeling they'll come today,' Gerard said thoughtfully. 'They don't have to start at dawn, you know. They could move in anytime and try to catch us out. How are you going, anyway?'

Linda stopped stirring her tea.

'I'm fine. I'm doing a supply run today, the dogs and the shopping. Need anything? Anything from the house?'

Gerard shook his head. 'You're doing a good job, you two.'

'I'd like a bit more action. All this domesticity, it's not what I expected.'

Bettina came bounding towards them, wearing what looked like a small squirrel on her head.

'What the hell is that?'

'Do you like it? Joel made it for me. It's a bandicoot. I found it on the road.'

She did a little twirl. It was a kind of headband tied at the back with two limp slivers of tail.

'It's very Daniel Boone.' Gerard smiled, fondling her neck.

'I'm off to feed your dog,' Linda said.

Bettina hugged herself. 'Wotan! Give him a cuddle from me.'

'No, but you can ask Mel if you like. She might do that for you.'

Gerard laughed and Linda felt a rush of satisfaction. He still had a soft spot for her sardonic side. She walked away with a nonchalant swagger of her hips and imagined he was checking out her arse.

They ripped through their list at the Balbirnie Cash 'n Carry and bought the rest at the fruit barn on the outskirts of town. By half past ten, they were on their way to the house to feed the dogs, driving along the river flats between the cattle yards.

Melanie was checking the list against their shopping dockets. 'Oh no, Mum, we forgot the rice.'

'Shit!'

'There might be some at the house.'

'Six bags of it? I doubt it.'

Donovan came running out to meet them, yapping loudly. A moment later Wotan emerged from under the house, his head down and heavy tail swinging. Melanie shovelled dry dog food into two ice-cream containers and set them at opposite ends of the veranda. Then she went round the back to fill the extra bowls and top up their various water containers.

'Cane toads!' she shrieked.

Linda looked out the kitchen window. Three toads were waiting on the porch for the marble-sized biscuits to land like manna from heaven. 'Put the garden fork through them!' she called, knowing full well how squeamish Melanie was. In the cupboard she found half a bag of brown rice, fastened with a clothes peg — nowhere near enough for the rice dish they were planning to cook that night.

'We're going back via Repentance,' she said as they climbed into the car. 'I'll try and get some white rice at the shop.'

Donovan was trying to squeeze his way into the passenger seat, and Melanie was making a half-hearted attempt to push him out.

'Mel, hurry up, shut the door.'

'He wants to come with us.'

'I don't care what he wants. Take him up to the house before I back over him, go on.'

Linda did feel apprehensive as they pulled in at the shop, but she crossed the road with her usual bravado. Glancing through the front window, she was relieved to see that Ray wasn't there, just the woman who worked there sometimes. It was only when Melanie mentioned it that she realised Joanne would be at school. She'd forgotten that school was still going. Today was the last day of term and she still hadn't rung to explain why Melanie was away. Oh well, too late now, there were more important things. She went straight to the grocery shelves without saying hello.

There were only two small packets of rice.

'Is this all you've got?' she asked the woman.

'How much do you need?'

Linda frowned and tried to remember what it said on the list. 'I'll take whatever you've got.'

The woman smiled obligingly. 'We might have some more out the back.' She went to the doorway that Linda presumed led straight through to the house. 'Ray!' she hollered. 'Have we got more rice in stock? There's a woman here wanting to buy the lot.'

Ray Parmenter appeared, a fit-looking man in long socks and neatly belted walk shorts. He peered at Linda as if his eyes were adjusting to the light. 'Is that so?' he said, folding his arms. 'And why would someone be needing so much rice, do you think, Mrs Blainey?'

They were both looking at Linda now.

'That's none of your business,' she said, making herself stand up straight.

'Now, you see,' Ray said, taking a step towards her, 'I disagree with you there. It is my business we're talking about. Mine and every other small business in this town. It's all of our businesses, what you're doing, you and your filthy friends.'

'You don't know shit about me.'

He strode across to the counter. 'You'd be surprised how much I know, Mrs Curtis.' He grinned as if using her name were meant to unnerve her. 'So I suggest you put that rice back where you found it and get the hell out of my shop and take your filthy welfare money with you.'

'So no rice, then?'

'No. No rice.'

Melanie shrugged and tapped an insouciant rhythm on her knees.

'I used to feel sorry for that creep,' Linda murmured, staring at the shop door.

'You did not.'

'I did. When he lost his wife, I did. Fucking prick!'

She replayed the scene in her head, shuddering at the memory of Ray Parmenter's smarmy smart-arse grin as they drove along the river flats north of Repentance and around the endless bends, through the sickening, flickering shadows of the trees.

Rounding the final corner before Joel Spender's gate, they found the road ahead of them blocked by a large herd of dairy cattle.

'Stinky!' Melanie squeaked, winding up her window. 'Why do we always run into milking time?'

'It's a bit early for milking. I wonder whose they are?' Joel didn't run a dairy, and neither did his neighbours.

'They might be dipping,' Melanie said, 'or moving them somewhere else.'

But these cattle weren't going anywhere. They were massed directly in front of Joel's gate, blocking the entire road and the verges on either side. A grizzled cattle dog was keeping them in check, running this way and that with his head and tail lowered. As they drew closer Linda saw people on the other side: a boy on a horse and about ten others, all of whom appeared to be women. Suddenly, with a jostling clatter, the sea of cattle parted, allowing a vehicle through from the other side. It was a blue ute driven by a man in an Akubra hat. He bipped his horn as he cleared the herd and accelerated past them.

'They're letting us through, that's good,' Linda said, inching forward in the car. There was shouting and a crack of a whip that sent the cattle into a skittering panic. The car was now surrounded by their wheezing, heaving bodies, their bellies swinging like waterskins from their bony spines. Linda kept nudging forward, her jaw set tight.

'Where are those people?' she snapped. 'They should be helping us.'

The cow in front of them lifted her tail and a torrent of hot piss went splattering onto the tar.

'Mel, you're going to have to get out.'

Melanie stared at her, aghast.

'You're going to have to open the gate. Do you remember the code?'

'I'm not getting out in the middle of this. I'll get trampled on.'

'Just shut up and do it!'

'You wouldn't.'

'I'm driving.'

'Those people have gone under the fence. They're coming down to the gate.'

'Well, thank God for that, but you still have to get out. They can't open the padlock.'

The drooling head of a jersey cow wheeled across Linda's window, its tongue leaving a green smear of slobber on the glass. It was like a scene in a horror film. Linda stared at the smear as Melanie gingerly opened her door and climbed out of the car. It was only then that Linda saw the women. They had ducked through the fence as Melanie said, come around through the paddock, and were now assembling in front of the gate. They were carrying sheets of cardboard. Fuck! They were protesting. They were purposely blocking the entrance to Joel's farm, and Melanie was walking straight towards them.

'Come back,' Linda shouted. Melanie turned, bewildered. The women started chanting, their placards in the air.

WE WANT JOBS, NOT HIPPIE SLOBS

Here they were, the good women of Repentance.

FORESTRY FEEDS OUR CHILDREN!

Here was Wayne Mackenzie's wife with her weather-beaten snarl, and that Parmenter woman, Joanne's aunt, in her sensible tweed skirt. Here they were with their mean sneers and their nasty, narrow minds, holding signs with bad grammar and stupid, clumsy verse.

HIPPIES ARE GREEDY THEY WANT THE LOT.
IF YOU ASK ME THEY SHOULD BE SHOT.

She could see Melanie trying to make her way back to the car. She saw the Parmenter woman rush forward and grab her by the arm. Linda wound down her window.

'Get your hands off her, you bitch!'

Melanie broke free and made a run for it.

'Holy shit!' Linda cried. 'Lock the door, good girl. What did she say to you?'

'She said she knew we'd be here.'

'What did she mean by that?'

'I dunno. What are we going to do now?'

Linda glared at the women. They were still standing across the gate in a straggly row.

'I could sit on the horn and wait for someone to come and help us. Or,' she said with the flicker of a smile, 'we could run the bastards over.'

Someone else was shouting now. Joel Spender was coming towards them, waving his arm in the air. He ordered the women away from the gate and said they were on his land. He drew an invisible line with his finger, and they shuffled back. They then resumed their invective, this time directed at him. He was a disgrace, he should be ashamed, betraying his own people. But Joel was a cool customer. It was water off a duck's back. Calmly he opened the padlock and waved Linda through.

'Go on, ladies, you've made your point. Time to move on. If these cattle aren't gone in the next ten minutes, I'll have to call the police.'

'We've got the right to protest too!'

'You're blocking a public road, and access to my land. You don't have the right to do that.'

There was something ironic there, Linda thought. Peg Parmenter saw it too.

'Blocking a public road, dear me. We can't have that, now, can we? We can't be stopping people going about their business.' She leered at him, looking like she might spit in his face. 'Your mother would turn in her grave,' she hissed. 'She was always so proud of you, Joel.'

This was her parting shot. They moved back through the herd to where the boy was waiting on his horse.

Linda looked at Joel. 'Would you like a lift back to the house?'

'No, I'll wait and see 'em off. You go. Are you okay?'

'We're fine,' Linda said. 'Melanie was a bit freaked out. It was pretty intense for a moment there. Thanks for coming down.'

'Huh, they're pretty harmless. I wouldn't worry too much.'

'Thanks all the same. Would your mother be ashamed?'

Joel rubbed at his whiskery cheek. 'Maybe, who's to say?' He cast his eyes over the hills and the paddocks on either side, nodding his head ever so slightly. 'She loved this place, I know that much. But then we all love this place, don't we, in our different ways?'

Chapter Twenty-four

It was break-up day, and the kids on the bus were euphoric and super rowdy. The Christmas holidays stretched before them like an empty plain, and they knew that there could no repercussions for them at school the following day.

Joanne felt none of this rush of possibility as she stepped down from the bus at the top of Main Street. It was just like the old days for her. Without Melanie she found herself once again following Tracy and Rhonda, holding on to the trailing threads of their conversation. As they passed the hairdresser she was gripped by a kind of nostalgia, that same aching awareness of the passing of time. Spring had drifted into summer. The jacaranda where Jane had spread her cotton rug on that distant afternoon was now in full leaf and casting an empty shadow on the ground.

'So what does your sister say?' Tracy asked.

Joanne raised her head. They were speaking to her about Barbara and the blockade in the forest.

'We reckon Melanie's gone out there. That's why she's been away. My dad says there's extra police coming up from Sydney. They're going to arrest everyone and put them all in gaol.'

Rhonda gave a skip and sang, 'Melanie's going to gaol.'

'We're going to Sydney for Christmas,' Tracy continued. 'We're going to David Jones. I'm going to get a pair of clogs, white ones with red anchors.'

'How do you know they've got them?' Rhonda wanted to know.

'They're in the catalogue.'

'Why don't you just buy them from the catalogue?'

Joanne looked down at her school shoes plodding along below her. The toes were scuffed at this end of the term, and the laces were frayed. She didn't like clogs, she decided. She didn't like Rhonda or Tracy. She watched the cracks in the footpath pass beneath her feet and waited for the girls to grow tired of her and leave her to walk on her own.

She had an hour to herself before taking Mrs Blainey's place behind the counter. There was time to eat a bowl of cereal in the silent kitchen and flip through the pages of her mother's recipe book, which Aunty Peg had left open on the table. It was an old exercise book, fat with clippings from the paper, its pages slightly crusty from the touch of floury hands. It was open at the pages dedicated to Christmas baking, recipes that Joanne had always found mildly exciting after all the casseroles and boring stuff like that. Spice biscuits, gingerbread, Jean Mitchell's rich white Christmas, all written in her mother's familiar hand.

Aunty Peg liked baking too. In fact, it was her passion. She kept the gas cylinders filled at her house on the other side of the showground so that she could continue to use her own oven, which, she maintained, was so much better for cakes and puddings than their electric one.

Both ovens had been in action for the cooking of the Christmas cakes. She made three fruitcakes in the end, and two large Christmas puddings. The puddings were now hanging in the Parmenters' pantry, dangling in their calico sacks like a pair of bull's bollocks. The cakes sat on the pantry bench in three big Tupperware containers, wrapped in layers of greaseproof paper fixed with rubber bands. Every Thursday Peg unwrapped two of them and spooned brandy over them in a process she described as 'feeding'. She didn't feed the cake she'd made using Delia's cookbook. Apparently their mother's recipe made no mention of doing this. Peg supposed that Delia had omitted it on purpose — you don't want to be giving children too much alcohol. Barb had been quick to point out that she was no longer a child, but Peg was doing her utmost to recreate Christmas as they knew it. Joanne had to concede this was nice of her, but there was something ruthless about her not feeding their mother's cake, as if she were purposely starving it while indulging her own babies.

Peg's two fruitcakes were destined for morning tea at the church on Christmas Day and for the Balbirnie Show at the end of February. She was hoping to redeem herself at the show next year, having failed to pick up a single ribbon at the last one. For the second time that afternoon Joanne contemplated the shrinking and stretching of time. Last February's show had coincided with Delia starting chemo. She remembered her mother sitting right here, at the kitchen table, while Peg went on and on about the inconsistencies of the fruitcake judging. Delia had given the impression of listening, leaning over her folded arms. Then she'd gone to the bathroom and been horrendously sick. Joanne and Peg had sat there shooting glances at each other, listening — the sound of retching from down the hall, the flushing of the toilet, the pipes hissing in the wall as Delia washed her face and hands. She returned to the kitchen table in a state of dignified dishevelment, oblivious to the string of phlegm caught on her cardigan. Peg tap-tapped at her own collarbone as a way of warning. What struck Joanne most was Delia's response, how little she seemed to care. She looked down at the mucous and, after a listless pause, slowly rubbed it into the wool with the palm of her hand.

'How are you, dear? How was school?'

Aunty Peg stood at the side door, wrenching a gumboot off her stockinged foot.

No mention of it being break-up day: she probably didn't know. There'd never been school terms in Peg's life, no calendar of that kind. She slipped her large, long feet into what she called her house slippers, and padded across the kitchen floor

'I've got to feed the cakes,' she said, turning on the pantry light. 'Doesn't the week go quickly? It feels like only yesterday I did it.'

Joanne heard the snap of rubber bands and felt the faint burn of brandy fumes in her nostrils.

'I've come from Joel Spender's place,' her aunty said over her shoulder. 'We've formed our own protest group, all the women with connections to the mill — you and Barb should get involved. We gave them a dose of their own medicine and blockaded Joel's gate. We were only there an hour or two, but it was quite satisfying.'

Peg dropped the rewrapped cakes into their Tupperware boxes.

'We stopped that woman, the red-haired one, the one that yells at you.'

Joanne looked up in alarm.

'They were sneaking supplies into the camp, her and her daughter.'

'What did you do to them?'

'Nothing. Just blocked the road, that's all. Peaceful resistance,' Peg proclaimed, raising a grandiose finger. 'The Byrnes brought their cattle down. That was a clever idea. We managed to stop four of their cars. Three gave up and went away, but then bloody Joel came out and let the last one through.'

'Was that Melanie's?'

Peg looked blank. She didn't recognise the name. 'Joel threatened to call the police. That was a bit rich, I thought. Anyhow, we made our point and put the wind up them. It'd be good to keep it going and starve them out of there, but you'd need a lot more people. It's not that easy for those of us who work.'

Wives ... mothers ... those who work. It occurred to Joanne that her Aunty Peg was none of these things, strictly speaking.

'And you're not to serve them in the shop, d'you hear? That's your father's orders. We're not feeding them while they're snatching the food off our plates.'

'How are we supposed to tell who they are?'

'Oh, for heaven's sake, Joanne, don't be so contrary. That woman won't be bawling you out, if that's what you're worried about. Ray dealt with her this afternoon just before we did. She was in here wanting to buy all our rice, the whole damn carton. Don't tell me that was dinner for two. Your father sent her packing.'

Joanne chewed on her thumbnail, aware of a queasy tension in her stomach. It was a panicky feeling, a confused blend of embarrassment and dismay. She recoiled at the thought of her Aunty Peg shrieking at Linda and Mel, of her father throwing them out of the shop. She tried to conjure up the anger she'd felt the week before, standing red-faced in front of the class as her plastic cows fell over. She thought of Mel and Linda mocking her over breakfast, but there was no heat left in that memory. It wasn't a memory at all. In the sullen light of the kitchen she saw the waterfall, the light fracturing in the cool uprush of air. She felt the joy of lying under that dome of stars, standing in a circle around the brush box tree, looking up at its crown of leaves and down at herself from above.

'What's the matter?' asked Peg.

'Nothing.'

'Here, make yourself useful.' Peg pushed Delia's recipe book towards her. 'I'm making your mother's golden-staircase pie for sweets. You read out the ingredients and I'll measure them.'

'I have to start work in a minute.'

'It won't take long. It'll save me going backwards and forwards. I've done the butter. How much sugar do I need?'

Joanne looked down at the recipe. 'Three ounces,' she said.

Peg tapped the sides of her mother's old measuring cone and tipped the sugar into a bowl on top of the softened butter.

'Aren't you going to use the Mixmaster?'

'No, I use a spoon. It's just as good and makes less washing-up.'

Drub drub drub went the spoon. It was just like Lena, that silly cup she used for washing-up. The recipe for golden-staircase pie was long and complicated. Over the page were instructions for a second and third layer, transcribed in Delia's cramped and careful hand. Peg had distinctive handwriting too, a bold, looping cursive that Joanne knew from birthday cards and notes on the kitchen table. There was no mistaking who was responsible for the asterisk on the second page and the scrawl at the bottom in red pen: *METHOD WRONG.

'What's this?'

'What's what?' Peg asked, scraping the sugary spoon once more around the plastic bowl.

'You've changed Mum's recipe.'

'Nah, show me. Oh, that's nothing. She put the cornflour in too soon, that's all.'

'How dare you write in her recipe book!'

'For heaven's sake, Joanne. I'm just avoiding lumps. You've got to be careful with cornflour, and that recipe is wrong.'

'You've got no right to change things here.'

Peg pursed her lips and reached for the book. Joanne snatched it away.

'So what do you want me to do, Joanne? Leave the pie half-finished?'

'I want you to go away and stop pushing in on us. I want you to mind your own business and stop fucking things up with my friends. I hate you and so does Barb. We don't want you living here.'

Something inside Joanne pulled as tight as elastic and sent hot tears tumbling down her face. Then, at the very crest of her rage, she saw the hurt in her aunty's eyes, saw her stumble back against the sink, her jaw working like a goldfish.

'Joanne? I'm off now, love.'

A bewildered Dawn Blainey stood at the kitchen door with her handbag over her shoulder. Joanne thumped the cookbook down and blundered past her, swiping at her cheeks with the snotty heel of her hand.

She hurried through the storeroom and into the shop just as Mrs Phelps came striding through the fly tapes, her timing impeccable as always.

'Hello, Joanne, happy holidays!'

If she noticed Joanne's tear-streaked face, she pretended not to. She picked up *The Sydney Morning Herald* and slapped it down on the counter.

'Just this and my mail, thank you, love, and I need insect repellent.'

Joanne pointed towards the toiletries on the opposite wall.

'Hah, look at that! It's made the Sydney papers.' Mrs Phelps was pointing to the photo on page one. 'Look there, in the middle. Is that our Melanie?'

The protesters were assembled among the trees like a ramshackle choir, carrying placards, drums, and guitars. Their faces were small and indistinct in the black and grey shades of the newsprint, but if you pulled back and looked again, Melanie was there.

'You should put a copy aside for her,' Mrs Phelps said. 'It's the kind of thing she might want to show her own children. In fact, I'll take another one now. I'm heading out there tomorrow.'

Joanne's heart lurched. She'd misheard that, surely. But no, here was Mrs Phelps, wearing the patient smile she always wore when preparing to launch into one of her lessons in life.

'It's not just hippies who think it's a crime to be chopping down old-growth forest. They've got a lot of support out there, I think you'd be surprised. I know where your family stands on this, Jo — I understand that too. And I'm sorry about your presentation, that was a real shame, but I didn't mark you down too much, I hope you noticed that.'

What did she mean, didn't mark them down? They got seventy-two per cent. It was the worst mark Joanne had received for any assignment all year.

'Melanie is exactly where she needs to be right now. I wasn't going to hold it against her. I'm hoping that this blockade might be turning point. As a history teacher I'm hardly going to penalise a student for being a part of history in the making.'

The newspaper, Aerogard, two large packets of chips. Joanne rang up the till with a trembling hand. Exactly where she needs to be, history in the making. Mrs Phelps left the shop without saying goodbye. The back flyscreen banged shut. Joanne pictured her Aunty Peg lugging a basket of wet clothes out to the washing line. There was no other noise but the buzz of the fridge and the distant whine of the saw and the tinsel spider rustling under the ceiling fan. Another door slammed, the kitchen door this time, and Aunty Peg's Triumph came backing out of the drive. Joanne watched her departure with a sense of relief. In five minutes she'd close up and have the house to herself.

From outside came a sudden flapping of bare feet, and into the shop burst a young woman, gasping for breath. It was Aurora from the waterfall with her mussy tresses of blonde hair and grimy fairy skirt. She did a double take when she saw Joanne, and her face broke into a smile.

'Hello,' she cried. 'I remember you. What are you doing in here? Oh God, look at all this chocolate! Cherry Ripes! Flakes!' she squeaked, shovelling chocolate bars into the sling of her skirt. 'I haven't had chocolate for over a week, I'm absolutely dying. I've been out at the protest camp. Have you been out there yet? You've got to come, it's great. The loggers didn't come this morning and we spent the whole day at the falls. Oh my God, I'm dropping them. Hang on!'

Joanne peered over the counter at Aurora crouched in a puff of dirty tulle, clawing around for the chocolate bars that had fallen on the floor.

'Did you see the *Herald*?' she asked her. 'Next to you, there, the photo.'

'Ahh, look at that!'

Joanne felt pleased. 'Are you in it?'

'I don't know.' Aurora scrambled to her feet. 'Let me see. Oh no,

I wasn't there that day. I got really ripped the night before, and no one woke me up. Remember when we hugged that tree? Wasn't that so special? Come with me now. I'm hitching. What time do you finish up?'

She seemed oblivious to the fact that Joanne was wearing a school uniform.

'Do you have to work tomorrow?'

'In the morning I do.'

'Come out after that. The nights are really fun. Although —' She pouted, glancing towards the window. '— they reckon it's going to rain.'

Aurora was still standing by the war memorial, waiting for a lift, when Joanne went outside to bring the headline cages in. As she watched, a car stopped, a grey station wagon, and when it pulled away the girl was gone. Joanne stared at the empty space and its cloud of settling dust. The jelly heat quivered on the road. It was like a vanishing act, she thought. *Mum calls her the Airy Fairy.* It was like she'd slipped through a magic portal into another world.

Chapter Twenty-five

It seemed to Sandy that these people hadn't moved since the previous Thursday. Here they were again, the motley mob, the same old cast of characters: Philip de Beer and his guitar, front and centre as always, with the scowling Mr Ansiewicz standing to his right. There was the little German girl and the crazy redhead and dozens of others crowding the road and spilling down into the trees. The 'concerned citizens' of the welfare state, making sure that no one else could go about their business. There were more of them this time, that was all. The singing and drumming was louder. Peaceful protest, Sandy scoffed. You could hardly hear yourself think.

The police moved in swiftly, and about time too. There was no point reasoning with these people; it got you absolutely nowhere. The police reinforcements had arrived. They had the manpower they needed to get in there and clear the way for the Komatsu. Pat Phelan and his men were raring to go. Once they reached the turning bay, it would be full steam ahead. If the police could hold the line and give them a bit of space, they could have the first load down by lunchtime.

They began with the small talk, with the sergeant explaining to the protest leaders in his slow, gravelly voice what was about to happen. He made a final plea for common sense and then walked back to Sandy, shaking his head as if to say, 'What else can a person do?'

In they went, the police up front and the tractor following behind. The officers worked in pairs, lifting the protesters by the arms and hoisting them aside. For a moment the music faltered, replaced by the rattling thud of boots and the grunt and tussle of people falling to the ground. Then the song re-formed, swelling beneath the shouts and screams and the wailing of the children. Men were dragged away by their shoulders, their heel bones bouncing along the ground. The crowd surged forward to surround the tractor, but the driver, Jerry Macklin, his jaw tight and determined, pushed through the middle of them.

Sandy walked back to his car. It was difficult to watch, hard to listen to, all those children crying. What were these people thinking, throwing their kids into something like this? There were women here with babies in slings, with toddlers on their hips. It was a worksite, for God's sake, dangerous at the best of times, and here were these poor little mites in the thick of it, watching their parents being dragged away and thrown into the slammer. Sandy leant against his car, his head resting on his forearms. Behind him, a man was being jostled into a paddy wagon. A woman who may have been his wife was shrieking at the two police, grandstanding about his legal rights.

Up the road the singing had become a toneless chant. It was time for him to head back into the fray. The rest of the crew was preparing to go in and join the tractor, which was now well inside the bay and surrounded by police. Poor old Jerry Macklin — it was so unfair. Here was a man simply trying to do his job, being heckled as a murderer and a rapist.

In the turning bay the police had formed a protective circle around the crew and their trailer of equipment. It was chaotic as all hell, like guerrilla warfare, without any clear frontline. The best they could do was clear enough room for the blokes to set up their gear, and keep the blasted hippies off the tractor.

The faller was Reg Velucci, a strong, stocky man, one of the best in the business. He came from up north, the descendent of Italian canecutters, and had been working with Pat Phelan for much of the past ten years. Like Pat he was a man of few words, thoughtful and self-contained. He took great pride in his work, in his skill with the saw, but he wasn't one for the spotlight and he looked distinctly unsettled as he oiled his chains. Any moment now he'd be hauling his Stihl down the slope to the big brush box, the first crown on his list. He and Pat had checked it out just after the marking was done. Back then he thought it looked straightforward, but he hadn't counted on having an angry mob breathing down his neck. The police were reassuring. They would clear and cordon off the area and make sure that no one got in his way, but it was nerve-racking, no doubt about that. Sandy felt sorry for him. These poor blokes were used to working on their own, in the quiet solitude of the bush. Reg particularly disliked being called a 'logger'. Sandy had heard him ranting to Pat about it the day before.

'*Logger* — what the fuck *is* that? What does a logger do? I'm a faller, you're a haulier: to them, we're all the same, like we don't have any special skills.'

The police were gradually gaining the upper hand, forcing most of the hippies to the edge of the turning bay. They did a sweep of the surrounding bush and pulled people out of the trees. Meanwhile Pat and Jerry created a kind of decoy for Reg, taking the tractor off in the opposite direction. They were just bringing down saplings to build the loading ramp, but the sound of the chainsaw was enough to distract the crowd and give Reg the break he needed.

Sandy went with him, along with a small contingent of police. They moved swiftly through the bush and a hundred yards down the hill to where the brush box stood. She was a beauty all right, ten foot across at the base and straight as a die. Forestry had blazed the fall direction on the lower bole, but Reg still took some time to consider his course of action. He checked the canopy for balance and the presence of troublesome vines. He cleared himself some space in the thick leaf litter and made sure that he could get away if the massive trunk should buck as it came down. The police cordoned off the area with a length of flimsy tape. It was starting to drizzle and Sandy glanced up at the sky. He could hear the soft prickle of rain in the leaves above his head, but it wasn't yet reaching the ground.

Reg started up his saw. He pulled down the visor on his hat, planted his stocky legs, and braced his back for action. Then he went to work, angling the spinning chain down into the wood. The noise of blade was jagged like an angry hornet as it sliced through the bark and into the spongey phloem. The hippies were pouring down the slope, whooping like a troupe of howler monkeys. Reg held his nerve and tightened his grip. The chain bit into the sapwood. Water gushed from the slit and he jerked back on the blade. The second cut was straighter and faster than the first. With one good whack of his axe, the wedge came out, nice and clean.

He staggered back and wiped the sweat from under his chin, the idling saw throbbing by his side. Sandy watched in admiration as he stepped around the tree and went straight in for the hinge cut.

There was a sudden commotion, and a shout went up for him to stop. Something was moving in the undergrowth below. A dreadful hush fell over the crowd. Reg flipped up his visor and swore. There was a child, a little girl, perched on the branch of a small foam bark further down the slope and directly in the path of the half-felled tree. Reg shut down the chainsaw, and Sandy turned to the people gathered behind him. They were quiet now, transfixed, and then from the foam bark came a voice that was harsh and strident, not the voice of a child at all. It was the German girl wearing denim shorts and sturdy walking boots and some kind of animal skin wrapped around her head. Slowly she pulled herself upright and bounced on the branch. Then, with a theatrical flourish, she turned her back to them all and, with one hand planted on her hip, gave a saucy wiggle of her bum. There was a ripple of laughter. Sandy heard the name 'Bettina'. She leapt to the ground, dusted her buttocks, and began to saunter towards them, yelling at the top of her lungs. Anger had thickened her accent and she was hard to understand, but it hardly mattered, given where she was, standing like an idiot in the path of the teetering tree.

The police looked to the sergeant. He nodded: down they went and grabbed her by the arms. She didn't resist but went as floppy as a ragdoll as they frogmarched her up the hill towards the vans. Hanging between the burly men, she looked so slight and vulnerable. Sandy felt a pang of concern. She'd sustained some nasty grazes on her legs, one of which was bleeding badly. They would hold her overnight. Would she be alone? Was she the only woman they'd arrested? As if she could hear his thoughts, the girl suddenly bucked around.

'And you're a dirty old man!' she shrieked. Sandy's stomach lurched. Her fierce blue eyes went through him like a lance.

In the end she only held things up for about ten minutes or so. The chanting of the crowd became a ululating war cry as Reg pulled down his mask and yanked at the starter grip. He blasted away on the northern side and hammered in three large wedges. With a deafening crack and a creaking sigh, the massive tree came down.

It crashed into the undergrowth, sending a wave of sound rolling around the basin. Birds shrieked. Branches and leaves showered down from the open sky, along with a gentle drizzle of rain. Reg was breathing heavily, adrenaline coursing through him. He knelt down in the rubbish beside the stump and, with enormous care, fitted the cap over the cutter bar of his saw. Sandy stepped forward and clapped him on the shoulder. On the slope above them the protesters were huddled in a wobbling line, their heads bowed, their arms around each other's waists and shoulders. They were sobbing, moaning, keening. They were singing a different song: a sad, defeated lament for the dying spirit of the tree.

Sandy helped Reg pack up his tools and offered to carry his fuel. He'd done a great job. The tree had fallen right on target. This was the turning point. They were underway at last, and despite the ridiculous antics of some, no one had been hurt.

Myrmecia

The clearing around the jagged stump was soon alive with ants. Bull ants came boiling out of the ground, jolted to the surface by the thud of the falling tree. They ran willy-nilly, carrying crumbs of earth, like emergency workers overwhelmed by the magnitude of the disaster. After a stunned pause, the arboreal ants emerged, crawling dazed from their bulbous nests that lay like bits of broken pot among the slump of branches.

It took just minutes for the first scouts to locate the sap, issuing from the edges of the stump. In their pheromone wake came ropes of ants, travelling up and down, business as usual, order restored, this is what we do. The gush of amber sap became a sluggish ooze, fringed with supping ants and small metallic flies. It dribbled down the sides of the stump and soaked into the sawdust, forming a gooey crust like blood on the floor of a butcher shop.

Twenty miles to the south-west, on the other side of Repentance, beside the road that ran through Wayne Mackenzie's farm, another line of ants was on the move. Tiny black sugar ants, drawn by the smell of blood, the congealing blood of an animal with a bullet in its head. A crow pecked at its sunken flank. The ants were unperturbed, labouring towards the glistening cavity in the creature's skull.

Chapter Twenty-six

Perhaps it was the sound of trudging feet and the absence of conversation, or maybe it was the dreary patter of the rain, but as they trekked back to the camp, Linda found herself thinking of that miserable scene in *War and Peace*, of Napoleon's troops in retreat from Moscow. How ludicrous, on this warm and muggy afternoon, to be imagining the bodies of men half-buried in snow. The giant brush box had gone to the mill. Just the one tree felled today, but the loggers had claimed the ground. They were setting up camp in the turning bay beside the Komatsu, with two police to guard them, night and day.

Many of the protesters had stayed on through the afternoon but with a burgeoning sense of helplessness and loss. There was nothing they could do but stand and watch as the massive tree was trimmed of its branches, cut into lengths, dragged up the slope, and hauled, log by log, onto the back of the jinker. They regrouped on the road as the truck pulled away, but the fight had gone out of them. The young truck driver only had to touch the accelerator to nudge aside the exhausted and dispirited crowd. The crazy guy with dreadlocks did manage to climb up onto the cabin, but he too fell by the wayside before they reached the bridge.

Linda's sandshoes were soaked again and rubbing at the back of her ankles. Below her, people moved in a broken line through the trees. Eight had been arrested in the end, including Bettina. Gerard had followed them into town to help sort out their bail. They were likely to be released until a brief court hearing. Linda imagined Gerard and Bettina retreating to one of Balbirnie's featureless motels, to the comforts of a warm bath and a bouncy double bed.

Back at the camp the women had managed to rekindle the fire. There was a lot of smoke and not much heat in the flames, but people still gathered around it, seeking refuge from the bleak fog that had settled on the low-lying paddock. There would soon be hot tea and plates of fruit and home-baked bread and butter, but the mood remained as sombre as the grey afternoon light. There was no music playing. Around the fire, women held their children on their laps, stroked their hair, and spoke in soothing tones. Jane fetched the first-aid kit and attended to their wounds — the scratches, cuts, and insect bites on their arms and legs.

The day's events had taken a heavy toll on the kids. Even the nine- and ten-year-olds stood before their mothers, twisting their fingers in their hair and whining for attention. Watching them as she waited for the camp kettle to boil, Linda saw that they were not just tired and hungry, but confused. Children have an unshakeable faith in their parents to set things right and ensure that goodness prevails. Until now this dispute had meant little more to these kids than painting bright pictures and singing songs about the trees and animals, but what they'd seen in the woods today was no teddy bear's picnic.

Linda looked around for Melanie. Did she need comforting too? She'd been panicked by Bettina's arrest and was upset about the tree. Linda had gone down to the stump with her after the logging truck left. Everyone went down there to pay their last respects. It was raw and suppurating, like the stump of an amputated limb. You could almost see the phantom tree quivering in the air above them. They clustered around, arms linked, faces averted. Phil de Beer stood like Jesus on the Mount and warned them against expressing their anger in non-peaceful ways. Again they sang the mournful song and came forward, one by one, to lay their hands on the hot, furry surface of the stump. You could see the cuts made by the chainsaw, and in the middle where they met was a tall, sharp bristle of splintered wood.

'It's bleeding,' someone whispered.

Linda felt Melanie flinch. It was only sap, she told her, but God it looked like blood. She wished Gerard were there to give them some scientific explanation for this awful sticky discharge seeping from the wood. It looked like it was pulsing. It puddled on the ground, attracting swarms of ants and tiny flies.

'Linda, did you want tea?'

Jane was standing in front of her, holding the handle of the big camp kettle with a pot mitt. Linda held out her mug.

'Where's Melanie?' Jane asked.

'I don't know. In her tent, I think.'

'I was walking with her on the way back. She seems really shattered. Why don't you go and get her? She should have something to eat. We're making veggie stew, I think, if anyone's got the energy.'

One of the children started to sob. 'I don't like veggie stew.'

'I'm not taking Mel back up there tomorrow,' Linda said. 'It's too much for these kids, too full on. We'll go and feed the dogs instead.'

She swirled the tea in her cup. There was something bothering her, something sitting heavily in her chest. It had been there all afternoon, or maybe even longer, ever since that Parmenter woman had leered through the windscreen at her, wielding her placard like a battleaxe. She was aware of it now, looking at the children's stricken faces. She saw the street, St George's Terrace, a big white house about halfway up the hill. Her memories were always of winter, in the early morning, of a grey drizzle or a freezing wind blasting off the Derwent. Sometimes it blew their posters away, flattened their sandwich boards. It whipped the pamphlets from her hands and sent them skimming along the footpath. She would run after them, trying to step on their corners, struggling to scoop them up in her gloved hands. There was always a sense of panic that somebody would come while she was scampering down the hill, that they would get through the gate before she got to them. *Think of the baby.* In her memory she was always breathless. There was always a scuffle of some kind, sometimes only brief, just a quick sidestep as the woman skirted around her or the boyfriend shoved her aside. Her mother would deliver a two-line sermon and attempt to press a Bible quote into the palms of their hands. Linda couldn't remember anyone changing their mind on the spot, but her mother used to tell her that it happened all the time: that girls might go inside the house, but they might not go through with it. It was possible that a baby was saved every time they were there.

Occasionally the police would come, responding to a complaint of trespass or harassment. 'So what about *murder,*' her mother would hiss under her breath. The police would have agreed, had there been any evidence, she knew that now. But the doctor was influential and respected and careful, and their congregation was not. The police never took much notice, just wrote down the names of the picketers and told them to move along. They never did more than that, but their visits always left little Linda shaken to the core. The officialness of it, the police uniforms, her mother being in trouble, the fact that babies were being killed and they didn't seem to care.

'Mum!'

She turned to see Melanie, wrapped in a blanket.

'Mrs Phelps is here.'

'Hello!' called the larger of two large women striding towards them. They were both wearing oversized jeans and carrying aluminium camp chairs.

'I'm Marj and this is Wanda. How are we all holding up? How are you, young Mel? One of my star pupils,' she announced to the assembly by the fire, 'when she bothers to come to school, that is. How are you, Melanie's mum?'

Melanie cringed with embarrassment. The women set up their chairs.

'You're getting plenty of coverage,' Mrs Phelps continued. 'You've got quite a bit of support in town, I think you'd be surprised. Among teachers, I know that much. You might get more of us out here now that the holidays are here. Which reminds me — Wanda, the biscuits? We've done some baking for you.'

'That's kind,' said Jane. She was holding someone else's child and had been very quiet until now.

'I know you, don't I?'

Jane smiled. 'You bought some earrings from me.'

Mrs Phelps nodded, her mouth full of crumbs. 'I did! That's right. I thought I knew your face. I was thinking —'

She stopped and squinted at someone coming across the paddock. 'Good God, it's Joanne Parmenter. What's she doing here?'

'For fuck's sake,' Linda groaned before she could stop herself.

'I've come to help,' Joanne said in a small voice. She was carrying an overnight bag and had a sleeping bag under her arm.

'How did you get here?' Mrs Phelps asked.

'I hitchhiked.'

'A girl of your age, in the dark, on her own. That was very smart. Does your family know you're here?'

'Oh, sweetie,' said Jane, taking her by the shoulders and leading her to the fire. 'This is the second time this little girl has run away from home in the rain. Make room for her, Mel, what's the matter? Let her share that log. Are you cold, honey? Are you hungry? Would you like a cup of tea?'

Linda knew she should be asking these kinds of motherly questions, but she was too pissed off to care. She didn't want this girl turning up again. She only brought her grief — from Gerard, from Ray Parmenter, from that awful aunt of hers. Linda hated the whole damned family and wished she'd go away. It didn't look like Melanie was too happy to see her either. She gave a huffy sigh as she shuffled along on the log. It was time to be practical. What could they do? How could they get her home?

'You can sleep the night in Melanie's tent. I'll drive you home first thing. You can't go up to the blockade, we've got enough on our plates without having to look after you. Mel won't be there anyway. She's coming with me tomorrow. We're going to feed the dogs.'

'No!' Melanie snapped.

'Mel —'

'Shut up! I'm not. I'll go with Jane if you don't come. I'll go with Mrs Phelps.'

'Oh no you don't,' said the Phelps woman. 'I'm not touching this one.'

Everyone was watching them, even the little kids lolling against their mothers, sucking on their thumbs. Linda shuddered with annoyance. Melanie was overwrought. She'd deal with her in the morning when they'd all had a proper night's sleep.

'So, Joanne,' Mrs Phelps said brightly, trying to lighten the mood. 'Who's your alibi this time? Are you spending another weekend with Tracy Willis?'

Melanie snickered. Joanne averted her eyes.

'Don't worry, I won't dob on you. I'm in the same boat. There's plenty of people wouldn't be happy to see me out here either. I'll tell you who's coming tomorrow.'

'Who?'

'William's family. The Robertsons, remember? We visited them when I picked you up, when Melanie was sick on the bus.'

Linda blinked. What was that about? The girls didn't seem to know either, but then something registered on Joanne's face.

'The Aboriginal family?'

'Yes, they're coming out tomorrow, or at least I think they are. Their mob knows this forest well. They come here for bush tucker. They told me women aren't meant to swim in the falls. I think we've all broken that rule. Anyhow, I thought they could do some kind of ceremony for us, tell us about rainforest foods and the Dreamtime stories of the place.'

Everyone else around the fire liked the sound of that, but Linda was finding the teacher rather wearing. Gripped by a sudden desire to lie down and close her eyes, she wandered off in the direction of her tent.

Melanie caught up with her.

'I've got to go to the loo. Can you come with me? I hate that toilet.'

'I told you, just go in the bushes.'

'You said only for wees.'

Linda sighed. 'Have you got your torch? I'll stand outside, but I don't see how it helps. Hey, what's with you and Joanne? Have you two had a fight?'

'No.'

'I think you have. I saw the look you gave her.'

'I think she might be spying on us.'

'Spying? Are you for real?'

'Her aunty said that thing to me, that she knew we'd be here.'

'That doesn't take much guessing.'

'But how did she know we were on Joel's farm?'

'I imagine everybody knows.'

'No, they don't. They didn't. I caught Joanne looking through Gerard's stuff in the lounge room. She saw Joel's name on a map and she made a comment about it.'

'What did she say?'

'That she knew him. I didn't think much about it, but now I think she went home and told everyone else.'

Melanie took the torch into the small bush tent, leaving Linda outside in the darkness. Rifling through Gerard's desk. Why was she doing that? It was certainly unnerving, but wasn't she too gormless to be playing a game like that? Linda thought of the girl sitting plumply on the log, listening to all their chat, her dark eyes shining the firelight. She didn't really buy it, but just for an instant there Linda wondered if the bandicoot might be a mole instead.

There was a light on in Joel Spender's shed. Linda walked towards it. It looked so bright and cheery in the evening drear. She could hear people talking and laughing inside. There was music playing. It was the Arty Smarts. They'd moved their workshop into the shed and were in a flurry of buoyant creativity. Joel was there too, smiling serenely. The boys called him Doc and he seemed very happy with that. He'd moved his skins aside for them and was letting them use his tools. They were working on two life-size puppets, to be lifted on poles, and his knives and blades had proved very useful for shaping the blocks of foam rubber.

The Smart brothers, Rob and Alan, formed the core of the group. Tall, thin, and frenetic in their movements, they reminded Linda of those lizards that dart across hot desert sands on their two hind feet. The rest of the group they'd collected on their way up and down the coast, guys in their early twenties wearing waistcoats with no shirts, sparking off each other with their zany and daring ideas.

Linda stood by the door. They took almost no notice of her, but she enjoyed watching them and listening to their screwball banter. One was using a sewing machine, making something from an old sheet. He worked intently, his face inches from the tiny light. An engineering problem arose with the poles that held the puppets' arms. The men all gathered in, relishing the challenge. One of the figures needed an axe and had to be able to hold it. Joel produced just the thing, a lightweight blade wedged into a handle of balsa wood. The music stopped. Linda went and turned the cassette over. Rob Smart grinned at her and asked if she wanted to help.

'Can you use one of these?' asked the guy on the sewing machine.

'No,' she laughed.

'Shame,' he said. 'You women are no help at all.'

Even here Linda felt like an outsider. She hung by the wall a bit longer and then decided to leave. If she was going to grab some sleep before dinner, she needed to do it now.

Chapter Twenty-seven

She must have slept for a long time. It was dark when she opened her eyes, and she felt that strange disorientation of missing the juncture between day and night. The air in the tent was thick and warm and smelt of khaki canvas. Outside, it was raining again, just lightly. She found it soothing, that tiny pricking of the rain on the roof so close above her head. What time was it? Her stomach growled. Had she missed out on the food? Could she be bothered to get herself dressed and go back to the campfire?

She dozed again. The rain grew steadier, and she imagined the field outside turning into a Sunbury quagmire. People would most likely have given up on the fire by now and gone back to their shelters, to baked beans heated in their tins on a primus stove. She thought of Melanie — and Joanne. They'd be hungry, poor kids, bunkered down in their little tent. She should go and see them. She found her torch in the corner, reached for her jeans, and then paused to inspect an insect bite on her thigh.

What was that? There was someone outside. The squelch of boots in the grass.

'Mel?' she called.

'Linda, it's me.'

She stuck her head out of the tent, holding the flaps closed under her chin, aware that she was wearing nothing but a singlet and undies.

'Thought you might like a drink,' Gerard said. He yanked a half-empty bottle of whiskey from the pocket of his army coat. His hair hung in wet ringlets, and in the reflected light of his torch his skin looked greasy and peppered with grit.

'You look awful,' she said.

'Thanks.'

She let go of the flaps. 'You'd better come in. Have you got any food? I don't have whiskey glasses.'

Glancing down, she considered her upper body to be half-decent, but she pulled the sheet around her hips and wriggled to the back of the sleeping mat.

'I thought you'd be staying in town tonight.'

He grinned and shook his head. 'Nah, Bettina's okay. There's eight of them there, she'll be right.'

'Are they in custody?'

'No, they're staying at someone's place. The court hearing's set for tomorrow morning.' He ducked inside the tent and sat down by the door, his knees drawn up inside his great wet coat. 'You did all right up there today.'

'Me? I didn't do anything. I stayed at the back most of the time, looking after Mel. You know me, Gerard. I'm a coward when it comes to things like this.'

She thought again of her talk with Jane beside the lily ponds. They'd been speaking about the Vietnam War, the moratorium marches, but it all boiled down to the same thing: some people have no stomach for conflict, the face-to-face, bone-on-bone, real-life shove and crunch of it.

'It was awful up there,' she said quietly.

He shook his head. 'It was.'

'That beautiful tree.'

'The arseholes. This could spell the end for us. A few blokes, a few months' work, and it'll all be gone.'

She noticed a tremble in his voice and saw that his hand was shaking.

'Are you okay?'

'Yeah, why's that?'

'You seem a bit antsy, that's all.'

'Antsy,' he snorted. 'Maybe, I dunno.' He turned the whiskey bottle in his hands and stared dumbly at the label. 'I'm angry, I know that much. I'm in a quiet rage. I said this would happen. I knew it. We were never going to stop them. All the talking we've done, all that bloody singing and dancing, and all it took from them was a bit of brute force in the end.'

But it wasn't the end, Linda thought. They'd be back up there tomorrow. It was just the one tree after all, and it had taken the loggers the best part of a day to get it out of there. Twenty foresters, forty police, seven paddy wagons — how long could they keep that up? It was like Phil said on the stump that afternoon: their power lay in perseverance. By simply hindering the operation, day in and day out, they had the power to destroy the economics of the thing.

This brief glow of defiance in Linda was quickly doused by guilt. Once more unto the breach was all very well, but she wasn't planning to be there.

'It's no place for kids, that's for sure, and it could be worse tomorrow. I'm not letting Mel go up there. We're going to feed the dogs instead.'

Gerard looked at her. 'No need.'

'What do you mean by that?'

'I went there today, on my way back from town. Linda, I've got to tell you — Donovan's dead.'

'No!'

'Wayne Mackenzie shot him. At least, I think he did. I saw the crows and found him in their paddock.'

Linda felt everything rising: the tears in her eyes, the gorge in her throat, the murderous cry of the crows.

'Have you told Jane?'

'Not yet.'

Then she remembered Wotan. She didn't really care that much, but it was only right to ask.

'He's fine, he was under the house. I was going to bring him back here, but I took him over to Bill's place instead.'

'Bill Parmenter?'

'Yeah, Bill's fine. He'll look after him.'

Perhaps this was the time to tell him about Joanne. But no, why bother? She'd be gone first thing in the morning. It would be like the first time, the night of the flooded causeway, when they'd managed to sneak her out undetected. Dogs or no dogs, Linda was taking her home. She had a mental picture of dumping her like a cat by the side of the road, of roaring away and hoping like hell that she wouldn't find her way back.

'Can you take off that horrible coat?'

'Why?'

'Because it's wet and it stinks and this is a very small tent.'

He complied without comment and tossed it into the corner. He was wearing his old Byrds t-shirt underneath, but the removal of clothing of any kind left Linda feeling suddenly awkward.

'I was about to have a smoke. Do you want some?' She grabbed the torch and began to rummage around in her bag. 'We'll have a joint and then you can bugger off back to the captain's cabin and jerk off or whatever you do when you haven't got your mate.'

She was aware of him watching her. She saw that he was smiling. There was something not quite right about him. He seemed almost feverish, breathing too quickly, blinking too much; his eyes were overbright. It might have been the alcohol — he had downed quite a bit of that bottle — but he seemed more wired than drunk to her. She found it a bit unnerving.

'Gerard —'

'What?'

'Jane and I were talking about Phil the other day, about LBJ's visit and him lying in front of his car. She asked where you were at the time, and I said I didn't know.'

Gerard looked at her darkly. 'I was overseas.'

'That's what I thought. In Asia, yeah? But she said you were there and got arrested.'

'Arrested? For what?'

'Arson.'

'Well, that's not true, is it? I'd skite about something like that.'

Linda lit the joint and took a long, eye-stinging drag, indicating with one hand for him to open the flap of the tent.

'Who told her that?'

'I don't know.' She lay back on the mat. 'Never mind. It's not even true. You're too enigmatic, Gerard, that's all. People start making up stories — it's like Jay Gatsby killed a man. That's what people do.'

She watched him suck on the joint, cupping his hands around it as if playing a mouth organ. It had always annoyed her, the way he smoked, such a bloody production.

'I might've done that, I suppose,' he croaked, holding the air in his lungs.

'Done what?'

'Killed a man.'

'When?'

'When I was in Vietnam, in the army.'

Linda sat up and stared at him, her mouth suddenly dry. 'But I listened for your birthday. I never heard them call it.'

'They didn't,' he said. 'I enlisted.'

'Fuck off, you did not!' She cast around, picked up a thong, and hurled it at his head. 'Tell me you're joking. Please. Why would you do that?'

'I dunno. You'd buggered off and I was at a loose end. I went back to Tassie for a while. My mates were signing up. It was just the one tour, not even that. I was discharged early. They said I wasn't well, but that wasn't true. I was just starting to see things as they were.

And they weren't good, not at all. Don't think I'm proud of it. It was fucked, what we were doing there. It was fucking awful.'

'And you killed someone?'

'Not directly, not as far as I know. Half the time we just sat around, or flew around in Hueys. But that's the thing —'

He broke off. She sat stock-still.

'— that's the thing I know for sure. I killed a lot of trees.'

It took Linda a moment to process this. She winced and shook her head. Then it came to her in all its horror: the steady beat of choppers, the trails of vapour drifting down on a sea of jungle green.

'I need to go outside,' she gasped, lurching for the door. Gerard moved across and blocked her way.

'You're angry,' he said. 'Of course you are. You think I'm a hypocrite. But you're wrong, Linda, I'm telling you, it's just the opposite. It made me a rebel for life, the things I saw over there. For a while I thought I might go back and help replant the mangroves, but then I came up here and saw what they planned to do in the basin and thought I'd be better off fighting my battles at home.'

Linda pulled the sheet more tightly around her.

'We've all got things to hide,' Gerard said. 'You've got your secrets too. I know that, and it's okay. I don't hold them against you.'

'What are you saying? That a child whose mother makes her stand outside the house of an abortionist is the same as fighting — *choosing* to fight — in a filthy foreign war? You think that's the same thing, do you?'

'I know you had an abortion. I know you went and aborted our child without even telling me.'

'Who told you that?'

'Your mother.'

'What? When did you see her?'

'When you were in Bali, I told you, I went back to Hobart. I loved you so much, Linda. It killed me when you racked off on me like that. And then I went and saw your mother —'

'Why?'

'To see if she'd heard from you. She told me you were pregnant before you left and you got a termination and she never wanted to see your face again.'

Linda's whole body slumped. 'Gerard, that's not true. That baby was Melanie and she was Tom's. I told Mum that, because — I dunno — because I wanted to hurt her. And because I was angry with myself. I wanted to get an abortion. I went to a place in Brisbane, but I couldn't go through with it. I felt so ridiculous. It was all because of Mum and those pamphlets, so many years of that shit. It got to me, can you believe? I was horrified. So I told her that I'd done it, and went and had the baby in Bali. And yes, I never saw Mum again, that much of the story is true.'

Was that why he went and joined up, because of what he, in his out-of-it mind, thought she might have done? She felt completely drained, all these revelations: Donovan, Vietnam, Agent Orange, Gerard's fucked-up opinions of her fucked-up choices in life.

Neither of them knew what to do next. He looked so dejected. She wanted to kick him out, but she couldn't.

'Do you want a massage?' she blurted instead.

That was all he needed. He obliged without a word, turning towards the door and dragging his t-shirt over his head. Linda groped around in the dark for her bottle of lavender oil. She flinched at the noise it made as she squirted it down his back. Then, as briskly as she could, she rubbed her palms together and set to work on his wretchedly tight deltoids. It was all she could do to keep her breathing calm and steady. She pushed his damp hair aside and saw the birthmark high on his nape. It was exactly as she remembered it. The beak mark of a stork. She clenched her jaw and kneaded into his shoulders.

Chop, chop, chop and slap, slap, slap. Another squirt of oil. Then all of a sudden she pulled back. 'Gerard, you've hurt yourself.'

On the underside of his arm was a bright red gash.

He lifted his elbow and looked at it. 'It's just paint.'

Linda laughed. 'Thank God for that. I thought it was some

horrible war wound you've been hiding.' She peered more closely at the paint. 'Where did it come from? It looks like roof paint, like the colour of the dairy roof in Melanie's school project. Is that what it is? Did you go out on the back veranda? They had a whole tin of it out there. They made quite a mess.'

It was he who turned and took her wrist, encircled it like a bracelet. But it was she who swept her fingers under his damp hair and laid her lips on the rosy birthmark. His skin smelt of wet wool. His breathing became ragged. And then a sighing collapse of limbs and fumble of clothing. His hand slid between her thighs, his tongue pushed into her mouth. At first it felt effortless, like a gentle, arching swoon, but very quickly, far too soon, Linda returned to her body. She lay like a patient awake under anaesthetic. She could feel the hard ground beneath her back. Their elbows were sharp, their teeth clashed, his mouth ground into hers. There was something rough and angry in the way he held her down. Her hair was caught under his hand. It pulled at her scalp and hurt. She pushed his arm but couldn't make him move it. When he finally came, she was relieved. He whimpered like a puppy, but, looking up, she saw that his eyes were firmly closed.

He slumped beside her and his breathing slowed to a tiny, rhythmic catching in his throat. Linda, however, was wide awake. She felt that her eyes were the only part of her body she could move. She imagined them, round cartoon eyes with black dot pupils, blinking and swivelling this way and that in the darkness of the tent. Outside, the neighbour's dairy cows had approached the fence again. She listened to their wet breathing and the soft knock of their hoofs. Everything was respiring, heaving up and down, while her thoughts turned in slow circles. The cows made her think of Donovan lying dead in the field, and of Wayne Mackenzie walking back to his dairy with his rifle. And now it was a spray gun and a bucket of herbicide, and Gerard was screaming at Wayne from their front veranda, ranting about the evils of fucking 2,4-D.

Anostostoma

By midnight a thin breeze was spilling over the escarpment, rushing behind the water now coursing down the rockface. The haunting call of a koel. The steady purr of rain. Palm husks lying in the gully below like discarded rowboats shifted on their moorings as the trickle became a stream.

The giant king cricket had been waiting for a rainy night like this, crouched in his burrow beside the bridge. He clawed his way to the surface, ready to feed, emerging from the silica grit like the prehistoric creature he was. Once clear of the burrow, he began to unfold, raising his enormous head and lifting his wingless abdomen on his angled legs. His long, fine antennae lay like wet threads in the mud. He dragged them a short distance and strained until they finally swung forward and lifted in the breeze.

The eardrums beneath his knees picked up the dreadful sound, a heavy thudding on the bank above him. There was no time to get back to the burrow. He scurried into a concrete pipe under the bridge, where he was struck and pinned by a blinding beam of light. The dark shadow of a man came forward and crouched before him, breathing heavily. The giant king cricket hissed at him, trying to scare him off, but, unperturbed, the man picked it up with a trembling hand and turned it in the torchlight. 'Cretaceous,' he said to himself in a sibilant whisper. The cricket shot a stinking tarry substance from its arse. The man's short, sharp laugh rang inside the pipe. He set the cricket down with the fastidious care of a child positioning his toy engine, and watched with satisfaction as it scuttled away.

Chapter Twenty-eight

Sandy had it all written down from his phone call with Jean the night before. So many instructions: not just which flowers to pick but how long to cut the stems and whether the ends should be bruised or blanched or plunged straight into water. He should have just given Peg Parmenter free range of the garden. She knew exactly what was needed. The rain had stopped in the early hours of the morning. Beads of bright water clung to the soft red foliage of the Christmas bush. This bush was the most important thing, being a key component of the Advent wreath on the altar. Jean had been refreshing the leaves in the church every week. Tomorrow was the fourth Sunday of Advent — they'd be lighting the Angels' Candle and having a special morning tea afterwards in the hall. Jean was sorry to be missing this. She was finding it quite a strain to be away from home at this time of the year, a guest in someone else's house and the grandmother of a baby weighing barely two pounds and breathing through a tangle of plastic tubes.

Little Rose. He'd had a nice idea for her, or for Jean at any rate. He'd found a small piece of rose mahogany in the shed and had spent the last few evenings at his workbench, shaping it into a palm-sized lozenge and sanding it silky smooth. The last coat of estapol had gone on last night, and this morning he'd given it a final rub with wet and dry. Next he was going to drop it down to Marie Willis to paint. She'd won prizes for her folk art, tole it was called. He would ask her to write *Rose's First Christmas, 1976* on the front, and on the back the words *Dysoxylum fraserianum — Rose Mahogany*. Might as well get her learning her timbers, heiress to the family business as she was at this point in time. Jean was going to love it. He'd even solved the problem of getting it down to her. Christmas was less than a week away and posting it was out of the question, but as luck would have it, the Willis family was going down to Sydney at the end of the week and staying in the vicinity of the Mater Hospital. Marie had kindly offered to take it to the maternity ward. She was hoping she and Tracy might get to see the baby, but Sandy wasn't sure if they'd be allowed. Either way, baby Rose would have her decoration and Jean would be as pleased as punch.

The woodwork had provided a welcome distraction for Sandy on these evenings, with all the stress of the forest blockade. Eight arrests yesterday, including his little German friend: forty police, and only one crown down. That was all, one brush box, a beauty though it was. Hopefully it represented a turning of the tide and Pat and the team would make better progress today.

The guile of that little German Miss. What kind of a stunt was that? Poor old Reg Velucci had nearly had a heart attack, believing for a minute there that someone was going to die. If not her, then the young policemen who had to go down and get her. Sandy snapped at a hydrangea bush with the secateurs. He wasn't going out there today. There wasn't a whole lot of point. He'd only gone yesterday to provide moral support. The police had control of it now, they had more reinforcements, and they'd be getting straight down to it, no mucking around. It was better for him to be down at the mill to receive the logs as they came. He was hoping for at least two loads today, although that could be optimistic. It wasn't just that they were working in a forest crawling with people. It was also that young Michael was new to the job and loading the jinker was going to take a bit longer.

But first things first. He had to get these flowers to the church. Peg Parmenter was expecting him at nine.

She was sitting out the front of the church when Sandy pulled in, her own buckets of flowers beside her. He found this surprising. Peg was an 'upright' sort of person, tall and solid. You didn't expect to find her sitting on a flight of damp wooden steps. She looked crestfallen and he wondered if she'd lost her key. If that were the case, he couldn't help. He didn't have the faintest where Jean kept hers. He would have to go back home and call her.

'Peg?'

'Sandy.'

'They're in the back, just a tick.' He pressed a button and popped the door of the Range Rover.

'Sandy —'

'What is it?'

'You have to come and see what they've done.'

He followed her down the side of the church and gasped in shock. There, written on the lower half of the white weatherboard wall, obscured from the passing traffic by a line of oleander bushes:

FATHER, FORGIVE THEM FOR THEY KNOW NOT
WHAT THEY DO — LUKE 23:34

The words were written in red paint and ran the full length of the wall, each letter standing over a foot high. Unlike the graffiti you often saw under railway bridges, the writing was not a hurried scrawl but very neatly rendered. Whoever it was had taken their time and considerable care.

'Wait, there's more,' Peg said.

She led him around the back to the square of weedy concrete that lay between the church and the hall. Both buildings were covered in the red writing, no longer down low but right up the walls and between the diamond-paned windows.

> THOU SHALT NOT DESTROY THE TREES THEREOF
> BY FORCING AN AXE AGAINST THEM ... THOU SHALT
> NOT CUT THEM DOWN — DEUTERONOMY 20:19

And there again, above the noticeboards on the cinder bricks of the hall:

> HOWL, FIR TREE; FOR THE CEDAR IS FALLEN;
> BECAUSE THE MIGHTY ARE SPOILED ... FOR THE
> FOREST OF THE VINTAGE IS COME DOWN —
> ZECHARIAH 11:2

So it continued, on the double doors, on the toilet block, on the wall behind the barbecue.

> HE SHALL CONSUME THE GLORY OF HIS FOREST,
> AND OF HIS FRUITFUL FIELD, BOTH SOUL AND BODY:
> AND THEY SHALL BE AS WHEN A STANDARD-BEARER
> FAINTETH — ISAIAH 10:18

'Jesus,' Sandy muttered. 'He certainly knows his Bible.' He rubbed at one of the letters with his finger. The paint was dry, which was strange when everything else was so damp.

Peg looked unimpressed. 'We should call the police.'

'If there's anyone there. It's all hands on deck up there in the forest today.'

Peg pressed her temple and winced as if she were getting a headache. 'Well, we can't leave it here for tomorrow, it's too upsetting, and we can't clean it up until they've seen it. It's a crime scene. It's a crime.' She cast her eyes around the desecrated walls. 'They should check under the church as well. Make sure they haven't left any bombs.'

'Bombs?' Sandy laughed, but he saw how rattled she was. He'd had his moments too, these past few weeks.

'Come on, Peg,' he said gently. 'Don't get yourself all worked up. It's just some nutter with a tin of paint, that's all.'

Peg unlocked the doors to the hall. 'I hope you've got someone watching the mill. It would only take one touch of a match to send that up in smoke.'

Jean had said the same thing. He'd put new padlocks on the gate, but what was there to stop someone tossing a piece of burning paper over the fence? Perhaps he should have had the place guarded. He stood in the middle of the church yard and reread the tracts on the walls. Selectively quoted they were, of course: you could do that with the Bible. There were probably just as many orders from God to take your axe, go forth, and clear the land. There was that thing in Genesis, right at the start, about man's dominion over nature. Someone should ask the minister to dig out a few good quotes as an antidote to all this.

Sandy took the buckets of flowers to the hall, where Peg was laying down newspaper on a trestle table. He asked her what Ray was up to today, whether he could help with the clean-up. And what about the kids on holidays, what about young Joanne? He could see a way of twisting this thing to their advantage, to play it the way the hippies did, make it a bit of a stunt. They should get the whole town mobilised to help them fix it up, and call up the papers to tell their side of the story. They should leave everything as it was until after tomorrow's service and then, instead of tea and cakes, hold a working bee.

'I'm not sure what Ray's doing,' Peg said. 'He could be stuck in the shop. Joanne's away for the weekend, she's gone to stay with a friend.' Peg then confessed that the two of them had had a blazing row and Joanne had taken herself off to stay with Tracy Willis. 'Teenage girls!' she sighed, stripping the leaves off a lily. 'She's such a handful, Sandy. I don't know what to do with her.'

Sandy was bemused. He had such a different impression of Joanne Parmenter. She always seemed so meek to him, so obedient and solemn.

'I'm on my way to the Willises' now, as a matter of fact,' he said. 'I've made a little something for the baby and Marie's offered to take it down to Sydney.'

'Well, there you go. You can ask Joanne yourself. I don't know about the Willises helping. They're not churchgoing people.'

'I'll drop in at the shop on my way and see if Ray's got a good ladder. But you're right, we need to tell the police. I've got to call them anyway to see what's going on.' He picked up his buckets and made for the door, then turned to her again. 'It'll need a couple of coats,' he said. 'It's a very dark colour, that red.'

Even from across the hall he could see that Peg was losing her composure. He came back, pulled up a chair, and sat across from her. Secateurs, wire, the spiky blocks that sat inside the vases: they were all neatly laid out on the table between them, but her hands remained in her lap and her shoulders were sagging.

'Graffiti's a rotten thing,' he said.

Peg nodded and sniffed.

He told her about the incident they'd had down at the mill a few months back. It was nothing, just an obscenity sprayed on the sign out the front, but the feeling of violation remained. Sandy had sent one of the young stackers out with a bottle of turps, but he never failed to notice the grey smear it left behind. Through the door the big red letters blazed on the white walls of the church. It's vandalism, Mr Mitchell, he heard a stern voice say — Gerard Ansiewicz, brandishing his big, long stick of bread. It was vandalism all right. It left a vibration, a trembling in the air, a blood-red angry aura of intent.

'That guy, Phil de Beer —'

Peg blinked and shook her head.

'The one from the commune, you know the one.'

'Tall, big mop of hair?'

'He was on the news.'

'Yes, I know the one.'

'You know what he told me once? He told me that the primary industries were finished in these parts, that the future of this town would lie in tourism.'

Peg stared at him blankly.

'We stop farming and harvesting timber and tourists will come flocking in.'

'And do what?'

'Bushwalking, that kind of thing. Swimming in the creek.'

'Oh,' said Peg. 'And how are people supposed to make a living out of that?'

'Food, cafes, souvenirs, all that sort of thing. They'll all come here to have their lunch and go on guided walks.'

'Well, that all sounds rather jolly,' Peg said. 'I can just imagine you.'

'Yeah,' Sandy scoffed. 'We've had a few laughs about that down at the mill.' He almost gave her the image of Fletch in a frilly apron but instead leant forward on his elbows and gazed intently at the freckled skin on the back of his hands. His nails were blunt and broken, and his knuckles nobbled with scars.

'These hands —' He sighed and shook his head.

Again Peg looked and waited.

'These hands have moved forests. They're the hands of a working man. They're not made for serving tea and cake to strangers.'

Chapter Twenty-nine

The first thing Joanne noticed when she opened her eyes was that the placard had gone. She turned over and, sure enough, Melanie had gone too, leaving only a rumpled sheet and the old t-shirt she slept in. It was still dark outside, but Joanne could hear voices: people moving past the pup tent, their torch beams sweeping through its thin nylon walls.

She and Melanie had barely spoken in the tent the night before. Melanie had given curt instructions as Joanne made up her bed and struggled into her pyjamas. *What did you bring pyjamas for? Nobody wears those.* There was no talk of the next day, no discussion of the evening's events beside the fire. As soon as Joanne had settled into her sleeping bag, Melanie had turned her back on her and promptly gone to sleep.

Joanne lay awake for a long time, pushed towards the tent wall by a kind of hostile forcefield. Propped in the corner above her pillow was a placard — SAVE THE TREES — hastily painted in dark-red capitals. She glanced across at Melanie, who was breathing steadily, and then, as quietly as she could, inched closer to the poster. She recognised the carboard by the price sticker in the corner. It was one of the sheets she'd bought at the newsagent in town. Melanie had used the paint they'd chosen for the roof of the shoebox dairy. In the darkness the dribbling letters looked like they were painted in blood.

Now both Melanie and the placard had gone and the campsite was coming to life. Did this happen before sunrise every morning or was something going on? Joanne pulled on her clammy jeans, searched about for her shoes, and without bothering to brush her hair headed for the campfire.

The sun was still a long way from rising above the range, but the light had increased to the point where you could see the surrounding clutter of canvas tents and vans. All but the very closest tents were drained of colour in the pre-dawn light, and Linda's on the far side of the field was still lost in the fog.

At the campfire Jane was on her knees, raking coals into a smoking pile. The rest of the fireplace was a ghost of its former self, a soft grey circle of ash dotted with charred wood and encircled with basalt rocks gathered from the paddocks.

'Hey there,' Jane said. 'How did you sleep? Would you like some porridge? There's some on the stove. Or there's that one there. That was Melanie's. She barely touched it.'

'Where is she?'

Jane sat back on her heels. 'She said not to tell anyone, but you can probably guess. Linda's going to have a fit, you wait. I should go and wake her.'

Across the creek, people were filing up the hill. Like ants they bobbed along in a thin broken line, lugging their placards as if they were fragments of leaf.

'Are the loggers coming?' Joanne asked.

'It makes no difference to you. You're going home. Have you packed up your things? Linda was wanting to get an early start.'

Joanne glowered at the discarded plate of porridge on the ground. She wasn't eating Melanie's leftovers. 'Can I have an apple?'

'Sure, they're here. I could offer you some muesli, except there's no more milk. I have to go and get some from Joel. Hey, why don't you fetch it for me — here — and some dry wood for the fire.' She held out a plastic bucket and a billy for the milk. 'Just some kindling to get things going until our wood dries out, there's a good girl. I'm expecting the next sitting for breakfast any moment now.'

'No,' Joanne said. 'I can't. I'm going up to the forest.'

Jane sighed and shook her head. 'You should let Linda know.'

'Linda's not my mother. And you let Melanie go.'

'Melanie snuck off on her own. I had nothing to do with it. Anyway, if you are going, you're gonna need some food. How about a sandwich? Do you like peanut butter?'

Jane went into a flurry of buttering slabs of bread.

'Are you coming up, Jane?'

'Maybe later. I was going to help with the creche. Andy's up there already. He went up first thing with Phil.'

'And Gerard? Is he there?'

'No, I think he stayed in town. You heard Bettina was arrested?'

'What's going to happen to her? Will she go to gaol?'

'Oh no, honey.' Jane smiled. 'I think that's very unlikely. I imagine they'll get a fine, or maybe just a warning. Have you got water with you? You have to take some water. Here, take mine. I've got another bottle somewhere.'

Eating the sandwich, Joanne walked down to the reedy creek, across the wooden footbridge and up the other side. It was the same cow track they'd taken when they went to the falls to swim. Joanne recognised things along the way: a rotting log, a termite mound, the collapsed rib cage of a long-dead cow lying in the grass. The people walking ahead of her were carrying lengths of chain. This was one of the tactics they'd discussed the night before, sitting around the fire in a circle. The talk had become quite heated, and Joanne had been surprised. Some guys wanted to hammer spikes into the marked trees to reduce the value of the logs and wreck the loggers' chainsaws. But someone else, a woman, got very upset about this, calling it an act of violence, not just against the logging crews, but against the forest itself. She went on to accuse some of the men of bullyboy tactics, of working as part of a secretive patriarchal posse that could undermine the spiritual unity of the group. Instead she suggested they follow Bettina's lead, but exactly what she meant by that, Joanne wasn't sure. There were people who thought it was dangerous, whatever it was Bettina had done, while others thought it a strategy worth consideration. It was Phil de Beer who suggested that they make more use of chains, that they climb or chain themselves to as many trees as possible, to those marked for felling and to others in their line of fall. Someone went off to Joel's shed to source more chains and locks. That was as far as the meeting got before the rain grew too heavy and everyone retreated to their tents and vans.

At the top of the ridge Joanne took the right-hand fork in the path and descended to the muddy clearing that was already swarming with people. She stood at the top of the steep embankment, looking down at the scene. It was not as she had imagined. A few policemen were already there, six of them in dark-blue jumpers and collared shirts. They were guarding a small bulldozer and a trailer of equipment. Beside their car Joanne could see the remnants of a campfire and a ring of fold-up chairs. Their presence didn't appear to cause much consternation. They were smiling and nodding with Phil de Beer as if exchanging pleasantries. Joanne had expected something more confrontational. She had envisaged two armies massing on either side, the protesters hurtling down the slope like a cavalry charge. What she was seeing was more like a friendly football match: the referee calling the captains together and requesting a good, clean game.

It was true that not everyone was friendly. There was some heckling going on, and people were chanting as they trickled down through the trees and onto the turning bay. The policemen made no attempt to stop them. Joanne wondered why not. Why weren't there more police out here, ready and waiting for them? The obvious thing would be for them to form a solid barrier, to block the path of the protesters coming down the hill. These policemen seemed reluctant, almost bored, as they stood in a huddle, chatting and blowing into their hands.

'There you are.'

It was Linda in a grimy singlet top and jeans, her wild hair bundled on the top of her head. She looked annoyed and haggard, like she'd just got out of bed.

'Where's Melanie?' she snapped.

'I don't know.'

'I'll go and look for her. You stay here. As soon as I find her I'm taking the two of you home.'

At that moment everyone surged towards to other end of the clearing, to where the road ran down to the bridge. Trouble was on its way. You could hear the distant growl of the approaching convoy, the whine of their engines accelerating out of the bends. Sensing a slackening in Linda's concentration, Joanne slipped her lead and ducked away.

The crowd swallowed her up: the dull thud of the bongo drums, the jostle and press of bodies. Joanne felt slightly sick. She was breathing second-hand air. She tilted her face to the sky, but it brought no relief. She scrambled back up the embankment, where she had a clearer view of the road sweeping down to the bridge and cars and trucks gathering on the other side of the gully. She could see the trucks from Forestry, the jinker and a ute, and a long line of cars and paddy wagons. Men gathered at the end of the bridge. Joanne narrowed her eyes. So many familiar faces: men from the mill, from the local police, from church, from table tennis. She knew their names, their kids, their wives, the newspapers they ordered. She couldn't see Sandy Mitchell, but Mr Phelan was there. Joanne slipped back into the crowd and hunched down low. If I can't see you, you can't see me. Isn't that how it worked?

The protesters got through two songs and started singing another. For a time it seemed as if their opponents were in retreat. The policemen gathered in a huddle near the cars, talking among themselves, now and then glancing across at the crowd on the side. Then all of a sudden, at someone's command, they charged across the bridge.

Joanne heard the rumble and crunch of their boots. The crowd braced itself, the pushing and shoving up the front travelling through it like a vibration. Drums pounded, whistles blew, the singing became more raucous. Joanne found herself at the back, surrounded by women and children. Now the jinker was coming through. Mr Phelan was driving. Michael sat beside him, looking down over his elbow at the people being wrestled aside. Just once, Mr Phelan raised his eyes and surveyed the crowd. Joanne felt his gaze swoop over her like the beam of a lighthouse. She ducked her head in panic and, bent almost double, joined the people heading back towards the turning bay.

The original group of policemen were still clustered around the bulldozer, grinning at a stocky woman in a funny hat.

'Just doing your job, are you, boys? Well, your job stinks. Look what you're destroying here. Look around you! Look up, go on! Look at this beautiful place! Can't you see it?'

The young officers stood, unmoved, their hands behind their backs. It was driving the woman berserk, their stupid impervious grins. She began to hurl expletives. The policemen squared their shoulders. The woman's friend took her arm and gently pulled her away.

On the other side of the clearing was a television crew. There was a man kneeling in the mud with a heavy camera on his shoulder, and another dangling a fluffy grey microphone on a pole. Clustered in front of them were Mrs Phelps, her friend Wanda, and a group of Aboriginal people: the Robinson family and several more, including one very old man. Mrs Phelps appeared to be organising them like a group of students about to perform in front of a school assembly. Joanne moved closer to hear what they were saying. The old man was speaking something that sounded like a foreign language, but then, in English, he clearly said, with a sweep of his hand, 'This here. Right across here. All of this, country. My people, we care for country.'

Care for country. Joanne found this an odd thing to say. Whose country: *my* country, *our* country? Was he making some kind of claim? And why were the journalists talking to these people anyway? They'd only just arrived. Why not talk to someone who'd been here the whole time?

Wanda caught sight of her and said something to Mrs Phelps.

'Joanne!' cried Mrs Phelps. 'Look at this, isn't it great? They've brought the whole family. And these people,' she said pointing to the television crew. 'They're from *This Day Tonight*. Do you ever watch that show?'

Joanne shook her head and backed away, fearing that the cameraman might turn his lens on her. It was then that she caught her first sight of Melanie that day, the flicker of her orange t-shirt moving through the trees. She was carrying her placard and heading down the slope. Not knowing what else to do, Joanne followed her, over the edge of the clearing and down a long, deep gash in the undergrowth. It was hard going, a slipping mess of churned earth and fallen branches. The air teemed with midges and smelt of vinegar. Suddenly, below her, in a patch of dazzling sunlight, she saw Melanie sitting cross-legged on top of a huge tree stump, looking for all the world like a gnome in a fairy story.

'Hello,' said Melanie solemnly, showing no surprise.

'This is the tree —' Joanne gasped. No one had told her this. It was the giant brush box they had encircled that afternoon, after swimming in the falls.

'Can I come up?' Joanne asked and immediately regretted it. There was no need to ask permission. It wasn't Melanie's tree.

'If you like,' Melanie said, neither moving nor offering assistance.

Joanne skirted the massive stump until she found a foothold and, with grim determination, hauled herself onto it. The sawn surface was a furry red-brown and warm from the sun. She ran her hands over it and touched her finger to the jagged wall of splinters down the centre. She peered at the sap oozing down the sides. It was tacky now, like half-set toffee, full of drowned ants and flies.

'It gushed like blood when they cut it down,' Melanie said softly.

'It was pumping, like a heart.'

Joanne swallowed. 'So what are you doing now?'

'I'm going to climb a tree.'

'Me too.'

Melanie rolled her eyes.

'Mel, what's the matter? What have I done? Why aren't you talking to me?'

'I'm talking to you.'

'No you're not.'

'I'm talking now, aren't I?'

'I'm the one who should be mad. I had to do our whole presentation on my own. It was so embarrassing. It was so — pathetic.'

'The project,' Melanie groaned, folding her arms. 'Is that all you care about, that stupid bloody project and your stupid marks?'

Here it comes, thought Joanne, like pus out of a pimple. Was she ready for it or should she back off now?

'I had to come out here,' Melanie said coldly. 'I didn't have a choice and we didn't get much warning.'

'You could've rung me.'

'What's the big deal? Mrs Phelps said we passed. I wasn't going to be here for it anyhow. We were meant to be up north by now, but then all this happened and we had to hang around.'

'That's not why you didn't go.'

'What do you mean by that?'

'Are you talking about Toona Bay? Don't you know what happened? It's not even there anymore, Melanie. The Queensland government bombed it.'

Melanie went to laugh, but her smile quickly faded. 'Who told you that?'

'Mrs Phelps.'

'And how does she know?'

'She said it was on the news. I thought that's where you'd gone when you didn't show up at school, but she said, no, you couldn't have, because they'd burnt the commune down and there's nothing left.'

Joanne was unprepared for the impact this had. Melanie's face grew pale and her jaw began to quiver. 'You're full of shit!' she spat, grabbing her placard and climbing to her feet.

'Where are you going?'

'None of your business. Stop following me. You don't belong here with us. Go home to your horrible family. What are you even doing here? These dickheads are your friends. You told them where we're camping. You saw it on that map. You told your crazy aunty and she attacked our car.'

Melanie leapt off the stump and blundered through the trees, dragging her battered placard with her. Joanne remained where she was, her breathing fast and shallow. The warm air was suddenly split by the deafening sound of a chainsaw, revving and juddering as its teeth began to bite. Almost immediately a second chainsaw started, this one even closer than the first.

Joanne slithered to the ground and headed for the same group of trees as Melanie. *Stop following me.* She stumbled and fell forward on her hands and knees and, on the ground in front of her, saw something small and shiny. The numbers 386/1, the letters REP. It was the tin tag that Aurora had wrenched from the bark of the giant brush box on that faraway afternoon. Joanne glanced behind her to where the tree had stood, her eyes travelling up the shimmering column of air and watering in the harsh glare of the sun. She slipped the tin tag into her back pocket and, dusting her hands on her jeans, decided to go up the hill instead.

Chapter Thirty

Ray Parmenter was crying. Joanne looked down at her father crouched at the base of the tree and saw him swipe at his cheeks with the back of his hand. He was wearing a short-sleeved business shirt, one that Aunty Peg had bought him, thick, ugly stripes of blue and brown. He looked like he was praying, but he wouldn't be doing that. Ray suffered church, or he did when Delia was alive. He wasn't one to turn to God, even at times like this.

There. He did it again. Joanne shifted in the fork of the tree, the knowledge of her father's tears only adding to her discomfort. She kicked her feet against the trunk to banish the pins and needles, and lifted her buttocks, one at a time, to allow the blood to flow back in and relieve the aching numbness. In nearly two hours she hadn't so much as glimpsed a bush crew, although there was an almost constant burr of chainsaws in the distance and, six times now, the awful pause and crack of a tree coming down. The falling sigh of the protesters, the rising shriek of bats.

And now here was her father. She had recognised the shirt, watching nervously as he waded towards her through the sea of bracken. He was livid by the time he reached her tree. He hammered his fists against the trunk and ranted. What the hell did she think she was doing? This blockade was killing the town. She ought to be ashamed of herself. You come down now, do you hear?

Joanne wondered how he'd found her, what he was doing here. Perhaps Mr Phelan had spotted her from the cabin of his truck after all and radioed down to the mill. Ray was offering no explanation. Since his initial outburst he had barely said a word. She could hardly hear him anyway, with the wind and the cicadas and being so far from the ground. Her climbing skills had surprised her. She hadn't climbed a tree since primary school, but she'd managed to get a fair way up in the end. You'd expect it of someone like Melanie. Even holding her placard she'd be able to swing up a tree like a monkey. Not that Joanne had seen her do it. There was no sign of her. Hopefully she was too far away to hear Ray shouting, to see him circling Joanne's tree like some crazed wolf in a children's book.

Joanne had only seen her father cry once before. It wasn't when her mum died as you might expect. It was sometime around July, just before they arranged for Delia to come home. It was in the hospital car park after their evening visit. Joanne and Barbara were waiting in the car. Ray had sent the two of them down in the lift on their own while he had a quick word with the matron. He took ages, and in the car they grew bored and silly. They played a rude version of I-spy to pass the time, lampooning the appearances of people walking past. The giggles stopped abruptly when Ray opened his door. He put his seatbelt on and the key in the ignition and then sat in silence, his head bowed, his feet on the clutch and brake. Barb looked at him expectantly; Joanne craned around the seat. Even now, she recoiled at the memory of his face that night, his wet cheeks shining in the green light of the dash.

Somewhere, a monotonous bird cried *womp womp womp*. A fruit bounced down from the canopy and fell with a thud on the ground. Joanne laid her cheek against the trunk and ran her hands around it. A bird landed on a nearby branch. It was smaller than a pigeon, a reddish brown, pale underneath, with a soft dark eye. Its beak was blunt and sturdy like a split peanut, and the whiskery legs of an insect were protruding from one side. The bird hopped twice along the branch and flipped around to face her. The insect whirred inside its beak, its legs clawing the air. The bird, annoyed, whacked it on the branch. Then, for no reason she could fathom, it suddenly flew away.

Someone else was coming through the bracken now, wearing an orange hard hat. It took Joanne a moment to realise it was Barb. She pulled off the hat and waved to Ray, but he didn't respond. She came and knelt beside him and took him in her arms. Joanne felt her own tears rising as she looked down at them. They were like a frozen tableau, Ray hunkered on one knee, Barbara leaning over him, her cheek against his back.

Eventually Ray got to his feet and brushed himself down. He glanced up at Joanne one last time, then turned and walked away. Barbara must have talked him into leaving them alone. She waited at the base of the tree until he was out of sight.

'I'm not going shout!' she shouted then. 'You're going to have to come down. Take your time, I'm not in a hurry.'

She made a show of being relaxed, sitting cross-legged, her back against the tree, nursing the orange hard hat on her belly. Something gave way inside Joanne, like a cake sinking in the middle. She was no longer sure what she was doing. Her thoughts were fuzzy and vague. What was the point of this tree-sitting thing when only her family knew she was there and cared about what she was doing? What difference would it make if she came down sooner rather than later? She had to come down sometime, she had no water with her. She had left the empty bottle at the base of the tree. Maybe this was making her fuzzy in the head. Perhaps she was dehydrated.

'Have you got any water?' she called down to Barb.

'There's plenty in the car.'

Joanne stared at a tiny black ant scurrying in circles in front of her. Then, slowly, she hoisted herself out of the fork of the tree and wrapped her arms around the solid trunk. It seemed like such a long way down, further than before, and the knots and branches that had been her footholds now seemed so far apart. Pressing her cheek against the bark, she searched blindly with one foot.

'Are you okay?'

She couldn't answer. Her heart was pumping like mad.

'Someone might have a ladder,' Barbara yelled.

Joanne was appalled. Imagine the loggers having to come and help her out of a tree. The very thought of that strengthened her resolve. She lowered herself to the branch below and continued like a slow animal to ease herself, hand and foot, all the way down to the ground.

'Dad was crying,' Barbara said.

Joanne rubbed her smarting palms.

'Do you remember that night at the hospital, Jo, in the car park?'

She nodded and then blurted, 'But why's he crying now?'

'Because of you, stupid. What are you doing here?'

Joanne sank to her knees with a sob.

'Oh no, not you too. Everyone's crying, I don't know, you're as bad as each other, you two.'

From far away came the quickening drums and rising wails of the crowd.

Joanne clutched her head in her hands. 'They killing the trees,' she whimpered.

'Oh, come on —'

'They are! They're cutting them down.'

'Yeah, and they'll grow back. Come back here in forty years and you won't even know this has happened.'

'Forty years!'

'It's not that long.' Barbara looked at her, perplexed. 'It's not even rainforest, they're not touching that. For God's sake, Jo. Look at this bush, it's not even that pretty up here.' The two girls looked around at the colonnade of trees, at the bird's nest ferns and bangalows and swags of woody vines. Above them sparks of sunlight flashed in the canopy. Joanne's head ached and her tears spilled down again.

'It will all die now.'

'No, it won't!'

'It will, the weeds will get in. And Barb, the trees, they talk to each other. They scream when you cut them down.'

'That is so much hippie shit.'

'They do — and they bleed.'

Barb stabbed at the dirt between her feet with a piece of stick.

'How did you find me, anyway? Who told you I was here?'

'Sandy Mitchell.'

'How did he know?'

'Tracy Willis told him.'

'Tracy.' Joanne frowned.

'Sandy went to her house this morning and then he came down to the shop.'

'But how did Tracy know?'

'She didn't. I put it together. Where *is* your hippie friend? They arrested that guy — what's-his-face?'

'Gerard?'

'No, the other one. The one with the guitar. It's finished, this blockade. They can't keep it up much longer. There's no point in you being here. Come back to the car with me.'

'Did you see Linda, Melanie's mum?'

'Yeah, she's still here. It was funny, I caught her eye and she gave me a filthy look.'

'Is Sandy here?'

'Yes. He came in the car with us. They vandalised the church, Joanne. Did Dad tell you that? They wrote all over it in red paint, all these Bible quotes.'

So much seemed to have happened at home in such a short space of time. Joanne felt frustrated, as though she'd missed out, as though she'd run away from the action, not towards it as she'd thought.

Someone called Barbara's name. It was Michael Phelan. She waved her hat, and he waved back and came up the hill towards them.

'You found her, then?'

'Yeah, we found her. She's okay, I think. A bit weird in the head, but then she's always been like that.'

'The truck's nearly loaded, Barb. Do you want to come with me? Dad wants to stay here with the crew.'

Joanne pawed at her sister's arm. 'No, Barb, don't!'

If Barbara went with Michael, Joanne faced the ghastly prospect of driving back, alone in the car with her dad and Sandy Mitchell. To her intense relief, Barbara read her mind.

'No thanks, Mick. I'll stay with Jo. I'll see you later on. Are you going to the pub?'

He shrugged and turned away.

'Maybe I should go with him.'

'No!'

Barbara winced with indecision. 'I really don't want to be in that truck — all those crazy people. Michael said one of them got on top of the cabin yesterday. Flopped down in front of the windscreen, like a madman in a movie, this guy with all these ropes of hair, it sounded horrible.'

'Do you want to just see him off?'

'Maybe. I don't know. No, I think I should stay here and keep an eye on you. Once the truck's gone, they'll all piss off and we can get to the car in peace.'

Joanne would always remember the things they talked about next. Trivial stuff like really, really wanting a drink of water, and look, here in my hair, Barb — do you think that's a tick? In science at school her teacher had said that gravity could bend time. She and everyone else in the class had struggled to comprehend this, even after he spread a silky black cloth on his desk out the front and tugged it down through the Bunsen-burner hole as a demonstration. But there, in that strange half-hour, or however long it was, Joanne felt the sagging grid of time. The descending mesh of cicada noise, the weight of the warm, still air, their voices deadened and hyperreal against the noise of the bush.

Again, from far away, came the jangle and whoop of the protesters, re-energised by the impending departure of the logs. Joanne imagined them all regrouping on the road above the bridge and Michael Phelan in the truck, facing them alone.

'I will go up,' Barbara said, getting to her feet.

'I'll come too.'

'All right, then. But you stay with me, d'you hear? No running off to join them.'

Joanne shook her head and trotted behind her sister like a chastened dog.

They found only a loose gathering of people in the turning bay. The truck had just departed, and with it the noisy throng. At the back of the crowd, a woman was dancing wildly, in a world of her own, her bare feet skipping on the spot. She wore a dirty yellow skirt, ruffled at the hem, and dozens of plastic Indian bangles stacked up her leathery arms. That's Marguerite, Joanne almost heard Melanie say, suddenly missing her whispered explanations. She's over sixty but really fit. She dances all the time. And the guy with the lagerphone, that's Rob. You met him at the falls. He's Tess's biological dad, and that's his girlfriend, Crystal. The whispering faded and the crowd became a mass again, a nameless rabble of hippies pressing around the truck. The police were in among them, pulling people off the rig and shoving them aside.

'If we climb up the bank, we'll be able to see,' Joanne told her sister.

But Barbara had resolved to get into the truck after all and drive to the mill with Michael.

'Are you crazy?' Joanne cried. 'How are you going to do that? He can hardly stop in the middle of this and open the door for you.'

Barbara frowned. 'If I can get to the bridge, I can wait on the other side. I should have gone with him before. He needs some moral support. Come with me, Jo, come on. Dad's there too, and Sandy.'

Hugging the hard hat to her chest, Barbara plunged into the crowd. Joanne lost sight of her almost right away. She didn't follow. It was a line she couldn't cross. She couldn't climb into a logging truck in front of all these people. Instead she resumed her gutless perch in the scrub at the top of the cutting, where she had a clear view of the bridge and the gully below. Barbara reached the line of police blocking entry to the bridge. She spoke to them. They let her through. Michael applauded with a quick beep of his horn.

There was a sudden surge of energy and movement in the crowd. Something was happening at the back of the blockade, near the bend at the top of the road.

The Arty Smarts had arrived. You could almost hear the bugles as they hoisted their puppets high in the air like wall-eyed battle standards. A pioneer man wielding an axe and his Ma Kettle wife. The protesters parted to let them through, clapping and cheering. The puppets ducked and bobbed and swayed to the rhythmic groove of the drums, their long arms wobbling on sticks. The pioneer man wore a puffy white shirt and waistcoat; the woman a long white apron. In the crush, the six men holding them struggled to move forward, but gradually they made their way through the jostling mob. The stuffed heads of the effigies passed Joanne at eye level: the man's leering grin, the woman's cockeyed stare.

Suddenly the female puppet swung around to face the other way, her long dress, until now obscured by the apron, catching the breeze and billowing out behind her. Joanne recoiled in horror and her hands flew to her mouth. Orange flowers, fluted crepe — Delia's maxi dress.

She slumped forward, her eyes pressed into the heels of her hands. She pressed so hard her eyeballs ached, but she wouldn't release the pressure. She couldn't bear to look again, and she didn't need to. Under her eyelids the orange dress jumped like a lick of flame. It spilled from the top of a garbage bag in the hallway at home. It burst from a plastic shopping bag in the back of the Smart brothers' van as they returned from Balbirnie with their loot from St Vincent de Paul.

Where was Barb? She needed Barb. She needed her to see this. Her sister was a tiny figure on the other side of the gully, waving her encouragement to Michael in the truck. He was still inching forward, still a long way from the bridge. As fast as people were pulled aside, others flooded in and sat cross-legged in front of him, their arms tightly linked.

Joanne withdrew into the trees and headed up the gully, driven by an impulse to move herself upstream. Travelling further from the noise, away from the chanting and drumming, she had a sense of going back to a place of safety. She was Joanne Parmenter. She was thirteen years of age. It was one week out from Christmas, her favourite time of year. She couldn't go back to the protest camp. She would not drive home with her dad. She would sit here, on this rock, in the middle of the stream, toss black bean pods into the water and watch them bob away. She would wait here, just like this, until everyone had gone, and then walk home on her own, all the way back to Repentance. She would take the much-vilified access road and then follow along the creek, past the mill, through the shop, down the hall to her room. She would take her place at the dinner table. Saturday. Corned beef. She would eat it all and then wipe up without complaining. The forest would once again recede to the edges of her mind, a frame of deep, woolly green around the bright-green valley. She would watch the trucks roar past the shop and not wonder where they'd come from, and life would go on to the whining song of the saw.

One black bean pod was now becalmed in the small pool below her. It swung slowly to one side and almost beached itself. Joanne cast around for a stick to nudge it free, but the water continued to tumble over the rocks behind it, gradually working it loose and sending it bobbing downstream. When she and Barbara were little they used to play with these empty pods, carefully loading each one with a cargo of berries and twigs. The idea was to trade with each other, but it never really worked, because the creek only ran in one direction and you couldn't send boats back. That inexorable trickle and flow. There was no moving upstream, no going back and unknowing the things that you now knew.

She felt the explosion before she heard it, a soundless blow on her chest. Then, on a great swoop of wind, came the deafening blast. A tearing sound and a clanking bounce. An eruption of bats and birds. A scream that was hardly human and the blaring of a horn.

It took Joanne forever to make her way downstream. The first thing she saw as she drew close was the bridge that was no longer there. There was a gaping fissure in the place where it had been, and a deep, scalloped gutter of mud running with yellow water. Joanne looked down the furrow of clay, over the scattered timbers of the bridge and the broken palms, over the logs that had burst their chains and tumbled from the jinker. The rig itself lay on its side, hissing like a punctured lung, its cabin twisted right around as if its neck too was broken.

Nephila

The derelict farmhouse on the hill takes the first buffet of wind as the change blows in from the south. The wooden windows rattle and the arms of Vishnu dance, hurling figs, as hard as bullets, against the iron roof. On the veranda, the swing seat creaks on its stiff ropes, but the little wind chime makes no sound at all. Swathed in thick cobweb, its shards of coloured glass barely move as the wind picks up, let alone tinkle.

The cool air somersaults over the ridge and tumbles down Main Street. Outside the trinket shop that once was Trisha's Salon, the strings of prayer flags jump about and the cheap dreamcatchers spin. A sandwich board collapses outside Rose's Cafe as the first drops of rain plash down on its coloured chalks.

On the northern wall of the basin, in a flat clearing of sunburnt bracken, across the overgrown road, above the burbling gully, a thousand golden orb weavers retreat for the coming storm. One leg protrudes from each curled leaf, hooked around the capture strand at the top of the spider's web, bearing witness to its destruction by the wind and rain.

After the downpour comes a softly dripping pause. Long wisps of water vapour rise from the valley below. The spiders emerge from their leaves and begin to rebuild, their bodies bouncing and jerking along the sticky thread, their sharp feet pulling and tugging and poking. From sapling to sapling, they spin their golden webs. Above the choke of spiny palms and scramblers, they make ready for the blundering insects of the night. They work to stitch the torn edges of the canopy back together, then brace like small black crosses against the open sky.

Acknowledgements

The road to *Repentance*, my first novel, has been long and winding to say the least. I have, however, been grateful for the support and encouragement of many people along the way.

To begin at the end, thank you to the team at Scribe, particularly David Golding for helping me overcome my aversion to conflict and make full use of my materials.

The Varuna PIP Fellowship I received in 2017 was another milestone, providing the impetus I needed to complete and submit the manuscript. Thanks to all at Varuna, The Writers' House, the Eleanor Dark Foundation, and my fellowship mentor Mark Tredinnick.

To my teachers and fellow creative-writing students in the UTS Masters program, thank you for your valuable feedback in the early stages of the project.

Turning north, I pay my respects to the people of the Bundjalung Nation, who, regardless of the perspectives of many in this book, always were and always will be the traditional custodians of the country where I grew up.

I am grateful to the many people — too many to name — who, over cups of tea in country halls and rainbow cafes, during evenings on verandas and long walks to waterfalls, shared the stories and recollections of a time and place that helped me create the fictional town of Repentance and its people.

I am indebted to Andrew, Gaela, and Lexie Hurford for bravely agreeing to help me with this book, taking me to the other side of the Great Divide and teaching me everything I know about sawmills and the generations of families for whom forestry is a way of life.

Thank you to Southern Cross University and Graham Irvine for access to the Aquarius Archive, and to the late Maurice Ryan for taking a keen interest in this book from the beginning and sharing with me his extensive knowledge of local history.

There are references I have kept close at hand throughout, including the works of Dr Nigel Turvey, Ian Watson, and Jeni Kendall on the forest wars of the 1970s and 80s, and my well-thumbed copies of *Australian Rainforest Plants*, vols 1–6, by Nan and Hugh Nicholson.

My love goes out to the Clunes girls — Lois, Sherrie, and Louise — and to Rachel, for the enduring friendships and childhood memories we share. Thank you to Catherine Marshall for her hospitality and her excellent suggestion that I spend a day hanging out at the Nimbin Show. Thank you to Leonie Huggins, my high-school English teacher, for lighting a spark in me, and my brother, David, who, years ago, first drew my attention to Genesis 1:26 and introduced me to the music of Joni Mitchell.

Heartfelt thanks to my sister, Rowena, who travelled so much of this road with me, particularly the last few rocky miles, and who, by gaslight in a camping ground in 2018, was the first person to read the full manuscript.

To my late father, Stan Gibbs, who instilled in me a deep love of language and literature. He read every story I wrote and, to the very end, never stopped asking how the novel was coming along. That he didn't live to see it published is one of my greatest regrets.

Finally, and first of all, I express my love and thanks to my sons, Lawrence and Francis, and my husband, John. Without their patient support and unshakeable belief, *Repentance* may never have been written.